ON BOOKS are published by

ublishing Corp.
enue
Y 10022

n Hardcover Printing: December, 1998
n Paperback Printing: August, 2000

6   5   4   3   2   1

nited States of America

ACCLAIM FOR RICK HANSON'S
ADAM McCLEET MYSTERIES

SPLITTING HEIRS

"The dialogue is sharp, the characters wonderfully eccentric, and the Pacific Northwest setting an effective backdrop."

—*Booklist*

STILL LIFE

"Delivers a thigh-slapping, comedic romp through the Old West. Keep them pages turning!"

—*Library Journal*

MORTAL REMAINS

"Howlingly funny. Hanson takes satirical shots at psychotherapy, peace demonstrators, yuppies, stern nurses and baton twirlers. Amongst all the gag lines, he offers a whodunit that'll keep you guessing."

—*Albuquerque Journal*

SPARE PARTS

"[A] smart, snappy mystery debut . . . a high-energy tale that will leave readers eager for a sequel."

—*Publishers Weekly*

EXTREME ODDS

"[Leaves] readers laughing and upbeat over the characters' shenanigans . . . well designed [with] an ironic twisting story line. Overall, this remains a unique, enjoyable series."

—*Harriet Klausner, BarnesandNoble.com*

P9-DZO-995

BOOK YOUR PLACE ON OUR WEBSITE AND MAKE THE READING CONNECTION!

We've created a customized website just for our very special readers, where you can get the inside scoop on everything that's going on with Zebra, Pinnacle and Kensington books.

When you come online, you'll have the exciting opportunity to:

- View covers of upcoming books
- Read sample chapters
- Learn about our future publishing schedule (listed by publication month *and author*)
- Find out when your favorite authors will be visiting a city near you
- Search for and order backlist books from our online catalog
- Check out author bios and background information
- Send e-mail to your favorite authors
- Meet the Kensington staff online
- Join us in weekly chats with authors, readers and other guests
- Get writing guidelines
- AND MUCH MORE!

**Visit our website at
http://www.zebrabooks.com**

EXTR
OD

An Adam Mc

Rick

KENSIN
KENSINGTON
http://www.

KENSINGT

Kensington
850 Third A
New York,

Copyright ©

All rights res
in any form (
of the Publis

If you purchas
that this book
and destroyed
Publisher has

Kensington an

First Kensing
First Kensingt
10 9 8 7

Printed in the

For Sandra and Janice—
the best sisters I ever had.

Chapter
One

When my time comes, I'd prefer an epitaph with a sense
of the absurd, something along the lines of: *Here Lies
Adam McCleet, Head in the Clouds, Toes on his Feet.*
Or a limerick. *There once was a man from Nantucket.* . . .

Such morbid ruminations weren't my usual preoccupa-
tion, but the man riding in the passenger seat of my '57
Chevy convertible was Max Faverman, and the last time I
saw Max was eight months ago when he commissioned me
to sculpt a memorial for his late wife, Selma.

When she passed away, five years ago, he erected a
simple marker without a date because Selma would have
died if anybody found out how old she was. Though friends
and family pointed out that, in fact, Selma was already
dead, Max remained true to her wishes. Selma had that
kind of clout. Four years ago, Max added a wooden seagull

Rick Hanson

to the marker because Selma loved the beach at Seaside, southwest of Portland. The next year, it was a replica of Selma's cat, who had finally passed on to the great litter box in the sky. Ditto for the dog. The latest addition, my work, was a stone bower of phlox and daisies, because Max's late wife was known far and wide for her gardening skills. Her gravesite was beginning to resemble a miniature golf course.

I glanced over at Max. "You must miss her a lot. Selma."

He turned his head skyward, checking in with the angels. "Every day, I miss her."

"That's why you keep adding to the grave."

"That's one reason."

"What's the other?"

He turned toward me. Max Faverman was a tall, elegant gentleman with fierce, hawk-like eyebrows that perched above his black sunglasses. Though his posture was somewhat formal and stiff, he was neither. "I was married to Selma for forty-five years, and lemme tell you, Adam, she wasn't an easy woman to live with. Demands? Oy, she had such demands! And she always wanted presents. Once I forgot Valentine's Day, and she made my life a living hell." He shrugged. "If I give her a gift every year on her grave, she won't come back and haunt me in my sleep."

"Ever think about remarriage?"

Again, he addressed the clouds. "I swear to you, Selma, there will never be another woman." To me, he added in a whisper, "But I might fool around a little."

Secretly, I'd hoped that after Selma passed away Max and my mother might get together. For as long as I could remember, the Favermans had been good friends of my family, and Max had taken on the role of surrogate father after my own dad died when I was nine.

I liked Max a lot and respected him. Though he owned

the largest shoe manufacturing plant in the Pacific Northwest, I always thought he had the heart of a warrior. He served proudly in World War II, and was possibly the only person who approved when I joined the Marine Corps on my eighteenth birthday. Just before I shipped out to Vietnam he gave me a twisted bullet that had been taken from his brother's leg after a skirmish on the Golan Heights. When I came back—roughly in one piece—Max encouraged me toward my job in the Portland Police Department, which had lasted fifteen years. He was less enthusiastic about my current livelihood.

"What about you, Adam? When are you and Alison going to tie the knot?"

I mumbled into the wind and gunned the Chevy's powerful V8 engine. The mid-June sunlight was warm and bright on the eastward route beyond the Columbia River valley. Unfortunately, the landscape in eastern Oregon near the Idaho border consisted mainly of farms and bland rolling hills which offered little fuel for diversionary topics. Still, I tried. "Hey, look at that old sod house. Probably built by the original settlers."

"Seen one sod house, seen 'em all," Max said. "So, what's the deal with you and Alison? You love her, don't you?"

"Very much." Alison Brooks was the light of my life, also the owner of Brooks Art Gallery, where many of my sculptures were displayed and sold. If she'd wanted to get married I could have been coerced, and we'd danced around the nuptial issue more than a few times.

"You're not getting any younger, you know."

"Thanks for reminding me. What's your point?"

"What about the children?"

"Whose children?"

"What am I talking about here? First the marriage, then

the children. The offspring of you, Adam McCleet, and
the incredibly gorgeous auburn-haired Alison. Lemme tell
you, if they got her looks, they'd be some handsome kids."

Panic tied my larynx in a knot. Marriage was one thing.
But children? I'd never been particularly fond of toddlers,
infants scared hell out of me, and I didn't even want to
think about purple-haired teenagers with Spiderman tat-
toos and pierced nipples.

"Urk." I pressed the accelerator to the floor and shot
past a semi on the narrow two-lane highway.

"It's time," Max said. "Are you making decent money
with this artsy schmartzy career of yours?"

"Decent enough," I said.

"God forbid you should settle down and give your
mother grandchildren. What are you scared of?"

"Genetics," I responded. "What if they took after
Margot?"

He shuddered. "Good point."

Discussing my younger sister was always a good diversion. The multi-married Margot had been an attractive
little girl who grew into a sleek mature woman who wasn't
bad-looking if you were given to thinking that Morticia
Addams was a babe. She gave new meaning to the definition of harpy. Margot the Malevolent struck terror when
she cast her web like a black widow spider, snaring innocent
males and leading them to the slaughter. The only intelligent response was to protect the groin area and run like
hell.

I confided to Max, "She has her eye on Buddy."

"My son? The *putz*?"

For as long as I could recall this had been Buddy's title.
My Son the *Putz*. He was almost my age, only two years
behind me in school. Though tall and lean like his father,
Buddy lacked the Faverman elegance. In high school, his

grades, although better than mine, were unremarkable. He didn't participate in sports or any other organized activity that the school had to offer. But he definitely had something going for himself, because Buddy always had beautiful females clinging adoringly to his bony arm. In high school it was the cheerleaders, the prom queens, and the college co-eds who came into our school to student teach. In later life, he dated perfectly groomed lady lawyers, a couple of film stars, and one renowned queen of grunge from Seattle.

I liked Buddy. He had an unconventional style that never failed to stimulate the creative side of my brain. And his quirky energy always charged my batteries. It was Buddy that Max and I were heading toward. His directions thus far had been easy to follow, all highway.

"I warned the *putz* about Margot," Max said. "Not that he ever listens to his father, but I told him that Margot might come after his skinny *tush* when word got out that he'd bought a country."

"But this isn't really a country," I said. Buddy was in real estate, and always selling chunks of property with names like Windsor Castle Estates or Tiffany Hills or Lakeside in the Desert. "This is another one of Buddy's developments. Condos?"

"The *putz*," Max said darkly, "calls it a country."

I was sure that there was a profit motive behind this development. That was another of Buddy's talents—if he stepped in dog shit he'd find a hundred dollar bill stuck to the sole of his sneaker when he scraped off the goo. "Why?"

"He gave me this song and dance about how the Favermans are the lost tribe of Israel that swam across the Atlantic and became native American Indians. Such a *putz!* I tell him his great-grandpa emigrated from England. But does he listen to me? No. He thinks he's some kind of *f'kactka* Hoolahoop Indian or something." Max looked up as if addressing his question to God or to Selma. "And what does he call this country?"

"What?" I asked.

"Bob."

"Uh huh." Bob wasn't a name for a country. Bob wasn't even a good name for a fast food franchise or a haircut. I figured Max was setting me up for a joke, and I didn't want to step on his punch line. "Did you say Bob?"

"You got it. Bob. Not even Robert. The *putz* is worrying me, Adam. He's on and on about Bob like it's really a separate nation, offered to make me the ambassador, but he hasn't even got a decent phone line for me to call him back."

"Seriously. Bob?"

"As in bob up and kiss my wrinkled ass. I should think Selma would want me to check out her only male child."

"How are the girls?" Buddy had two older sisters, both married and active in Portland charities.

"How should they be? They're fine." He sighed heavily. "Thanks for driving me all the way out here. I would've come alone, but I had this cataract thing on my left eye, you know?"

I knew. Max's physical condition was incredibly good for a man his age, but some of the more vulnerable parts were beginning to wear out. I had to wonder if this whole Bob scenario was a result of hearing loss. Though Buddy generally operated on a high weirdness frequency I'd never known him to take on a venture that lost money, and a country named Bob sounded about as lucrative as investing in Beta videotapes.

A metal sign, similar to the standard green highway

markers except that the background was purple, indicated the turnoff.

"Bob next right," I read. The sign said: Bob. Maybe there was nothing wrong with Max's hearing.

"The sun is bothering my eye," he said. Taking off his dark glasses, he replaced them with a black patch over the left eye. "What do you think?"

"Very dashing. You look like Moshe Dayan."

After about four miles on the graded dirt road we came upon a gated chain-link fence with barbed concertina wire stretched across the top. A small, red and white striped guardhouse stood next to the gate. A sign on the gate, resembling the great seal of the U.S., read: Independent Republic of Bob.

I parked at the gate and honked twice.

The beefy guy who emerged wore beige camouflage, similar to the combat fatigues used in Desert Storm. It was a uniform of sorts, probably the latest in wacked out paramilitary gear. On each shoulder there was a winged insignia. Beneath the discreet but noticeable row of decorations on his chest was a name pin that spelled out VAN GLOCK in capital letters. He had a black beret, wrap-around sunglasses, and an AK-47 slung over his shoulder with a leather strap.

"Welcome to Bob." He swaggered over to my side of the convertible. "State your business."

As a general rule, I try to be courteous to anyone who carries an automatic weapon. I grinned.

Max was incensed. "My business is none of your business."

"It is if you and your partner plan to enter this country, pops."

"Now you're calling me pops?" Max unfastened his

seatbelt and tilted sideways in the passenger seat so he could better focus his eye. "Who told you to call me pops?"

"I calls 'em like I sees 'em."

"Me, too." Max's eyeball glared. "So you won't mind if I call you shit-for-brains."

The pseudo-soldier made a rumbling noise in the back of his throat, and I figured it was time to defuse the situation before Max bolted from the car and strangled Van Glock with his own rifle strap.

I said, "We're here to see Buddy Faverman. This is his father."

"Buddy never said nothing about no father."

"Use your last living brain cell," Max said. "You think the *putz* was hatched from a turtle egg? Of course, he's got a father. Me. God help me, I am father of the *putz.*"

"Nobody crosses this border without my authorization. You two birds look like undesirables. Therefore, your entry is unauthorized."

Before I could talk sense to Van Glock, Max leapt from the car. Over six feet tall and solidly built, he was impressive. His steel gray hair bristled like a Brillo pad. Though he wore a salmon-colored Mr. Rogers type of cardigan over a golf shirt, he looked more like a retired prizefighter than a kindhearted grandpa. Actually, both were true. In his youth Max had spent his share of time in the boxing ring. When I was a small boy he'd taught me how to bob and weave, and Max still had the fastest hands I've ever seen. He could catch a fly in midair.

Dignified, Max stated, "I don't need your permission to enter."

"Back off, pops."

"Again with the pops!" With a flick of his arm he

reached out and patted the other man gently on the cheek. Before Van Glock could react, Max had pivoted and was on his way to the gate. "I'll open it myself."

Van Glock whipped his AK-47 into firing position and chambered a round. "This is your last warning. Don't touch that gate."

"Whoa." I climbed quickly out of the car. A goofy situation had suddenly escalated to lethal, and I had to do something. "There's no need for that," I said. "Can't we all just get along?"

Slowly, Max turned to confront him. With the eye patch and the scowl on his lips, he looked like a bloodthirsty pirate.

"You're going to shoot me, you Nazi shmuck?"

"I will shoot."

Carefully, Max unbuttoned his sweater. A little smile curled his lip. I could hear him humming, "It's a Beautiful Day in the Neighborhood."

"Max," I called to him, "don't push it."

"Who, me? I'm just a little old man. But this person? This person needs a lesson." He raised his eyebrow at Van Glock. "What do you say? Put down the gun and I'll show you a thing or two."

"You're on, pops." Van Glock's naturally ruddy complexion was beet red. If Crayola had a color in that shade, it would be called heart attack. He propped the gun against his guardhouse wall, yanked off his beret, and spun around. Crouching, he made an impatient "come on" gesture with his hands.

Max circled around him.

I assessed the situation. Though Max was quick, he was a few years past seventy. Van Glock, moving with the delicate grace of a drunken rhino, looked clumsy but dangerous. I didn't want Max to get hurt.

"Let's calm down. How 'bout we just call Buddy and straighten this whole thing out?"

Max slapped Van Glock twice. When the younger man charged, he lightly stepped out of the way and kicked him in the butt as he passed by. Then he offered advice. "Always protect the *tush.*"

"Okay, Max," I said. "You've made your point."

"Stay out of this, Adam."

He feinted like a matador, tripping Van Glock as he made his next blundering advance. This time, however, the trigger-happy guard doubled back quickly. He caught hold of the back of Max's collar.

"Watch the fabric," Max yelled.

"Watch my ass."

Ducking, Max pivoted to face him and grabbed him by the lapels. They were locked in a strained embrace, snarling in each other's faces.

I sighed, went over to the AK-47 leaning against the guardhouse, picked it up, and fired a three round burst into the dirt. "Playtime is over." I held out my hand toward Van Glock. "Phone," I said.

"No."

"If you don't give me the phone I'll put a couple of rounds through the steel toes of your boots."

"Those aren't steel toes," Max said, his expertise in the shoe business coming to the fore. "Not even well-constructed. I bet they leak like a son of a bitch in the winter. Am I right?"

"Yeah," Van Glock admitted.

"I could give you some advice on footwear."

"I'm listening."

"Phone," I repeated.

Van Glock grasped the modular phone, punched in three numbers, then rudely tossed it toward my feet. From a distance, I heard a high-pitched whine which, I assumed, had been triggered by the numbers Van Glock coded into the phone. No doubt an alarm was sounding in the land of Bob.

Max continued his conversation with the paramilitary Van Glock. "No wonder you move like a crippled bear. Your feet hurt?"

"Sometimes."

"I could fix you up with decent boots," Max offered. "For you, wholesale."

"Yeah? How about boots for the rest of my men?"

"There's more of you?"

"Eighteen," Van Glock said proudly. "Protectors of Bob."

And here they came. Careening down the road from the forest was a HumVee. Three men in camouflage fatigues stood on each running board on either side, clinging to the rollbar and trying to balance their weapons while keeping their berets on their heads. They looked like a military version of the Keystone Cops.

Van Glock held out his hand. "Gimme my gun."

"Only if you promise not to shoot yourself in the *tush.*"

"Now," he demanded.

The odds on escaping eighteen paramilitary loons who appeared to be heavily armed were not good. I had no choice but to hand the weapon back to Van Glock.

He snatched the rifle and glared at me. "You pissed me off, mister. Think you're pretty smart, don't you?"

"Not necessarily pretty," I said.

The troops spilled out of the HumVee. Tripping over each other, they lined up on the opposite side of the fence in a formation that looked like pins at the end of a bowling alley. A flying wedge? What the hell kind of strategy was that? When the going gets tough, the tough shoot each other in the back?

The man in the front was skinny and gawky, with a droopy face and bulging eyes. Smartly, he took two wide paces forward and juggled his rifle so that he could salute without shooting himself in the head. I recognized him immediately. He'd been a security guard at a hotel in Seattle where I'd had some trouble a couple of years ago. "Fishman," I said. "Is that you?"

His eyes bulged even further. "McCleet?"

Van Glock thundered, "Sergeant Fishman! Do you know this man?"

"Yes, sir. He's a sculptor." Fishman's loose lips drooped into a frown. "Or a Secret Service agent."

I groaned, regretting for the ten thousandth time that little white lie I'd told Fishman about my affiliation with national security protecting then Vice-president Quayle.

"Secret Service." Van Glock sneered. "We don't much care for government agents around here."

Max beamed at me. "Is this true, Adam? Are you back in the law enforcement business?" He turned to Van Glock. "Ten years, Adam was in the Portland Police Department."

"A cop." Van Glock spoke in a disgusted tone that another person might have used to say: a cockroach. "I hate cops."

"That's right," Max continued. "Maybe you should think about that before you give him trouble. My friend, Adam McCleet, he knows people."

"Please, Max," I said. "Don't help me."

"You're under arrest, McCleet."

Van Glock unlatched the gate and the troops, led by Fishman, circled around me. I had the feeling we weren't getting set for a game of dodge ball.

"What are the charges?" I asked.

"Spying and counterintelligence."

Chapter Two

This wasn't the first time I'd been incarcerated. Ever since I left the Portland PD, my position with cops and other authority figures could be described in two words: Spread 'Em. I wasn't comfortable with the idea of being locked up, especially not in Buddy's new nation, where the legal system probably made as much sense as a country named Bob.

Fishman drove me, handcuffed, in my own car to the jailhouse, a shiny Air Stream trailer in the middle of a forest clearing. Nearby, a couple of trucks were parked outside another long flat-roofed building, probably a bunk-house for the militia. A couple of them, dressed in camouflage, sat in lawn chairs, playing with their guns and listening to the radio, which was tuned to a station which was appropriately named K-BOB.

The husky voice of a female DJ said, "I'll be here with you, for your intense listening pleasure, until five o'clock. Then we'll be taking a break for the funeral of Roger Engersoll. Y'all come. Old Rog is the first death we've had here in Bob, and everybody should turn out to pay their respects."

"Party on," I said to Fishman.

"What?"

"The funeral." I nodded toward the radio.

Fishman scowled and pointed me toward the trailer. "This way."

The female announcer continued, "This is Vikki Ramone on station K-BOB with an uninterrupted half hour of Wayne Newton's greatest hits. Sing it, Wayne."

At the end of the narrow hall inside the trailer was the holding cell, formerly a bedroom. There were heavy iron bars bolted across the tiny windows, presumably to keep any midget miscreants from staging a jailbreak. The real punishment in this low-ceilinged room was the decor: paisley foil wallpaper, matted orange shag carpet, and a leopard print blanket at the foot of an aluminum frame camping cot. Warmed over disco.

As Fishman unlocked the cuffs I asked, "Can I use the bathroom?"

"Oh, I don't think so, McCleet. My recollection is that you're a slippery one."

I handled the situation with my usual stoic maturity. "If you don't let me use the bathroom I'm going to pee on this god-awful carpet."

Consternation flooded his face. Once he'd been a nervous little man in charge of hotel security. Now he was a nervous little paramilitary wing-nut with an automatic rifle.

"Okay," he said, backing down the narrow hall and

pointing toward a minuscule toilet. "But I'm going to stand right here and keep an eye on you."

"Whatever blows your dress up." I went to the bathroom and unzipped. "So, Fishman, tell me about Bob."

"I shouldn't be talking to you."

"What about interrogation? Isn't that part of the job when you arrest dangerous criminals like me?"

"I don't really know. I've only been here for two weeks."

"And you're already a sergeant. Way to go."

"I had experience," he said. "Also, enough money set aside to buy my own plot of land."

I suspected that the second qualification carried more weight than the first. "And you haven't arrested anybody in two weeks."

"Only one perp." Fishman loved his cop speak. "A public nuisance. But when he sobered up, we let him go."

That sounded like par for the course in law enforcement: Serve, Protect, and Babysit the Drunks. "How'd you end up in Bob?" I asked.

"About six months ago I saw a flyer at the place where I take target practice. Elite Commandos Wanted, it said. And I was getting pretty darned frustrated at the hotel."

"Are you guys survivalists?"

"Oh no," he assured me. "We're law-abiding, and we don't mean to harm anybody."

"Hence the machine guns," I said.

"I have an inalienable right to bear arms. Are you done?"

I nodded and obediently went into the bedroom, where I stretched out on the cot and closed my eyes against the glare of the wallpaper. As I always did when in a prone position with nothing else to do, I thought of Alison, her smooth skin and her thick auburn hair. Before I could really get into a fully developed fantasy of a black lace bra, matching garter belt, silk stockings, and three-inch high heels, the door to my holding cell swung open and Buddy Faverman strolled in.

He was casual to the point of boredom with a cigarette held between his thumb and third finger. His eyebrows, not yet as ferocious as those of his father, were cocked high above his round, silver-frame eyeglasses. Though Buddy was in his forties his lanky body had changed very little since high school, and I wondered again why beautiful women went crazy for this guy who dressed like an unmade bed in baggy corduroy slacks and stretched out T-shirts.

"Adam." He stood over me, peering down, and I couldn't help staring up into his cavernous nostrils. His nose had always been his most prominent physical feature, as far as I knew.

"Buddy," I said.

"You look like shit. Have you been taking your medication?"

"Whenever I can get it." I sat up on the cot. "Where's Max?"

"I left him in capable hands. Her name is Vikki Ramone."

"The radio announcer?"

"The very one."

"What's with the Wayne Newton?"

"I said she was capable, not tasteful." He glanced toward the door. "Let's get the hell out of here before the carpet attacks."

I followed him down the narrow hall to the exit. As we stepped into the sunlight Fishman and two other guards snapped to attention and performed a salute that looked vaguely like the hand motion of the giant neon cowboy who welcomes the suckers to Reno, a touch of the eyebrow and a wave.

"Sir," Fishman said.

Wincing at the official tone, Buddy inclined his head toward Fishman. "Is that me? Sir?"

"Yes, sir."

"How about you call me Buddy?"

"Okay, Buddy sir. We have orders from Commander Van Glock not to release the prisoner."

"And you're familiar with the concept of bail?"

"Sure."

"That's what I'm doing. Bailing out this wretched male-factor. He's my responsibility now."

"Yes, sir," Fishman stammered, "B-b-buddy."

Shaking his head, Buddy steered me away from the aluminum trailer toward a waiting Beamer. "We're going to have to get some laws around here. You know, Adam, you've had experience as a cop. Maybe you could help out with making up laws and procedures and stuff like that."

"No thanks."

I slid into the passenger seat and reveled in the cool of air conditioning as Buddy drove through the forest on a winding two-lane road of graded gravel. The eastern border of Oregon was far more arid than the coast or the magnificent Columbia River gorge. Vegetation on these rolling hills was scrubby, and dust hung in the air. "Okay, Buddy. Tell me about this country."

He lit a cigarette and exhaled long streams of smoke. "I sent Max a prospectus."

I couldn't remember ever hearing Buddy call his father anything but Max. "Apparently," I said, "Max didn't read it. He was worried about you."

"Don't give me guilt, Adam. It didn't work with Selma. And it won't work with you."

"Come on, Buddy. You can understand why your father is concerned. A country named Bob?"

"It's not so much a country as a golden investment opportunity. About fifteen years ago, I bought several lots here, about twelve square miles. Undeveloped land. It was cheaper than Uncle Lou's polyester suits."

When the Beamer crested the hill he pulled over and parked, offering me a panoramic view of a valley where clumps of trailers surrounded a single asphalt paved street with wood frame buildings on either side.

"I paid cash," Buddy said. "I could see potential after the developer showed me architect's drawings of a resort hotel and gambling village he had planned."

"You had to know that gambling was illegal in Oregon back then. Still is, just not so you'd notice."

"It's not illegal here. This land was given to a small tribe of Indians by government treaty. The last known member of that tribe was the developer, whose name, by the way, was—guess what?"

"Bob?"

"Chief Bob. He's been dead for eight years, but the treaty still stands."

This sounded like an obscure loophole. "Are you saying this country, Bob, is an Indian reservation?"

"Technically, yes. Part of the purchase deal with Chief Bob was for me to swear allegiance to his tribe, which I had no problem in doing. I see a lot of similarities between the Jews and the Indians."

Buddy was beginning to worry me. Though I'd never thought of him as an excessively ethical person, this logic was bizarre. "I'm only guessing here, but I'll bet you don't have taxes in Bob."

"Only profit." Buddy ground out his cigarette in the ashtray, cracked the window, and pitched the butt into the forest. "I sell off the lots, plus farming acreage, and the entire profit comes to me. It's a sweet deal, and that's not the best part."

"What is?"

He flipped the Beamer into drive and cruised down the hill. "I'm going to show you, Adam. You came at a good time."

We drove through a cluster of five ratty, beat-up trailers, circled like a wagon train. I couldn't believe that people would actually choose to live there. "What's your water situation?"

"Not bad. It's not the Willamette, but we've got a couple of creeks," Buddy said. "Enough for some irrigation and farming. The groundwater is okay. We've got wells."

"What about power?"

"Our own electrical generators. Propane heaters and stoves."

Though I'm not a fan of big government, I'm aware of life's necessities. A country needs street crews, garbage pickup, postal service, infrastructure. "Have you got any governing body?"

"My first four investors got cheap deals because they wanted to pursue their own thing in a place where the feds wouldn't bother them. Those four plus me are the Council of Bob, so to speak. We run things."

"To pursue their own thing," I repeated. "Are we talking about criminal activities?"

He shrugged. "Let's just say that we're not breaking any of the major commandments."

"Uh huh. And what minor federal regulations are you ignoring?"

"Well, you've already met Van Glock, who's into bearing arms in a way that would freak the NRA. Then, there's Vikki—the woman keeping an eye on Max. She's in charge of setting up the gambling casino. Her payoff is to make

herself the star performer. Then, there's Bambi Stokes.
She's a hemp grower.''

"Hemp? As in marijuana?''

"Whatever,'' Buddy said. "And there's a reverend with
a congregation that believes in polygamy. They call themselves the followers of Gee-Oh-Dee.''

"God?''

"It stands for Geo-political Omni Doctrine.''

Visions of Waco flashed through my mind. "Those religious fanatics can be dangerous.''

"Not this bunch. Their plan is to repopulate the world.
Half of the women are already with child.''

"I've had dealings with pregnant women before. Scary
beasts. One of them commissioned me to sculpt her.'' I
shuddered at the memory of a bulbous creature who could
laugh and cry at the same time. She was stubborn,
demanding, obsessive, and nearly bludgeoned me to death
with a parasol because I didn't have peanut butter in the
studio. "Like I said. Dangerous.''

On the main street of Bob there was no moving traffic.
Pedestrians lined the wooden sidewalk on either side of
the extremely wide asphalt street. Except for the cars and
trucks, it reminded me of a set for an Old West movie.
"High Noon," I said, remembering my favorite Gary
Cooper western.

"Are you crazy?'' Buddy checked his wristwatch. "It's
almost five.''

"Is something happening at five? It looks like these
people are waiting for something.''

"Shit.'' Buddy pulled over to the curb and parked. "I
forgot about the funeral. As a member of the council, I
ought to be involved. You mind?''

"I've got no problem with funerals.''

He climbed out of the car and came around to my side.

At the far end of the town, near a whitewashed church with a short, fat steeple, a crowd dressed in black had gathered in the street.

Wherever Buddy went people greeted him by name. Most of the Bobites were friendly, but others spoke through clenched teeth. All in all, they seemed like a fairly normal group.

Buddy found us a place to stand in the doorway of a shop with the word *Sprouts* over the door. In a low voice, he said to me, "I can't believe I forgot. I felt real bad about this guy's death. Roger Engersoll. He was one of the first people to move here. Kept to himself, and he had a prime piece of property next to the creek."

"What happened?"

"Fire," he said. "It was a wood cabin. We're lucky it didn't spread."

The door in the storefront behind us opened, and an incredible woman carrying a small paper sack stepped through. She was at least six feet tall, and her long black hair fell to her waist. She wore cutoff jeans, high-top black sneakers, and a lowcut T-shirt. No bra. I could see cleavage and the outline of nipples on a young, firm set of breasts.

"Hi, Buddy." She hugged him, then turned to me. Her eyes were translucent blue, pale as a waterfall, a little bloodshot. "And who might you be?"

"I might be Adam McCleet," I said.

"I'm Bambi."

"The hemp grower."

"Organic farmer," she said. "Dedicated to the proposition that all Bob should be vegetarian."

"I think so, too," Buddy said. "Except for the meat."

She took the cigarette from Buddy's lips, dropped it to the boardwalk and ground it out under the heel of her sneaker. Then she shook hands with me. She had calluses, which struck me as both incongruous and adorable.

"Are you here for the funeral, Adam?"

"I drove out here with Buddy's father for a visit."

"Way cool." She dug into the sack and pulled out a small bottle. Expertly, she twisted off the childproof cap and tapped out a couple of capsules. "St. John's Wort. It's good for stress. You want one?"

"Sure, why not?" I accepted the pill and swallowed. It was always good to be prepared for more stress.

From the end of the street the funeral procession was getting underway. A man in a black suit played "Amazing Grace" on the accordion. The instrument lacked dignity, but the volume was good.

"You know," Bambi said, "he was murdered."

"Stop that," Buddy said. "It was an accident."

"Yeah? Well, how come the only room in his cabin that burned totally was the bedroom?"

Other people had begun to gawk at us, and Buddy said in a hushed voice, "I've been over this with you before, Bambi. The fire was started by the Franklin stove. It spread to the wall that separated the living room from the bedroom."

"And why didn't Roger wake up?"

"He was in his sixties, and losing his hearing."

She tweaked Buddy's nose. "Why didn't he smell it?"

"The windows were open."

Bambi rolled her eyes. "If he had the windows open, he wanted to cool off. So. Like, why did he have a fire?"

The funeral procession drew even with us. Six men dressed in black carried a poorly constructed pine box at shoulder height. The lid slipped back and forth precariously, threatening to spill open and dump the charred remains of Roger Engersoll right there in the street. Apparently, there were no professional undertakers in Bob.

I overheard a few more whispers about murder. From the brief description Bambi, had given I tended to agree, and I wondered if the council had done any sort of investigation. If not murder, arson seemed like a clear possibility. Did they even have a coroner in Bob?

Though I reminded myself that Roger's death was none of my business and I'd only driven out here as a favor to Max, an unsolved murder bothered my sense of symmetry in the universe.

At the end of the street, the procession made an about-face. A redhaired man wearing a black suit and a clerical collar came to the front of the group. Impatiently, he gestured for the accordion player to stop.

"That's Reverend Mike Petty," Bambi whispered to me. Her breath was warm on my ear.

I remembered Buddy's description: the man of Gee-Oh-Dee. "He is one major cartoon."

His dark eyes stood out in a heavily dotted freckled pale face. His mouth arched in a frown. He waited until he was sure we were all watching, then took a huge breath, puffing out his chest, and spoke in sonorous tone.

"Roger Engersoll was a quiet man. He lived alone. Some say he was murdered. We know he is dead."

Beside me, Bambi stifled a giggle.

The reverend continued. "Today we pay our respects to the first man to die in our chosen country. Though we don't know whether Roger was a Christian or a Jew or a Buddhist, he died a free man in Bob, free from the conspiracies of trilateral satanists who would enslave the earth by implanting ISBN codes at the base of our spines. Even now, they're watching us from their satellites, recording our every deed. And I say to them, on behalf of

Roger and all the faithful dead who will rise from their
graves when Gabriel blows his silver horn, I say to the
forces of evil—Beware. For the followers of Geo-Political
Omni Doctrine are ready for your assault, and we shall not
perish. Amen."

Dramatically, he bowed his head.

There was a smattering of applause.

I leaned close to Bambi and whispered, "Cuckoo."

The accordion started again, playing "Onward Christian Soldiers" as the funeral procession returned to the
church. When they had passed, the Bobites returned to
what I presumed were their daily activities—mostly jump-
ing into their cars and trucks and driving like lunatics
along the asphalt main street, which did not have a center
dividing line or marked slots for parking at the curb.

Bambi dug into her paper sack again and pulled out a
small plastic bag with green stuff inside. She took a single
leaf, placed it on her tongue, and chewed thoughtfully. "I
still say it was murder, Buddy."

"How about a motive?"

"How about this? He left his land to the reverend."

Buddy sighed. "What do you think, Adam? You were a
cop. Does this sound like murder?"

I bit my tongue. The smart thing was to say nothing
and avoid getting involved, but Bambi was watching me
with rapt attention, as if she really cared about my opinion.
"If there's any question, you should investigate."

"Are we talking fingerprints?" Buddy asked. "Because
after we got done putting out the fire, the cabin had been
tromped to shit."

"You could still take statements from witnesses," I said.
"You could call in an arson investigator."

"Wow," Bambi said. "I never thought of that stuff."

Encouraged, I continued, "The most important evi-

dence is, of course, the corpse. A pathologist could tell
you exactly how and why Roger died."

"He was charbroiled," Buddy said. "The cause of death
was fire."

"Okay, but maybe he was unconscious before the fire
reached him. Or maybe somebody tied him down so he
couldn't get away. An expert could tell you."

"Excuse me," Buddy said. "You think we've got a spare
forensic pathologist hanging around in Bob? We don't
even have a regular doctor."

"Who signed the death certificate?" I asked.

"We need a certificate?"

Buddy was so far beyond the realm of proper procedure
that he wouldn't find his way back with a map. "There's
a lot of stuff you have to do in the case of any death, much
less a possible wrongful death. If you contact the Oregon
criminal investigation department, they can help."

"We're not part of Oregon," Buddy said.

"Does Oregon know that?"

"We've sent them notice. They don't respond. Therefore, we are a nation by default."

"A separate nation," Bambi said. She took a few strides
away from us and waved cheerfully, sending tremors
through her grapefruit-size breasts. "Catch you guys later."

"The delivery is today," Buddy said. "In a few minutes."

She flashed a white-toothed grin. "I'll stop by."

The backside of Bambi walking away was nearly as entic-
ing as the front. "Very nice," I said.

"Yeah, she's something to look at," Buddy said. "She
tastes like peaches."

Of course, he would know. He was probably having an
affair with Bambi. "You and a vegetarian? I don't get it.
You smoke, you drink, and you eat everything. Why do all
the women go crazy for you?"

"What can I say? It's the Faverman curse."

I fell in step beside him, and we proceeded down the main street of Bob. There was a quaint saloon with swinging doors, a cafe named Mom's, and a general store. The storefronts lined up in a coordinated style. "Who designed this street?"

"It was Vikki's idea. When she's not doing neon and spangles which, I might add, she does very nicely, she's got a nice sense of kitch. You think this is homey?"

"Cute," I said. We'd come to the church at the end of the street. On the opposite side, surrounded by an ocean of parking lot, was a warehouse-size structure with no windows. "What's that?"

"The Thunderbird," Buddy said. "The future casino."

"I assume the hotel goes on the other side. How are you getting all this stuff constructed?"

"Give me a little credit, Adam. I've been in real estate and development for twenty years. I hired contractors. Some of them even settled here."

"What's your population?"

"Two hundred and seven, with more arriving every day. After the first five investors, I upped the land prices significantly."

"And you own all the land?"

"Every inch. I've only got twenty more lots on level ground, then I start selling the rock pile right up to the border of the Wallowa Forest."

He stopped in front of a neat wood frame building with white siding. On the front, there was an impressive double door. "You know, Adam, I'd give you a deal if you wanted to live here. We could use a former cop."

"I'm retired from that business."

He didn't let that stop his sales pitch. "So, be an artist.

We don't have an artistic element, and you could set the standards."

Though I was a long way from the upper echelon of sculptors, I had a fair enough reputation and I made a living. I really didn't need to be a big man in Bob. "I don't think so, Buddy."

"Wait until you see what I've got planned. There's some serious money to be made here. Big bucks, and I'm not talking about deer which Bambi wouldn't eat and Van Glock wouldn't hunt without a bazooka."

He fitted a key in the front door lock of the building, pushed it open, and stepped aside so I could enter.

Inside, the walls were matte white. The only windows were high, at the edge of the fifteen-foot high ceiling. Buddy flicked a switch and fluorescence shone down on walnut wainscotting, matching desks with computers, and a long counter. In spite of the plain looking exterior this was a modern, attractive office.

I was intrigued. As always, Buddy had offered just enough information to raise questions without giving away the ultimate surprise. This emphasized something I'd known about him since high school. To the naked eye, Buddy appeared to be an average nerd, but he had the heart of P.T. Barnum.

With his long, spidery legs he stepped onto a chair, and from there to the center of the counter. He spread his arms, encompassing the room. His eyes, behind his round glasses, were wide and excited.

"Welcome," he said, "to The Bank of Buddy."

Chapter
Three

I've never pretended to be a master of high finance, but there had to be more to opening a bank than putting up a building and a counter. The Bank of Buddy reminded me of an elaborate version of burying cash in the backyard in tin cans.

Buddy was still standing on the countertop, posed like a monument to himself but much more animated. He tippytoed to the end and back again, raised his skinny arms over his head, and shimmied. "I'm going to be so fucking rich!"

"You can't just call yourself a bank," I said. "You've got to have something to back up the money. Isn't there some kind of gold standard, a federal depository?"

"Not in Bob." He hopped down. "That's the beauty part."

With more energy than I'd ever seen from him, Buddy loped to the rear wall behind the desks. He yanked open double oak doors to reveal the stainless steel door to a walk-in safe.

"What's the first thing a civilized nation does?" he asked.

"Schools," I guessed.

"Nope."

"A library? A hospital?"

"You're hopeless, Adam. Don't even guess. I'll show you in just a minute."

After a few cranks of various knobs and dials on the face of the safe, he flung open the door. Then he checked his wristwatch and went to the rear of the bank.

His wild-eyed enthusiasm was having an opposite effect on my mood, or maybe it was the St. John's Wort that Bambi had given me. In the pit of my belly I had a growing sense of dismay and indigestion, underlined by the suspicious death of Roger Engersoll. One person had already died. I had an uneasy feeling that there'd be more.

"Ready?" Buddy said. "You're about to witness a milestone in the history of Bob."

"Imagine my delight."

"We should have a holiday for this date. Maybe call it Buddy Day."

At the back door of the bank, he fiddled with locks. He also turned on a computer and pulled up a video image. "Surveillance," he said. "This shows who's at the door. There's also a camera at the front. And a scanner on the roof."

"Thorough."

"Gotta be. It's a bank." He turned toward me and wiggled his eyebrows. His glasses slipped down on his nose. "Are you ready?"

"Do I have a choice?" I felt like a passenger on the Titanic, trying to identify that huge white thing looming in the mist.

Buddy opened the rear door to admit two armed guards, real guards, who came from an armored truck.

"Sir," one of them said. "I don't advise unloading until we have dispersed several individuals in camouflage fatigues. They appear to be dangerous."

"They're on our side," Buddy explained. He stuck his head out the door and yelled, "Van Glock!"

The commander appeared, aggressively shouldering his way past the legitimate guards. "I'm here."

"That's the problem," Buddy said. "I hired this truck and these guys to make the delivery. That's their job. After the delivery, your guys take over guard duty. You got it? *After.*"

Van Glock eyed the other guards suspiciously. "I don't like it. You can't trust outsiders."

"I'll take full responsi—"

"You're damn good at doing that, Buddy. Taking full responsibility. First, you spring this guy from the jail." He pointed at me. "Now this."

Buddy's narrow shoulders lifted in a shrug. "I'm a responsible type."

"So far, you've been real goddamned lucky. But, sooner or later you're going to get your dick caught in a wringer."

"My dick?" He looked down at his crotch. "But I'm so fond of my dick. It's my favorite appendage."

"You just better watch out. You hear?"

"Loud and clear. Now, Van Glock, I want you and your men to disappear for a while."

"I'm in charge of security. You've got nothing here. A couple of cameras, but nothing else. I should set up booby traps around the perimeter."

"Maybe later," Buddy said.

Beneath his black beret, his beet red face twisted in a petulant scowl. "I should be overseeing this operation."

"That's a negative, commander. This is my bank. Bank of Buddy. And we're doing this my way. Otherwise, I tell these guys to go and we forget this whole operation."

Van Glock considered for a moment, then nodded. "If anything goes wrong it's not my fault. I wash my hands of this."

"Fine. I'll call when I want your men."

He drew himself up. "We'll disperse."

"Do that," Buddy said. He was skating close to an insult. Obviously, he didn't take Van Glock seriously, which was, in my opinion, not a good attitude to take with an erratic commando. "Dispersing is a good thing. Very strategic."

"Then," said Van Glock, "we'll regroup for guard duty."

"Regrouping is also good."

As soon as he'd departed, Buddy instructed the men from the armored truck. "Put the cargo in the walk-in safe."

After making sure the area was secure, they unlatched the rear of the truck, where there were two more armed guards. The four of them began unloading heavy canvas sacks, dozens of them, onto the shelves in the safe.

If this was money, I was impressed. If it was Buddy's money, I was amazed. I eased closer, to watch, mesmerized. Was it money? There had to be several million. My immediate reaction was shock, then a cold sweat, then itchy palms. All that money. Was Buddy a gazillionaire?

He pulled a few of the sacks aside and opened them, then called to me. "Come on over here, Adam."

I joined him.

"So," he said, "what's the first thing a civilized nation does? It prints money."

From a banded stack of notes, he peeled off one bill and held it out for inspection. It was orange. In the center was a seal with the likeness of an Indian Chief. In the corners were the numeral one. It said: In Bob We Trust.

"This," Buddy said, "is a bob."

I exhaled slowly, still recovering from the moment when I thought I was surrounded by more cash than I could earn in several lifetimes. "Jesus, Buddy. This is Monopoly money."

"Tomorrow, it won't be. Tomorrow morning, starting at nine o'clock, the residents of Bob will be required to turn in their U.S. currency for Bob bucks."

"There's no way," I predicted, "that you'll get people to give up cold, hard cash for this."

"Au contraire, my brother. All the local merchants have agreed not to accept anything but Bob money, which will also be the only cash recognized at the casino when it opens. Plus, I'm offering them a deal. Double your money. One dollar, U.S., equals two bobs."

He picked up another stack of bills. This one was pink. "There are five bobs in a glock, which is named for our commander. See, it has a cannon in the center. And two glocks in a mike, which is Reverend Petty's first name."

Another stack was blue. The number in the corners was twenty-five. "This is a bambi. I considered decorating with a set of hooters before I settled on a little hemp leaf. A bambi is twenty-five bobs."

A purple stack of bills had a musical note in the center. "A half bob is called a vikki."

Triumphant, he pointed out the color most resembling green. The beak-nosed profile in the center was unmistakable. "A hundred bobs equal a buddy."

I stared at the weird currency. "You can't just print up your own money. There's nothing to back it up."

"Don't be naive, Adam. You think there's enough gold in Fort Knox to cover all the U.S. dollars in circulation? Our monetary system is way out of hand. Thank you very much, Mister Greenspan. Why shouldn't we have our own money?"

There was a hammering at the front door. Buddy checked the surveillance computer. "Ah, we're being paid a visit by the delectable Bambi herself."

He opened the door for her and locked it behind her.

She stood in front of the counter and turned in a complete circle. "Wow. This really looks like a bank."

Buddy came up beside her. "You were expecting maybe a car wash?"

She hugged him and bounced back a few paces. "Can I see how it turned out?"

Buddy gave her the handful of bills which she held up to the light, crinkled in her hand and stroked. "Excellent."

"The fibers in our currency," Buddy explained to me, "are made partly from Bambi's first harvest. Her brother runs a paper mill near the coast, and he agreed to process the hemp, turn it into paper, and have it engraved."

"Let me get this straight," I said. "This paper is made from marijuana?"

"Hemp," Bambi said.

"So, theoretically, you could roll one up and smoke it."

Bambi looked thoughtful. She curled the currency named for her into a tube and eyed it.

"Definitely not," Buddy said. "This is the stuff used to make rope, and you wouldn't smoke a rope."

I was about to contradict him when Bambi said, "Can I keep these two bambis?"

"You'll be my first transaction," Buddy said. "A bambi

is twenty-five bobs. And you get two bobs for a U.S. dollar. So two bambis are twenty-five bucks."

Her shining blue eyes clouded with confusion. "Huh?"

Apparently, math was not her strong suit. But I was willing to forgive her. Her long legs were tanned and firm, but not too muscular. The cascades of black hair longed to be stroked. Bambi was enough to make me give up meat on the spot.

Slowly, Buddy said, "Those two bambis cost twenty-five U.S. dollars."

"Okay." She reached into the pocket of her snug cutoffs and pulled out a roll of cash. She peeled off a twenty and a five. "Here you go."

"The bambis are yours."

"Groovy."

In an aside to me, Buddy said, "One born every minute."

After carefully wrapping her bambis around the roll of real money and sticking it back in her pocket, Bambi looked at me as if she were noticing me for the first time. "So, you were a narc, right?"

"A cop," I corrected. "Not any more."

"Are you moving here? We could use a cop. You know, like to do all that investigating stuff about Roger Engersoll."

"Give it up," Buddy said brusquely. "Roger's death was an unfortunate accident."

She shook her head slowly. "What if it wasn't?"

"What are you saying, my little fawn?"

"If somebody killed Roger, they might kill again. Especially now because we've got all this money stuff going on. As soon as you have capitalism, you have crime."

I wasn't following her spaced out logic. "How do you figure?"

"Agrarian societies where it's all farming don't have robberies," she said. "I mean, why should anybody steal from anybody else when all they need to do is grow some more?"

"And what does this have to do with the murder of Roger Engersoll?"

"The possible murder," Buddy said. "The unlikely murder."

"Greed," Bambi said. "I was thinking about what Buddy said. You know, about motives and stuff. And Roger couldn't have been killed because he pissed somebody off."

"Why not?" I asked.

"He kept to himself. He was kind of grumpy, but not enough so that anybody would kill him. And he wasn't having a sex thing."

Following the way her mind worked was a trip into the tropopause. "What does sex have to do with anything?"

"It has to do with everything." Her smile was sultry. "But Roger wasn't killed by an angry husband because he was having an affair with the angry husband's wife. You know?"

"Are you sure?"

Scornfully, she said, "He was too old."

Buddy and I, two males on the brink of fifty, harmonized. "Not necessarily."

Buddy added, "Mid-sixties isn't old."

"Whatever," Bambi said. "Damn, why don't you guys understand what I'm saying?"

"Try again," I encouraged.

"All this money stuff can only lead to trouble. We're creating a class system where none needs to exist. The dream of Bob is pure and good. We shouldn't pollute our dreams with money."

"But we can't finance our dreams with pinecones and berries," Buddy said. "You like the way the money looks, don't you?"

"It's very cute." A beautiful grin stretched her full lips. Her teeth, despite the lack of carnivorous exercise, were straight and white. "Maybe you're right, Buddy. Maybe the fire was an accident."

"That's better," he said. "Why don't you come over to my place tonight? You can meet my father."

"Sure. I wanted to check on the construction for my house, anyway. The crew isn't making too much noise for you, are they?"

"Not so I'd notice. I'm only home at night." He caught hold of her hand and gallantly lifted it to his lips. "So? You're coming?"

"Yeah, Buddy. And I'll bring brownies."

"I hope you won't be insulted if I make hamburgers?"

"I'll be totally disgusted, you piglet."

But she was still smiling at him. How did Buddy manage this magic act? Why didn't I have women melting over me like hot fudge on a sundae?

He took Bambi by the arm and led her to the front door. "Now, I have to ask you to leave while I get this counted and sign the receipts."

He escorted her outside, then returned to me. "Give me a hand on this, Adam. We'll just do a quick inventory."

Of course, there was no such thing as a speedy count of millions of dollars in fake money, but Buddy was willing to believe that the individual sacks had been properly packed so we could just count the sacks without opening them. "After all," he confided, "this money isn't worth shit outside Bob. If a sack comes up short, I'll just make the adjustment."

He signed off on the acceptance and the armored truck

drove away. After Buddy locked up in the rear, we went to the front door together and exited.

Van Glock and three commandos were waiting.

They saluted.

Van Glock stepped forward. "Reporting for guard duty. Now, here's my plan. I'll leave three men. One at the front. One at the back. One inside."

"Nobody inside," Buddy corrected. "The keys stay with me, and the combination to the safe is locked in my head."

Van Glock glared at me as if this were my idea, then turned to Buddy. Officiously, he said, "My men require internal access to the banking facility in order to protect it properly."

"Translate," Buddy said.

"We gotta get inside."

"No way, Van Glockenspiel. And don't piss me off or I'll hire my own security."

Red-faced, Van Glock issued orders to his men, who trotted like robots to do his bidding. If they were all as incompetent as I knew Fishman to be, I predicted a bank heist within twenty-four hours.

Buddy and I strolled down the main street of Bob. Night had settled and the overhead streetlamps were mostly dark. The boardwalk was illuminated sporadically by the glow from the saloon, which was doing a brisk business, and Mom's cafe.

Buddy was hyped by his windfall of funny money. He talked fast, with lots of arm waving. "Okay, it's all set. Tomorrow is the big switcheroo. Two bobs for every buck. It's genius, Adam."

"I still don't understand how you're going to make any money from this."

"Service charges. To start with, I'll charge a half of a percent for the cost of the cash exchange, which means that for every million dollars I make five thou. Then people need a place to keep their money. Where better than The Bank of Buddy? And I charge on their accounts. Then they need loans and—"

"I get it," I said. "Like Bambi said, it's your basic capitalist pig routine."

"Barbecue my rump and call me Porky." As he climbed into the Beamer he squinted back at the bank, the only place in town where the outdoor lights worked. "Next stop is Casa Del Buddy, otherwise known as Maison d'Faverman or Der Buddy Haus. A humble abode which is not yet on the Life-styles of the Rich and Famous tour."

"It's good to know the Bob bucks haven't gone to your head."

He snorted a laugh. "I miss being around somebody like you, Adam. Somebody who appreciates sarcasm."

"Somebody sane," I suggested. "When you live in a nuthouse, it's hard to avoid the filberts."

"Even harder to not become one of them." He pushed his glasses up on his nose. "Could be that this is a midlife crisis for me. Did you do one?"

I nodded. Quitting my job on the Portland PD and diving headfirst into a new career as a sculptor qualified as a major switch in later life, but I was beginning to think that changing the source of my paycheck was only the beginning. For most of my adult life I'd been face-to-face with violence, first in Vietnam, then as a cop.

But when I was younger it was different. I never really considered myself a part of the horror and mayhem. Whether I was attacking the enemy or chasing the bad guys, it was only a job. I didn't personally know or care about my adversaries. They didn't have faces or names.

I'd changed a lot since then. I was different, more serious. A couple of years ago, I'd witnessed the bludgeoning murder of one of my best friends. I'd watched the death of the man I considered a mentor. The brutality had been personal, and so was my response. My grief came from a dark place in my soul that needed vengeance. When I took after those murderers it wasn't a job. It was almost a passion. My aggression drove me, controlled me. It made me feel alive.

When I was a younger man, I saw death from a distance. Now I was shaking hands with my own mortality and thinking about my tombstone. Maybe I should sit down and make out a will while I was still of sound mind.

"Yoo hoo. Adam?" Buddy snapped his fingers in front of my eyes. "So, tell me about this midlife crapola. What do I expect?"

"Danger," I said.

Buddy was taken aback. "You're talking about some kind of psychological crisis, right?"

"No, I mean danger. When you're really a grown-up, you've got to confront the probability that, someday, you're going to die."

"You think I'm in some kind of real physical danger?"

"It's possible," I said. "You've got a troop of lunatic commandos, armed to the teeth. That reverend, with his eulogy about trilateral satanists, is a prime example of a delusional paranoid."

"How do you know that?"

"It's not a mental stretch. A first year psychology student could see it." I kept going. "Bambi, who is possibly the most fantastic woman I've ever seen, is a space cadet, but she might be right when she worries about how the Bobites are going to handle this new money. People get real hostile when it comes to taking, giving, and protecting wealth."

"But everybody here loves me."

"Uh huh." Was he blind? Van Glock was a time bomb

about to go off, and he obviously hated the dismissive way that Buddy treated him. "Didn't Van Glock just mention something about a dick in a wringer?"

"Merely in jest."

"Van Glock doesn't strike me as someone with a sense of humor," I said. "In my experience, the only reason to walk around with a fully automatic assault weapon is because you want to shoot something or somebody."

Buddy shrugged.

"There's a good possibility," I concluded, "that you've already had one murder here."

"So maybe I should get my *tush* out of Bob while I still can." He plunged the Beamer into gear and took off. "Actually, that was my plan. Right after I make a killing on the Bob bucks, I'm history."

"Don't wait too long. I don't want to be sculpting your memorial."

It was a short drive to Casa del Buddy, a triple wide trailer faced with slate blue siding and white trim. It backed up to a hillside and faced south. There was a wide covered porch and a nice little flower garden that Selma Faverman would have been proud of.

The only apparent drawback that I could see was the development going on around him. The hillside above Buddy's house was being terraced into another lot. Though the bulldozers and backhoes were parked and quiet in the night, I suspected that in the morning there would be serious noise.

"What do you think?" he asked.

"Very nice."

"And you want to know the best thing about this location?"

"What's that?"

"The view." He pointed toward the Caterpillar equipment. "That's Bambi's new place."

"So she'll be on top."

Frankly, I was glad to know that Buddy wasn't living in a ramshackle trailer like most of the Bobites. He wasn't the kind of guy who would be content in cheesy living quarters. Max and Selma had made sure that their children were introduced to the arts, opera, and ballet. From early childhood they knew the difference between Gucci and Kmart.

As soon as we left the Beamer we heard the harmonizing of Vikki Ramone and Max Faverman as they sang, "Oh, What a Beautiful Morning."

Buddy paused to light another cigarette. "This could be a very unfortunate evening. Vikki has the collected works of Rodgers and Hammerstein on karaoke. You remember the freakin' show tunes, Adam? Every family event ended up with Selma banging the ivories and Max belting out, 'There's No Business Like Shoe Business.'"

An unfortunate evening would be the perfect ending to this long day. I concentrated on the bright spot. "When do you think Bambi's going to get here?"

"You're smitten?"

"Of course not. I love Alison. But as a sculptor, I naturally take an interest in the female form."

"Naturally," Buddy said.

"Artistically, she's . . . something." At best, I was rationalizing. At worst, I was lying to myself about my carnal urges regarding an extremely tall, healthy, nubile woman with breasts like ripe mangos. "Are you and Bambi an item?"

"I wish. We're friendly, but I haven't *schtupped* her."

For some reason that pleased me. Not that I was thinking of Bambi that way. Alison was the only woman for me.

"Vikki," Buddy said, "is another story. I was thinking I might give her a nudge toward Max. It'd be good for him to get back into the game."

I doubted that Max would succumb to any woman's earthly charms. He'd been married too long. "Your father seems to think that Selma is watching from beyond the grave."

"She probably is."

When we entered Buddy's house Max was down on one knee. This dashing white-haired gentleman with an eye patch was vigorously singing "Some Enchanted Evening" to a well-endowed platinum blonde wearing painted-on jeans and a gingham bra top that fairly screamed, "Look at us."

Vikki was only the second woman I'd seen up close and personal in the land of Bob, and both of them had astonishing, firm, rounded breasts. I wondered if it was something in the water. Could it be bottled? Could I be the distributor?

She rose slowly, sinuously, and sashayed in her high heeled sandals to the karaoke machine, which she turned off with the stab of a long fingernail, enamelled red like blood. She tossed her head, causing nary a ripple in her short, sassy blond hair.

It was a devil-may-care gesture, but I wasn't fooled. There was a frantic intensity that radiated from her. When I looked closely, I could see the wrinkles around her eyes and at the corners of her lips. She was probably in her late thirties or early forties, and her age worried her. She was walking on a thin tightrope, teetering and fighting gravity every inch of the way.

In a throaty voice she said to Buddy, "Max knows all the words."

"Does he?"

"And he told me that you know all the words, too."

"Sure he does," Max said. "His mother and I took him to all the Best of Broadway at the VFW. He used to get dressed up in a little sailor suit and sing 'Yankee Doodle.' "

"You told me," Vikki said to Buddy, "that you didn't know the words, and that's why you wouldn't sing along with me. God, Buddy. Did you have to lie?"

"Trust me, Vikki doll," Max said. "It was for the best that you didn't have to sing with the *putz*. Buddy isn't exactly Wayne Newton, if you know what I mean."

"I adore Wayne," she said. "My goal when we open the Thunderbird Casino is to get Wayne Newton for a limited engagement."

"I met him," Max said. "Nice shoes."

Slow and slinky, Vikki surrounded Max. "Tell me." She arched her back. "Tell me all about Wayne."

Max blushed. He was breathing harder than was healthy. His eye bulged, his fierce eyebrows lifted, and I suspected those weren't the only body parts affected by Vikki's blatantly seductive assault. Maybe I'd been mistaken about Max Faverman's readiness for sex.

When he cleared his throat, his Adam's apple jogged up and down. Softly, he said, *"Oy."*

Since Buddy seemed disinclined to come to his father's aid, I stepped forward. "Hi, I'm Adam."

She patted Max's cheek and turned to me. Her eyes assessed me like a balance sheet. "What do you do for a living, Adam?"

"I work with rocks and metal."

Her smile was condescending. "I could tell that you did something physical. Your forearms are well-developed. But what exactly do you do with your . . . rocks?"

Buddy stepped in. "Adam is being modest, Vikki. He

owns a diamond mine in South Africa and a gold mine in Australia.''

She glanced from Buddy to me and back again. Clearly not falling for Buddy's line, she smirked. "And I suppose Adam's last name is Trump."

"Would you believe it?" Buddy asked.

"I don't believe anything you say." She stepped forward and shook my hand. She had a no-nonsense grip. "It's nice to meet you, Adam. And it doesn't matter to me whether you're a diamond miner from South Africa or a sculptor from Portland, like Max told me."

All in all, I thought Vikki was a perfect match for Buddy. Cynical, nervous, and acquisitive.

She followed him into the kitchen, where they made plans to burn some meat before Bambi arrived. I sat on the fawn-colored leather sofa beside Max.

He leaned back and closed his eyes. "That girl makes me feel like I'm sixteen again. Such a beauty. Like a rose waiting to be plucked."

"Trust me, Max. She's been plucked."

"You think she and Buddy might get together?"

"I think they already have."

"This is going to sound crazy, but she reminds me of Selma. When she was young, my wife was a looker." He opened his eye and nodded at the ceiling, where Selma apparently resided. "Not that she wasn't always a handsome woman, even when she was over seventy."

"Selma was over seventy?"

"You didn't hear that from me," he said.

"Of course not."

"I'm old, Adam. Getting older every minute. I'd like to see the *putz* find a good woman. Is it too much to ask that I see my only son married and settled down before I die?"

Being unmarried and unsettled myself, I couldn't drum up much enthusiasm. "Probably not."

Max glared. "Look who I'm asking. Mister Peter Pan. Am I losing my mind?"

"A rhetorical question."

He closed his eye again and sighed. Resting quietly, Max Faverman was a pale shadow of the vigorous man who had slap-boxed Van Glock and sung show tunes with Vikki. When he dropped the facade, I could see his age. He was tired but peacefully resigned, as if he were ready to pack up his bags and follow Selma into the last good night.

"Nineteen sixteen," he said.

"What?"

"That was the year Selma was born. When I die, I want you to put her year of birth and death on her gravestone. People should know she lived a long life."

Again with the tombstones and thoughts of mortality. This was becoming a major theme for me, a depressing one, and it gave me another reason to be pleased when Bambi showed up on the doorstep with an eggplant casserole and a tray of brownies.

Given Buddy's earlier prediction, the evening progressed pleasantly. Vikki was a skillful hostess, frequently refilling the wineglasses. Everybody laughed at Buddy's jokes and listened politely when Bambi launched into a plea for protecting the spotted owl. We even sang a chorus of "Oklahoma!" with the karaoke machine.

Buddy was in the middle of his version of *The King and I*'s "Shall We Dance?" when we heard cars pulling up outside.

"Shall we belch," he sang. "Burp, burp, burp. On a bright cloud of—"

"Buddy," Vikki interrupted. "There's somebody at the door."

"Who cares?" He sang, "Shall we fart?"

"Buddy! It's Reverend Petty and some other people."

"Shall we clap? Tum, tum, tum. Who's got clap? Tum, tum, tum."

Vikki opened the door. Reverend Mike Petty, still wearing his black suit and a clerical collar, braced himself in the doorway. With one hand on either side of the door frame, he looked like Samson ready to push down the beams supporting the house.

"This time," he intoned, "Van Glock has gone too far."

Chapter Four

A group of followers stood behind Reverend Mike Petty on the doorstep, nervously twittering among themselves. Two of the women were hugely pregnant. Though it seemed only courteous to invite them inside to sit down and plead with them not to go into labor, I understood Vikki's hesitation. Led by the redhaired reverend, this crew couldn't be anything but harbingers of bad news.

Buddy was, however, oblivious to the signals of impending disaster. "Rev! Come on in. Bring the flock."

Buddy introduced me and his father to Petty, who greeted Max first, then turned to me. He sandwiched my hand between both of his and made disconcertingly direct eye contact. In spite of his red hair, his eyes were dark, almost black. His voice modulated to a low level so only I could hear. "Pleased to meet you, my son."

Earlier in the day, Max had been outraged when Van Glock called him pops. I had the same instantaneous antipathy to being called son by a man who was probably younger than I was.

When I tried to pull my hand away, he tightened his grip.

"I sense that you're troubled," he said. "We live in treacherous and problematical times."

"I've got no problems, Petty."

"Perhaps . . ." he dropped in a long, overly dramatic pause, ". . . you live in Portland?"

"So?"

Petty continued, "Within the year your city will be attacked by the infidel submarines of the Ayatollah's navy and enslaved. The assault is already underway, and has been approved by the supreme highest levels of our own so-called government."

Though I should have expected something nuts I was blindsided by the breadth of his weirdness. "Huh?"

"They're working with the Red Army out of Tiajuana," he said. "I have documented proof of involvement, including a photocopy of a memo from the Attorney General and the Joint Chiefs."

"Why would our government agree to—"

"Black gold, as black as the heart of Satan. Oil. Our government wants oil. And you may rest assured that they have already accepted the initial bribes, the bait. Our only salvation is to form our own nations and set about repopulating the earth with enlightened thinkers."

I surmised that this was the rationale for polygamy. "To get as many women pregnant as possible."

"It's our duty."

Decisively, I whipped my hand away from his clammy grasp. Reverend Petty was the scariest kind of fruitcake, the kind that really believes what he's saying.

He remained close to me. "Have we met before, Adam? I never forget a face."

"You might have seen mine earlier today," I said. "I was at the funeral."

A feisty looking blonde tugged on his sleeve. "We need to get moving. We need to rescue my husband."

"I'm busy, Lois," the reverend said.

He was beginning to look a little bit familiar to me, a fact that worried me since nearly half of my acquaintances from my cop days were convicted felons. "Are you from Portland, Reverend?"

"I've spent time there."

"Spent time or done time?"

His forehead creased with hostility, but he didn't deny my accusation. "We're all sinners, Adam."

"Tell me about the death of Roger Engersoll. Was it murder, Reverend Petty? I heard that he signed his property over to you before he was burned to death."

"A most horrible fate," Petty intoned. "At least, Roger will be spared the ultimate indignities when the—"

"Reverend!" The blonde, Lois, stamped her foot.

"Let's get this straightened out," Buddy said. He clapped the reverend on the shoulder with a friendly blow that was hard enough to make Petty wince. "So, Petty, you were saying something about Van Glock."

"He arrested one of my elders. Jethro Kowalski. Do you know him?"

"Jethro? I see him first thing every morning. His crew is doing the excavation work on Bambi's property above my house. A big guy."

"A former Seattle Seahawk," said Lois. "My husband."

"Right," Buddy said. "We'd talked about arranging a loan so he could add on to his property. What did Jethro do?"

"His only crime was coming to the door of The Bank of Buddy and knocking."

"What was the charge?" I asked.

"Resisting arrest," Petty said. "Though I did not witness this heinous assault myself, I've heard that Jethro fought back when Van Glock's thugs foolishly tried to handcuff him. As you heard, Jethro is a former professional football player. He weighs over three hundred pounds, and can be quite a handful."

"We've got an easy solution to this problem," Buddy said. "We'll go over to the jail and get Jethro sprung."

"Wait!" Petty raised his hand as if holding back the demons of hell. If the guy was this dramatic in a conversation, he must be hellfire and brimstone in the pulpit.

"What?" Buddy asked. "Why wait?"

"Brother Jethro is not in the jail."

One of the pregnant women started wailing, and Petty went to her, circling her shoulders protectively with his arm. "It's all right, my dear, we'll bring Jethro home to you."

"What about me?" Lois demanded.

"He'll also come home to you," Petty promised. He nodded to another woman. "And you."

Bambi rolled her eyes. "Only three wives? Maybe I should whip up a batch of industrial strength ginseng for Jethro."

The reverend glared at her.

"I have an idea," she said. "Would you ladies like some of my brownies?"

"Shame on you," Petty snapped. "These women are pregnant. They shouldn't indulge themselves."

"How about it?" Bambi asked them. She picked up the tray and waved it in front of them. "Delicious. And they're totally organic."

The women were tempted to disobey their leader. Their eyes, barren of makeup, glittered. But they stood together, strong and united. "No, thank you."

"Could we back up a minute?" Buddy asked. "I must be going deaf, because I thought you just told me that Jethro was arrested."

"He was."

"But then you said he wasn't at the jail."

Petty left the women and came toward him. "I went to the jail to have Jethro released, and he was nowhere in sight. Van Glock's men told me that he'd escaped. But I saw evidence of a struggle. There was blood on the ground."

Buddy exchanged a glance with me. "What do you think?"

"You got trouble, my friend, right here in River City."

"Okay," Buddy said, "let's go find out what happened to Brother Jethro, former Seahawk and husband of three."

We poured out of Buddy's house—Bambi, Vikki, Reverend Petty, Max, me, and the flock—determined to rescue Jethro from whatever fate may have befallen him at the hands of Van Glock's overzealous commandos.

As the mob started piling into vehicles, Buddy called a halt, "Wait a minute! Everybody stop!"

Immediately, they halted mid-stride. These might not have been the brightest people on earth, but they were really good at following instructions. As one, they turned toward Reverend Petty for the last word.

"Onward," he shouted. "We must rescue poor—"

"Yeah, yeah," Buddy said. "But let's assume, for starters, that this isn't really a case of persecution but—"

"Persecution! That's exactly what has happened here.

I wonder who, among Van Glock's men, is really a federal agent."

"Maybe nobody," Buddy said. "This could just be a misunderstanding about guard duty."

"All things happen for a reason," Petty said. "Make no mistake, Buddy. There are no coincidences."

Though he stood no more than two feet away from Buddy, his voice projected as loudly as if he were yelling through a bullhorn. Petty's speech was meant to be overheard. It was practically a sermon. He looked skyward, toward the bulldozer on the hill behind Buddy's house, then his eyes darted left and right.

"The recent hurricane in the Bahamas," he said.

"What about it?"

"That was no random weather. The machines that control the precipitation and winds in the Atlantic are located in Iceland."

This was too much for Max. "What kind of nonsense is he spouting? Where did you find this guy?"

"Max!" Buddy interrupted. "Let me take care of this."

"Your father is right," Petty said, far more quietly. "Sometimes my words sound crazy, but remember—above all—I am completely, utterly sane."

Dangerously sane. I had a bad feeling that he knew exactly what he was doing.

Once again, Buddy tried to organize the situation. "All I'm saying is that, until we know what happened we shouldn't create a disturbance. We really don't want to drive twenty cars through town."

"If Jethro has been harmed," Petty said darkly, "there will be an uprising."

"You're not listening," Buddy yelled. "I'm just saying we should carpool. Take only a couple of vehicles through town."

"But the people should be alerted to what has transpired," Petty said. "We must not harbor secret alliances."

"Reverend," Vikki said. "You want justice, don't you?"

"Of course."

"And you want what's best for Bob?"

"Yes."

"Then tonight, you need to be cautious. Tomorrow, after the bank opens, we'll really be a nation with our own separate monetary system. And we'll make our own laws. Our own organization."

Petty nodded his approval.

Bambi added the final note. "We should always seek peaceful solutions to our differences. Like the animals, who live together in harmony."

"Mutant beasts," Petty said.

Given Petty's leaning toward paranoia, I was pretty sure that the word "mutant" was key to another wacko conspiracy theory. Therefore, I was grateful when Buddy pushed for action.

"I suggest," Buddy said, "that we take only three cars and we drive through town at a safe, sane speed. Our destination is the jailhouse. Okay?"

The reverend considered for a moment. His gaze rested on the several pregnant women surrounding him. "That seems prudent."

After a lot of jockeying around, we crammed ourselves into three vehicles. I ended up in the backseat of a Yugo, squished between two largely pregnant women, a blonde, and a brunette. Lois, the most vocal of Jethro's wives, was behind the steering wheel. As far as I could tell, she wasn't pregnant. A man filled the front passenger seat.

Though the Yugo was at the rear of the convoy, Lois attacked the road like Marissa Andretti on acid.

"Spawn of Satan," she muttered under her breath.

I wasn't sure to whom she was referring, so I kept my mouth shut.

"My poor sweet Jethro," she continued. "If anything's happened to him, there'll be hell to pay."

The blonde on my right said, "You go, girl."

Lois zipped around the last turn before Main Street. Since there were virtually no shock absorbers on the late model Bosniamobile, we jolted over every pebble on the unpaved road and the women on either side of me groaned loudly with every bounce.

"Ma'am," I said to the driver, "you might want to slow down."

Paying absolutely no attention to pedestrians, curbs, and meandering traffic, she whipped around in her seat to glare at me. "Don't you understand? He's my husband, and he needs me."

From what I'd seen thus far, the only thing Jethro needed was a vasectomy. "I'm sure he wouldn't want you to speed. Especially not with other people in the car."

"The Lord will protect me." She turned her attention back to the road just in time to swerve around a couple who were blithely crossing the street with no regard for traffic. "That's what Reverend Petty tells us. We have the Geo-political Omni Doctrine on our side."

"Amen," said the pregnant brunette.

"You go, girl," the blonde repeated.

"Oh, Lord," Lois said. "I wish I'd eaten that brownie."

We caroomed over a huge bump and the backseat maternity ward wailed.

I appealed to the man, another of the Reverend Petty's congregation, who sat in the passenger seat. "Tell her. We need to slow down."

"How come?"

"If we keep bumping around, these ladies are going to give birth right here and now."

"That'd be swell," he said with a particularly stupid grin. "They're both mine."

"You don't want them to go into premature labor," I said. Not with me sitting between them.

"Wouldn't be premature," he said. "Junie, the blonde, is nine months, and Janine is nine months and two weeks. They're in a race to see who's going to be first."

"Why?"

The brunette, Janine, explained, "One of us is going to give birth to the first real natural-born citizen of Bob."

"Hospital," I said. "Don't you want to be in a hospital when you go into labor?"

"I don't need a doctor. The reverend says that in the Garden of Eden Eve didn't have a doctor, and I believe every word he says."

"Even the part about the submarines attacking Portland?"

"Especially that," Janine said. "He's got letters on Pentagon stationary. And there was a real good article in the *Supreme Territorial Imperative*. That's the only newspaper in America that isn't controlled by satanists."

Oh, man, I couldn't wait to get the hell out of Bob.

We'd left the populated area and were weaving through spastic roads that went through the trailer clusters. On the unlighted road, the only directional cues came from moonlight and the taillights of a mini-van in front of us.

The Yugo driver sped up to pass him.

"No!" I yelled.

"My husband needs me."

She swerved wildly to the right, completely misjudging the width of the road. The Yugo clung to the edge, wobbling precariously on the shoulder, then careened into the ditch at roadside. Our forward momentum continued. The tires tore into the soft earth. With a final pathetic fishtail, the Yugo halted just short of a scraggly pine tree.

The engine coughed, sputtered, and went dead.

The women on either side of me screamed in gulping sobs. Religious decorum was forgotten in a rain of curses that would have made a gangsta rapper blush.

Fortunately, we were all packed so tightly in the backseat that I didn't think any real physical damage had been done by the jostling around. I tried to extricate myself from between the two bulbous women. At the same time, I gallantly offered comfort. "Shut up," I said.

"Fuck you," said the perky blonde Junie.

"You aren't hurt, are you?"

"Not that I can tell."

But I felt a wetness on my left leg. Had Janine been injured? Was she bleeding? I wrenched a shoulder free and turned toward her. "Ma'am? Are you okay?"

She panted like a marathon runner. "My water broke."

"Wow," Junie whispered. "You go, girl."

Though I had heard the phrase, "My water broke," in movies and on television, I never bothered to pay much attention. Now, my trousers were drenched in a flood of viscous liquid. This wasn't good. This was an ocean.

Sticking my arms straight out in front of me, I rammed the front seat. "Let me out."

Both the driver and the husband in the passenger seat had turned around and were making demented cooing noises at Janine.

I roared, "Let me the fuck out of here."

Janine threw back her head and screamed. Her pitch was at least an octave above high C. At the same time, she grabbed my wet leg and dug her fingernails through the material and into my flesh.

I sucked back a scream of my own.

"Oh my Lord," she shrieked. "It hurts."

"It's okay, Honey," her husband said. "You're in labor."

"But it hurts!"

She'd cut off the circulation in my leg, and I was feeling my own pain. Why did it always come as such a big shock to pregnant women when labor hurt?

Her grip subsided. Her mountainous breasts heaved.

I figured I had a few minutes to escape. "Okay, she's relaxing. Let's give her some room."

They all looked dumbly at me.

Speaking slowly, I instructed, "Open the doors. Get out of the car."

They responded. Lois and Janine's husband left the front seat. With some difficulty, Junie then maneuvered until she popped free of the backseat, like a cork from a bottle. I'd almost fought my way to freedom when the next labor pain struck.

Janine grabbed handfuls of my Oxford cloth shirt in her fists and let go with another bloodcurdling wail.

Struggling to get out of the car, I tore the seams on my shirt. The sleeve ripped off as she dragged me back with the kind of strength expected from an Olympic wrestler. Her fingers clenched around my arm like a vise.

"Bastard!" she yelled. "All men are bastards."

It seemed like an unfair generalization, but I wasn't about to argue with her.

When she released me, I leapt from the car.

The night air was cool and tasted good. There was enough moonlight to see the faces of the other three people gaping at me. Without their leader, they didn't have a clue.

The man asked, "What are we going to do?"

"I'll go for help," I said.

"Nope," he said. "That's my job."

He took off running, leaving me with rampaging Lois, a bouncy blonde prego the size of Shamu and a brunette in labor. I looked toward Lois. "I guess you're going to have to help her."

"Me? But I'm not a midwife."

"Neither am I."

There was another scream from the back of the Yugo.

"I heard that you used to be a cop," she said. "Don't they teach emergency birthing procedures?"

Though I had attended several mandatory First Aid classes and was pretty good at dealing with a sucking chest wound, I didn't know "nothin bout birthin" no babies. "Oh, no," I said. "I'm not doing this."

She pressed her palms together and lowered her head. "Oh Lord," she said, "you've sent Mister McCleet to help us. Let him know thy will."

"Don't start," I said.

"For if he refuses to come to our aid," she continued, "poor Janine will surely die."

From the car came a pitiful plea. "Help me. Somebody please help me."

These women were clearly idiots, duped into a mindless reproductive state by the sermons of Petty and a vague fear of being attacked by the forces of Iceland and the Ayatollah. They hadn't even considered the implications of giving birth without medical attention. They were counting on the diety to protect them without thinking that God might be busy elsewhere, maybe tending to lepers.

But I couldn't turn my back and walk away.

"Okay," I said to Lois. "She can't stay in the back of the car. There's no room. Do you have something you can spread on the ground?"

She looked up at me and smiled. "No."

The Yugo had a hatchback. "Open the trunk."

With Lois's help, I got the backseat opened out and Janine turned around so she could lie with her head against the driver's seat and her legs dangling over the rear gate.

She was gasping in some weird pattern.

Reluctantly, I leaned inside. "What are you doing?"

"Lamaze," she said. "This is happening too fast. The other women told me I'd be in labor for hours with my first baby. But it feels like it's ready to come out."

"Not yet," I said.

"Oh, yes. Right now."

Junie piped up, "You go, girl."

When Janine's gigantic body spasmed in another labor pain, I climbed into the rear of the car beside her and held her hand. This wasn't any medical procedure that I could think of, but it seemed to help. Together, we went through another labor pain.

When she'd calmed, I said, "Janine, you're going to be all right. Just hold on. Your husband has gone to get help."

"Not enough time. I want to push."

"Push what?"

"Push the baby out. I've got to."

"No, no. Don't push."

She braced her feet against the rear gate of the car and spread her legs. "It's time."

"You want to wait," I told her. "Just hang on. Come on, we can do this."

"Mister McCleet, I'm scared. I'm not ready to have this baby now. I hate living here. I hate being one of two wives. Junie is an idiot. My hubby is a jerk. How did I ever get into this mess? How could I—"

She broke off in a scream.

I figured that now wasn't the best time for a lecture on why she shouldn't be in Bob following a fruitcake reverend and being married to a polygamous coward. "Everything is going to be okay, Janine."

"I've got to push."

I let go of her hand, climbed out of the car and took a look at the other end of Janine. It was not a pretty sight.

Turning to the other two women, I said, "I could use some help with this."

"Of course."

In unison, they dropped to their knees and began to pray.

Okay, this was my show. My obstetrical debut was in the back of a Yugo with the tire iron to the left and a discarded McDonald's sack to the right.

Gingerly, I touched Janine's thighs. There was something going on down there, but I didn't see a baby.

"Look," Lois said. Excitedly, she pointed. "Here comes somebody to answer our prayers."

In the soft glow of moonlight, I saw a man riding a magnificent white stallion with white tail and mane. He drew to a halt beside us. "You need some help, pilgrim?"

"This woman is in labor. She's ready to push."

"Got it."

He dismounted. In contrast to the horse, he was dressed in loose-fitting black pajamas, like a ninja in cowboy boots. He had dark smears under his eyes and across his forehead, possibly as camouflage. His three-day growth of beard was black with flecks of silver. His eyes were cold and empty.

If I'd met this guy on the street I'd have run, not walked, in the opposite direction. However, right then I would have accepted assistance from an eight-legged alien.

He peered into the rear of the Yugo. "What's the matter with you? That's not even sanitary."

While Janine let out another shriek, he returned to his

horse, a remarkably well-behaved animal, and got a blanket from the saddlebag and spread it on the ground.

Together we lifted Janine from the Yugo to the earth. She was trembling all over. Her dark hair clung to her cheeks in sweat-drenched strands.

The stranger said, "You're going to be all right, little lady. What's your name?"

"Janine. What's yours?"

"I'm a friend."

He arranged her legs and soothed her forehead and gave me orders to fetch water from his canteen, another blanket from the saddlebag, a pillow for her head.

Moments later, he gently told Janine that it was time. "This is going to be rough work," he said, "but you can do it. You've got to be strong."

"Okay, friend."

"Now, Janine. Push."

After another three fierce efforts, I could see the baby's head. Janine was yelling, straining every muscle. The stranger gently encouraged her. And the baby slipped out.

He handed the little red creature to me. It was tiny with perfect little fingers and toes. A boy. The arms and legs twitched, and the infant broke into a wail. The little round face twisted as it cried.

"My baby," Janine gasped. "Is it all right?"

I was speechless. The baby had stopped screeching and seemed to look at me through scrunched up little eyelids. It was the most awesome moment in my life.

"Incredible," I said. "It's a boy."

The stranger snipped the cord and tied it while I gave the baby to his mother. She cradled him against her breast while the stranger managed the rest of the job.

"Ladies," he called to the other two. "Get over here and make Janine and her son comfortable."

He stood and faced me. "See you around, pilgrim."

He returned to his horse and mounted. Before disappearing into the forest from whence he came, he turned to me. His voice was low as the wind. "McCleet," he said, "take care of Buddy. He's in danger."

Chapter
Five

Truculent, Junie lumbered over to the new mother and child. The still pregnant blonde lowered her bulk beside Janine. "Not fair," she said, pouting. "You got to be first."

"Look at him, Junie. Isn't he precious? Maybe you'll have the first girl baby in Bob."

"I could." Junie visibly softened as she touched the infant's fingers. Within seconds, she was making goo-goo noises and playfully poking at the baby.

Lois stayed by my side. Like me, she was watching as the stranger on horseback weaved through the trees into the deeper forest. "Who was he?" she asked.

My question exactly. Who was that unmasked man? He knew the basics of delivering a baby, which made me think he had a paramedical background, but he dressed in black

karate pajamas. How had he known my name? Why did
he think Buddy was in danger? "Good thing he showed
up," I said.

"Yeah," she said. "You weren't doing so hot."

I shrugged my shoulders, and the night wind swept
across my mostly naked back. In the throes of labor Janine
had demolished my shirt. One sleeve was completely gone.
My trouser leg was still damp from the fatal moment when
the water broke.

Lois snickered, and I was beginning to detect a mean
streak in her. "You should have seen your face when she
spread her knees and said she was going to push."

"I thought you were too busy praying to see anything
else."

"At least I got results." She pointed toward the forest
where the man on the white horse had vanished. "I prayed
for help, and he came."

Though I doubted that the arrival of our gynecological
saviour was the direct result of divine intervention, I didn't
bother arguing with her. Religious fanatics, especially those
who believe that hurricanes come from a machine in Iceland, are notoriously difficult to dissuade. "With all you
pregnant women waddling around, you might want to find
a more reliable way of contacting that guy."

"Waddling?" She took offense. "I'm four months along,
and you can't even tell. I'll never let myself turn into a
cow. Not like these women."

"You need prenatal care. Aren't you concerned, Lois?"

"A little." She spread her fingers across her belly where
there was a small, barely discernible bulge. "You don't
really think I'm fat, do you?"

From a lifetime of associating with women, I knew there
was only one correct answer to that question. "Of course
not."

But she was still frowning. "We don't need establishment doctors. We help each other."

I'd seen how effective that was. "What about a midwife?"

"We'll learn. How do you think the pioneer women did it?"

"A lot of them died." All these pregnant women walking around were like volcanos on the verge of eruption. "What if there are complications? I don't know much about this, but what about breech births and stuff like that? What if somebody needs a Cesarean?"

"Whatever happens is the Lord's will."

"Horseshit," I said, exercising a blatant intolerance. "If you have access to modern medicine and don't use it, the good Lord ought to consider you too damned stupid to reproduce. How many of you are with child?"

"Eighteen." She planted her fists on her hips. Though she wasn't showing, she had the hormonal insanity of a pregnant beast down pat. "You think you're real smart, but you don't know what you're talking about. We've figured everything out. If there's a serious problem, Van Glock has a helicopter, and he can airlift us to the hospital at Maryvale."

The helicopter was a good start.

Janine called to me. "Adam. Adam, please come here."

Like a shot, I responded to her voice, an instinctual reaction. During the last half hour Janine and I had bonded at a level heretofore unknown in my experience. We'd suffered through labor together. We'd screamed in each other's faces, and I'd seen a human being emerge from her.

I squatted down beside her and she beamed, exhausted but happy. The baby boy wiggled in her arms, already nosing at her breast.

On Janine's other side, Lois joined the blonde, and they harmonized on coochie-coochie sounds.

I smoothed the hair off the new mother's forehead. "Congratulations, Janine."

"I've decided what I'm going to name him," she said.

After me? Aw, shucks, she didn't have to do that. I swelled with undeserved pride. I hadn't done any more than any other standard, red-blooded American hero would have done. I grinned. "What are you going to name him?"

"Bob."

I should have known.

"Isn't that perfect?" she asked.

"Easy to spell," I said. "And he only has to learn one word for his name and his address."

The blonde tickled the little critter under his chin. "You go, boy."

From the direction of the jailhouse, I saw headlights. It was the mini-van. Apparently, Janine's husband, alias the Chickenshit Bozo, was returning belatedly to help with the birthing of his son. I could've cared less about seeing him again, but when the car parked and I saw that his helper was Bambi, I was instantly alert.

She rushed toward our little group. When she saw the infant and his mother, she sighed. "Wow. One of life's miracles."

It pleased me that her whisper was melodic and soft without a hint of goopy baby talk. From her jacket pocket she produced another plastic envelope with leaves in it. She gave one to Janine. "Chew on this. It'll help the pain."

"I don't know if the reverend would approve."

"Trust me on this. It's something only women know about." She stood. "I'm happy for you."

Obediently, Janine chewed. "Thanks, Bambi."

"No problem." She stepped back, giving the father and other wife more room. "You're both beautiful."

"Amazing," I agreed.

I followed Bambi, drawn like the proverbial moth to her flame. Her translucent blue eyes were glistening in the moonlight. "So, Adam, you're a man of many talents. Did you deliver the baby?"

Though I would have liked to bask in her admiration, there were witnesses to refute my story. "I wasn't much help."

"Women's work?"

"Actually, this guy appeared out of nowhere on horseback. He performed the delivery."

Her smile went from soft to megawatt. "A white horse?"

"Do you know him?"

She pulled me aside, several yards away from the others. The night closed around us, and I felt like we were completely alone. I was acutely aware of my ripped shirt and wet trousers. Sucking in my gut, I gave her my full attention.

"Which way did he go?" she asked.

I pointed, and she peered toward the forest as if she hoped to catch a glimpse of the mystery man. Her breath speeded up, and her slender hand rose to her cheek. Though I couldn't discern details in the darkness, I had the impression that she was trying to conceal a blush. I jumped to the annoying conclusion that the mystery man was Bambi's number one fantasy.

"Tell me about him," I said.

"He lives around here, but nobody knows where. Rumor has it that he was a mercenary in Vietnam or an assassin, or maybe somebody from the witness protection program. One of the farmer dudes, a guy who's planting apple trees, said he saw the stranger kill a mountain lion with his bare hands."

"Not a good vegetarian," I said, casting an aspersion. "But way cool."

Of course, his reputation would be macho in the extreme, and I figured that was part of the attraction for Bambi. She was hempish but basically wholesome. It only made sense that she'd have the hots for a bad boy.

If I hadn't been in love with Alison I might have reinvented my own image to suit her ideal. After all, I'd been a marine and a cop. I could slip on the mantle of danger if that was what she liked.

"My baby!" the errant husband loudly proclaimed. "Bob!"

I glanced over my shoulder at him as he babbled delightedly about the honor of having the first Bob citizen, and I experienced a tightening in my chest, something like heartburn. Regrets? I had a few. At my age, it was unlikely that I'd ever have children. Alison and I had talked about it in one of those rambling relationship discussions where the topic of marriage got batted around. Neither of us were real excited about raising a herd of little McCleets.

Fathering was something I wished I'd already done, so I could look back with pride and have heirs to mention in my will.

Recruiting the other two women to help, the new father got Janine to her feet and half-carried her toward the mini-van. They didn't seem to need my help, and I wasn't inclined to offer. Instead, I kept an eye on Bambi, who was still searching the forest for a sign of the mysterious stranger.

"He comes and goes," she said, "like the wind. A couple of times I've seen him at a distance. It was like he was watching over me."

If he was keeping an eye on her, he at least had good taste. "And he doesn't have a name?"

"Once, some of the kids were goofing around in the forest. A little girl tripped over a log and fell. Her ankle was badly sprained. From out of nowhere the stranger appeared, comforted her, and made a splint before taking her to her mother on horseback. Wow." Her eyes were all soft and dreamy. "He told the children to call him Spanky."

That rascal! "Spanky?"

"That's right," she said. "I think he's kind of a spirit guide who comes when we need him."

More likely, he was another anti-government knucklehead lurking in the land of Bob. If he was into spying and surveillance, that explained how he knew my name. He could have been listening outside Buddy's house. "Before he rode away he told me that Buddy was in danger. How seriously does one take a man in black pj's who calls himself Spanky?"

"Duh, Adam! Of course Buddy is in danger. After tomorrow, when he gathers up all the moolah, he'll be the richest dude in Bob." She bit her lower lip, a charming expression of concern. "I'm worried. I want Bob to be a Xanadu, but things are getting way out of hand. First, Roger Engersoll. And now, there's this mess with Jethro."

I remembered. The disappearance of Jethro was the reason I'd gone on the Yugo roller coaster ride with the pregnant women. "What's happening at the jailhouse?"

"A lot of yelling. Basically, Van Glock says that his men told Jethro that they were guarding the bank. He got freaked out, and it took three of them to subdue him. But he escaped before they got him to the jail."

"And Jethro is still missing."

"Right." She was tall enough to look directly into my eyes. "Buddy could use your help right now."

"Buddy could use a straitjacket for even starting this idiotic country."

"Don't be totally hard on him, Adam. He means well."

From what Buddy had told me, he meant to make a killer profit on Bob before the feds moved in and shut the whole thing down, then to move on to other ventures in other venues. It wasn't in his interest to establish the ideal meatless society where marijuana grew free and disillusioned extremists gambled for Bob bucks.

But I didn't inform Bambi of my old friend's cynical agenda. Let her, and the other citizens of Bob, believe that Buddy was their kindly, altruistic banker.

I followed her to the mini-van, where the Bobites had come up with a plan. They would take me, Bambi, and Lois to the jailhouse. Then the husband would trundle home with his wives and new baby boy.

During the ride I gave myself a stern lecture about not getting involved with Buddy's twelve-square-mile domain. Whatever happened in Bob wasn't my problem. Due to my experience with Janine, I had a humanitarian interest in seeing that these morons found a medic to look after them, but that was all. I sure as hell wasn't going to get involved in investigating Jethro's disappearance or Roger's suspicious death.

At the jailhouse, Buddy welcomed me with open arms. "Adam, we've elected you sheriff."

"Not a chance."

"You look like hell. What happened to your shirt?"

I gave him the *Reader's Digest* condensed version: "Dead Yugo. Labor pains. Spanky. The miracle of birth. And everybody lived happily ever after. Have you got a jacket I can borrow?"

Van Glock marched up beside us. "I don't trust you,

McCleet. Not no how. Not no way. I refuse to acknowledge your authority as sheriff."

"Fine, because I'm not—"

"Hold it," Buddy interrupted. "Commander Van Glock, would you excuse me and Adam for just a minute?"

"I don't like this."

Apparently Reverend Petty was similarly disgruntled. Some distance away from us, he stood glaring like the wrath of Geo-Political Omni Doctrine while his congregation crowded around the mini-van to *ooh* and *aah* over Janine's new baby.

Buddy dragged me to neutral ground between Van Glock and the flock. "Here's the deal, Adam. You're the only one around here with cop credentials. If this turns out to be a murder investigation—"

"Stop right there," I said. "If Jethro was murdered, you can't wave your wand and play like all is well in the magical land of Bob. You've already got one probable arson and suspicious death on your hands with Roger. It's time to call in the Oregon Criminal Investigation Department."

"Van Glock would go berserk. He won't even let the Highway Patrol cross the boundary into Bob."

Buddy didn't have to tell me about Van Glock and his sentryhouse. I'd been there, done that, and bought myself an hour in the Bob jail. "Buddy, I've got one word for you—lawsuit."

"It's different here. We've got frontier justice with no attorneys and no courts."

"Yeah? Well, I just spent an hour with Lois—one of Jethro's wives. She might look like a wide-eyed drone following the word of Petty, but she's not an idiot. If her husband has been murdered, there's a chance she'll cross the border and sue your skinny ass for every bambi, buddy, and bob that you have stashed in your bank.''

''I'll make you a deal, Adam.''

''No.''

''If you listen to the facts and think we're really looking at the possibility of murder, you can call in the Oregon CID. I promise.'' His eyebrows raised and he nodded, encouraging me toward lunacy. The glasses slipped down his nose. ''Come on, Adam. I need some support here.''

In spite of everything, I really liked Buddy. I didn't want to see him go down in flames, if for no other reason than I owed it to Max to make sure the *putz* didn't get himself locked up in a real jail. I clarified, ''If there's any reason to believe this is murder, we call the real police. Right?''

''You have my word.''

That was probably worth two vikkis and a glock. ''Okay, I'll pretend to be sheriff. But I have one more condition.''

''Name it.''

''Get me a damned shirt.''

''Done.''

Buddy went to Van Glock, who spoke to one of his men, who returned with a camouflage jacket that was roughly my size. It had been a long time since I'd worn fatigues. I peeled off my shredded shirt and slipped it on. The fabric was slightly starched, the way any uniform ought to be. It felt good against my skin.

Fastening buttons, I joined Buddy and the commander.

Buddy was explaining to Van Glock. ''You and your boys are the commando unit, like the army or the marines. Right?''

''Right.''

''But we also need a civilian authority to handle the everyday infractions, like parking tickets. You don't want your men to waste their time with meter violations, do you?"

"You're saying the problem is jurisdiction," he said.

"Exactly." Buddy lit another cigarette. "You understand?"

"As long as I'm the top man, we're okay." The bright lights surrounding the jailhouse compound shone red on Van Glock's face. "Nobody—especially not this guy—is gonna tell me and my men what to do."

"Absolutely not," Buddy assured him. "Think of Sheriff McCleet as an advisor."

Sheriff McCleet? I didn't like the sound of that, but a promise was a promise. "Let's get started, Van Glock. What happened with Jethro?"

"There was an altercation in town. My men cuffed him," Van Glock said. "When they got here to the jailhouse, they took off the cuffs. Bad procedure. Against my directives. Jethro took off running."

"What did your men do?"

"Fired warning shots over his head, but let him go." Van Glock winced at this breach in the performance of duty. "Even though they should have fired low and disabled Jethro so he could be apprehended, they didn't. Judgment call. My guys didn't want to shoot anybody in the back."

"Honorable," I said. "Which one of your guys fired the gun?"

He stiffened his back. "You talk to me. I'm fully responsible for the actions of my men, even if this was dereliction of duty."

He was stonewalling, the first step in a cover-up. Though I wouldn't have believed it possible that Reverend Petty and I would agree on any subject, I was leaning toward his theory that something unfortunate had befallen Jethro.

I turned back to Buddy. "And Jethro still hasn't been found?"

"He's not at his house. He's not around here."

"Any evidence that he was shot or injured?" I asked.

"There's some dried blood on the dirt near the entrance to the jail," Buddy said. "Petty claims it's Jethro's blood."

Van Glock said, "We slaughtered a deer a couple of days ago. That's all it is."

And, of course, there would be no forensic lab to test the blood. Any kind of investigation in Bob would be right out of the dark ages. "Any other witnesses?"

"Only my men," Van Glock said. "And they all saw the same thing. Jethro running off into the forest."

Like Spanky. If the mysterious Spanky had been bivouacked in this area for several months and had remained hidden, there was no reason to believe that it would be easy to locate Jethro. Much of this land included rocky foothills, and it was thickly forested. Bob's borders adjoined millions of acres of Wallowa National Forest.

"So, Sheriff McCleet?" Buddy said. "What comes next in the investigation?"

"You've got no evidence, no witnesses, and no body. I'd have to say this isn't murder."

Buddy smiled. "Good. No need for further investigation, right?"

"We still have a missing person," I said. "More than likely, Jethro ran off into the forest, and he's hiding out. If he's a sensible man he won't come out until he's sure nobody is going to shoot at him."

"Very good," Buddy complimented. "I've never seen this side of you, Adam. You're a regular Columbo."

"Tomorrow morning," I said, "we'll wait and see if Jethro shows up at work."

"Which will be easy to check," Buddy said, "since he supervises the crew of guys who are working on the hill behind my house."

"If he's not there," I continued, "we gather here and pair off. Then, we search until somebody finds Jethro."

Van Glock clicked his heels together, obviously pleased to have a course of action. "We'll start at zero six hundred hours."

"How about eightish?" Buddy said.

"Eight o'clock," I confirmed. "And if we're lucky, Jethro will come home tonight."

When Buddy presented the plan to Petty the reverend seemed oddly cooperative, which made me think he had something to hide.

The only objection came from Vikki. "The bank is opening tomorrow. We can't be out here, *schlepping* around in the woods. Everybody has money to exchange. This can't wait."

"Shame on you," Petty thundered. "Shame, sister. Our monetary system is unimportant compared to the life of one of our brethren."

"Your brethren," she snapped. "I don't even know the *schmuck!*"

Lois stomped forward. "How dare you call my husband a *schmuck!*"

"Ladies, please." Buddy stepped between them. He was a far braver man than I. "It's late. We're all tired."

"Schmuck," Vikki hissed. *"Schmuck, schmuck, schmuck."*

"Bite me, sister."

"Nice talk."

Their catfight was interrupted by the popping of distant gunfire. Van Glock's mobile telephone sounded and he answered, "Commander Van Glock here."

Silently, we waited. Had Jethro been gunned down by one of Van Glock's men on patrol?

He pulled the phone away from his ear and addressed the gathered crowd. "Bad news. The FBI is at the front gate, and they're demanding entry."

Chapter
Six

Having learned my lesson about getting stuck in a small car with Petty's crazoids, I claimed shotgun in Buddy's Beamer. In the back, Max rode between Bambi and Vikki.

Buddy snapped the car into gear and took off like a Scud Missile. This time I was at the front of the convoy. Behind us were all the cars and trucks for the flock and Van Glock's HumVee.

Buddy was seriously cheesed off. "What the fuck is this all about? The FBI? I'm trying to start a peaceful little country here. Who do they think we are, a bunch of extreme fringe wing nuts?"

"It's Van Glock," Vikki said. "Running around with his idiot commandos. That *schmuck* is nothing but trouble."

I heard Max chuckle. "You got a new favorite word, huh? *Schmuck?* You like that?"

"I like you," Vikki said.

"This is all Petty's fault," Bambi said. "He's always freaking people out with his conspiracy theories."

"We're not doing anything wrong," Buddy said. "Are we more dangerous than an Indian reservation? No, we're not. If the FBI sets one cheap wing tip into Bob, I'm going to—"

"What do you know?" Max reached between the seats and whacked his son on the back of the head. "I knew this place was trouble. Don't be such a *putz*. You can't start a country when you already live in a country."

"Thanks, Max, for clearing that up. It probably didn't occur to you that I could use a little support right now."

"You want to talk support? I'll give you eighteen years plus college tuition worth of support."

"Would it hurt to tell me I'm doing okay? How many sons are capable of founding a whole new country? Of starting a bank, The Bank of Buddy? How 'bout that, Max?"

"You should have been a dentist," Max said stubbornly. "You make good money. People always need dentists."

The two Favermans strung a sticky web of guilt. When Buddy parked at the front entrance to Bob, I couldn't jump out of the car fast enough.

The situation at the sentryhouse looked nasty. On the other side of the chain link fence, I counted three unmarked cars and two vans with tinted glass windows. My guess was that each of these vehicles was bulletproof. Fifteen or more government agents, male and female, ranged around their vehicles. They wore a variety of flak jackets, helmets, and caps that would certainly make Van Glock drool with envy. Though most of the feds had holstered their weapons, four men in body armor had M16's trained on three of Van Glock's men who stood behind the closed gate with their weapons aimed and ready. It didn't appear that either group was interested in a healthy, nurturing relationship

Headlines featuring Waco and Ruby Ridge flashed through my head like a newsreel. Though my shiny new title of sheriff was mostly a joke, I decided to place myself in the front row of negotiators. If I left the talking to Van Glock and the reverend, this confrontation might easily turn into a bloodbath of biblical proportions.

"Shit," Buddy said softly.

"Ditto."

"What do we do next, Adam?"

"Disarm everybody. The feds don't want to start shooting any more than we want to get shot."

"Right." Buddy left the Beamer and approached Van Glock's men. "How's about if you guys put down the guns?"

I could tell that his approach wasn't going to work any more effectively now than it had on the playground when we were kids.

One of Van Glock's men said, "No way, Buddy. We don't take orders from you."

"Fishman," I said, "who's the ranking officer here?"

"Me." His bulging eyes blinked furiously. I expected that he was coming to terms with the stark contrast between playing at being an elite commando and actually being face-to-face with heavily armed federal agents.

"Fishman," I whispered, "are you nuts? These guys will shoot you 'til you're dead."

Fishman stammered, "G-g-gentlemen, lower your weapons."

Rifle barrels slowly, reluctantly, were aimed toward the ground.

I had hoped that the government sharpshooters on the other side of the fence would do the same, but I must have been dreaming.

Blustering like a bad wind from the north, Van Glock joined us. His jaw stuck out, fierce as a rottweiler's, and his eyes were glowing like the headlights on his HumVee. It was obvious that he loved this shit.

To Buddy and me he said, "I can't believe it. They're all here. FBI, DEA, FWS—"

"FWS?" I questioned, unfamiliar with that acronym.

"Fish and Wildlife Service," he said. "And the FCC."

Vikki popped up beside me. "The FCC? Oh my God, they'll want to shut down my radio station. This is terrible! I want to expand to a wider area so we can publicize the casino."

"Calm down." I patted her arm. The least of our worries was the FCC. As far as I knew they seldom went in with guns blazing to eliminate airwave pirates.

Van Glock hitched up his trousers. "You'd better let me handle this, Buddy."

"No. You and your men need to be ready in case they decide to open fire." Buddy glanced over his shoulder. "We've got women here."

"Pregnant women," I added.

Buddy turned to Van Glock. "You've got to keep everybody else back. Especially Reverend Petty."

"You're right," Van Glock said. "He's a hothead."

But Petty and the others had already swarmed around us.

Petty was almost as excited as Van Glock. "I knew this day would come. One day, I knew I would meet the dark satanic forces of the Antichrist, these agents of the Devil." He took a long stride forward. "Let me be the first to die."

"Nobody's going to die," Buddy said. "You need to tend

to your people. Look at them, Reverend, they're scared prayerless."

The mob looked anything but frightened. A couple of the pregnant women had picked up rocks.

"We're ready," Petty said in his loudly projecting voice. "We are ready to defend our Geo-political Omni—"

"Enough," Buddy said. "Here's what's going to happen. I'm going through the gate. Me and Adam. The rest of you stay back."

"Why should you speak for us?" Petty demanded. "You're only the banker. How can you express our religious principles?"

"Buddy is the best one to talk." It was Max. The old warrior stepped among us, squinting behind his eye patch. His bearing was heroic, immediately commanding respect. "Let me explain something to you, Reverend."

"What?"

Max stood shoulder to shoulder with his son. "Buddy and me. We are of the Chosen People."

Petty scowled.

"You want to talk persecution?" Max said. "I give you the Holocaust. I give you thousands of years defending our homeland. Not to mention all that wandering in the desert. Buddy is the negotiator. He's the best. End of discussion."

Petty's brow wrinkled in concentration, and I bolstered Max's logic. "This isn't the final battle, Petty. It's the first skirmish. Our troops are exposed. We don't want to lose our whole army in the first confrontation. Drop back. Regroup. It could be a long war."

Petty cocked his head to one side, thinking. Again, I had the sense that I'd seen him before.

Finally, he said, "The patriarchal father of Buddy makes sense. We will defer to his judgment. But it's just this once."

He stepped back, allowing Van Glock and his men to herd him with the others.

Before Max joined them, he whispered to his son, "I love you, *putz.*"

"Thanks, Max."

Buddy and I went through the gate and locked it behind us.

In a normal voice Buddy asked, "Who's in charge here?"

A man wearing khaki Dockers and a striped golf shirt under his FBI windbreaker stepped forward, holding out his badge. "I'm FBI Special Agent Richard Gosinia."

Buddy glanced at the badge then at the man. "What's the problem, Dick?"

"Don't call me Dick." His grin was tight-lipped. His pointed chin was straight out of the Dick Tracy comics. "We've got a couple of problems here. We heard gunshots from inside your compound, and we want to know what's going on in there."

"You've been watching us?"

"That's right. You're under surveillance."

"Why?"

"It's our job. We keep an eye on things."

I elaborated. "They take photos, make tapes, collect fingerprints, talk to friends and family. Then they compile all this data. Then they file and cross-reference. The 'B' in FBI stands for Bureaucracy. Is that about right, Gosinia?"

"You forgot wiretaps," he said. "The main thing, though, is we don't want any trouble."

"We're on the same page," Buddy assured him.

"Okay, good. So I showed you my badge. Who are you guys?" I would've been surprised if he hadn't already known Buddy's identity. The fibbies might be a pain in the ass, but they were thorough when they started in with surveillance.

Buddy shook hands with Gosinia. "I'm Benjamin David Faverman. Call me Buddy. And this is my friend, Adam McCleet, who used to be a cop in Portland."

I also did the handshake. Though Gosinia was giving an excellent impersonation of a friendly presence, he still hadn't ordered his cohorts to lower their weapons. He said, "Tell me about this place you got here. What do you call it? Bob?"

"That's right," Buddy said. "Named for Chief Bob, the founder of this twelve-square-mile Indian reservation where, I might add, the United States government has no jurisdiction."

I added, "Not that the people of Bob don't respect the U.S. government."

"Yeah?" Agent Gosinia looked dubious. "Then how do you explain the armed guards? They look dangerous."

"Hunters," I said and quickly segued to a less confrontational topic. "Here in Bob, the goal is to live peacefully and to open a gambling casino, just as many of the other Native American tribes have done in Oregon. And this won't really even be gambling, because there isn't U.S. currency involved."

"Bingo?"

I launched into a convoluted discussion of bobs, bambis, glocks, mikes and vikkis. By the time I was finished, Gosinia had a blank stare pasted on his face. His sharp chin softened as he gaped, slack-jawed.

"So," I concluded, "you can see that Bob isn't a militia. I think we'd all feel a lot better if you told the sharpshooters to put their weapons down and relax."

"Two bobs make a buck," he said. "And there are five vikkis in a bob?"

"And a hundred bobs in a buddy."

He waved to the men who were standing behind him. "Take a break, guys."

I breathed easier when the muzzles of several high tech weapons were lowered. As Buddy had said earlier, the people of Bob weren't breaking any of the major commandments. There shouldn't have been anything to fear.

Gosinia remembered, "What about the gunfire?"

"No big deal. A couple of the guys messing with their weapons. Nobody has been shot." As far as I knew, that was the truth. Roger Engersoll was killed in a fire. And we didn't know what had happened to the excessively fertile Jethro Kowalski.

"We've had communication," Gosinia said, "with one of your people. The nature of this discussion causes us to believe there might be illegal substances available in your community. Now, even if you guys are some kind of separate nation, the U.S. government takes a real dim view of drug trafficking."

Which explained the presence of the DEA. Bambi and her hemp growers needed to get their act together.

"Organic farming," I said. As a further distraction I pointed out Bambi, who was standing in the front row of observers with her arms folded beneath her breasts. "You see the woman with black hair?"

"It's hard not to notice her."

"She's in charge of the farming. Now, I ask you, Agent Gosinia, does she look like a drug trafficker?"

As he scanned the people behind the chain link fence, Gosinia's eyebrows lowered. "How many pregnant women have you got back there?"

"A lot."

He exhaled heavily. "I want to assure you guys that

we're not looking for a standoff, and we don't want the media involved."

"Sure." Buddy nodded. "I think our discussion here is going well, Richard. But it's late, you know? Why don't we set up a time when we could sit down and talk? We'll have a little *nosh*, get to know each other, and I'll tell you everything you ever wanted to know about Bob."

"Tomorrow. Oh-nine hundred hours."

Buddy shook his head. "Tomorrow's not good. Look, I don't have my Day Timer, but—"

"Tomorrow," he repeated. "Make it noon."

"Noonish," Buddy said. "I'll meet you here. We'll talk."

Agent Richard Gosinia frowned, probably wondering if he'd been conned. I gave him another reason not to change his mind, "You're doing a good job of negotiation. Much as I hate to mention Waco, Ruby Ridge, the Freemen, and that group of nuts in Texas who had their embassy in a Winnebago, this is totally different. You'll probably get a promotion for handling this so smoothly."

"As long as we can keep the media out of it," he repeated, "we'll be fine."

"See you tomorrow," Buddy said as we took a step back toward the perimeter. "By the way, who was the person who contacted your guys?"

"That's classified information."

"Well, of course it is."

We waved and went back toward the gate. Behind us, Gosinia ordered the assembled agents to do the same. By the time we were safely inside Bob the bulletproof cars and vans were driving away.

I patted Buddy on the shoulder. "You done good, kid."

He was looking toward his father and smiling broadly. "I know."

Max gave him a thumbs-up signal.

In spite of being surrounded by a confederation of fools, I felt warm inside. The Favermans, father and son, had come to a different level of understanding. Though Buddy had technically been a man since his *bar mitzvah,* this was the first time his father acknowledged that the *putz* had grown up.

When we got back to Buddy's house I took the cell phone into my guest bedroom and punched in the long-distance number for Alison. When I got the answering machine I listened to her voice and hung up without leaving a message. How could I explain that in the course of one day I'd been arrested, gone to a funeral, witnessed the founding of a bank, and assisted at the birth of the first natural born citizen of Bob?

I stretched out on the bed and thought about women, all kinds of women. There were the healthy, tall women like Bambi. And the hard-edged blondes like Vikki. Pregnant women. Ghost women like Selma, who still haunted her husband, Max. None of them were Alison, and for some reason that pleased me greatly. When I fell asleep, I dreamed about her.

My pal Buddy had eightish and noonish commitments for the following day. First, he'd promised to search for Jethro Kowalski. At lunchtime he would negotiate with the feds. Throughout the day there was The Bank of Buddy money exchange.

Fortunately, I had no such obligations. Though I'd agreed to be sheriff, the position actually had no defined duties or job description. I could have hung back in the wings. I've always been good at maintaining a low profile, a skill that has contributed more than once to my survival.

Nonetheless, I joined the others for an early breakfast, prior to the Jethro search. Max, Buddy, and I sat around the

table in an attractive breakfast nook while Vikki Ramone
poured coffee and set out a spread of stone-cold muffin
lumps and runny eggs. I amused myself by gazing into
Vikki's cleavage, one of the natural wonders of Bob. In
spite of the hour, she wore a Las Vegas business suit—hot
pink mini-skirt and a bolero jacket over a sequin tube top.
She'd taken the time to apply her make-up with careful
precision. Her blond bouffant was artfully tousled.

"No bagels?" Max questioned.

"We don't have a bagel shop," she said. "There's only
one bakery, and the woman who runs it is pregnant, so
we have whatever she feels like making for the day."

I shuddered, convinced that the entire country was con-
gealed in the grip of rampaging estrogen, enslaved by a
herd of thundering pregzillas.

Max raised his thick eyebrow. "You got a deli?"

"The general store has a delicatessen section," Vikki
said.

Across the table from me, Buddy snorted, "It's pathetic.
No *knishes*. No *latkes*. We're talking packaged bologna and
turkey with yellow mustard."

Max shook his head sadly. "You need bagels in Bob."

In spite of this tragic deprivation, I was unable to work
myself into a sweat regarding the lack. No bagels was the
least of their problems. "So, Max, you want to leave around
noon?"

"How can I abandon this *putz* in a place where he can't
get decent food? I'm calling a friend of mine. A caterer."

I didn't like the sound of that. "Wait a minute, Max. If
you start trying to fill in the stuff they need in Bob, we
could be here forever."

"What's that supposed to mean?" Vikki demanded.
When she planted her fists on her hips, her breasts did an
attractive little shimmy. "What else do we need in Bob?"

"A doctor." I was distracted by her hooters, but I only needed a small portion of my brain to think of dozens of other life necessities that were absent in Bob. "How about schools? You don't have a library. There aren't even stop signs on the street corners."

"But today," Buddy said, "we'll have money."

"That's right," Vikki put in. "The Bank of Buddy opens today."

Instead of offering an opinion I sipped the coffee which appeared to be the only palatable item on the table.

Vikki continued, "As soon as we get the new money in circulation, everything is going to be fine. I can even open the Thunderbird Casino on a limited basis. We've got twenty slot machines that just need to be adjusted to take Bob bucks."

Twenty machines did not a casino make. "What about poker and blackjack?"

"No problems there," she said. "I used to be a dealer."

"In Vegas?"

"Not exactly. I performed in Vegas, of course. And I once dated Frank Sinatra's bodyguard."

"Were you a dealer in Reno?"

"Actually, it was after I went back home to regroup after the neon lights and glamour."

She sat down at the table and sipped at the coffee. Her expression was pensive, and I suspected that Vikki had the kind of personal history that might have filled several Jackie Collins novels.

"Where's home?" I asked.

"Boise, Idaho. I was a dealer during Riverboat Gambling Nights at St. Elmo's. I don't suppose you think that qualifies me to run a casino and maybe it doesn't, but poker is poker. No matter where you play it, the cards are still the same."

"Opening a casino is a big operation, Vikki. Maybe you'd be better off sticking to your illegal radio station."

"Don't be a *schmuck*, Adam. I can handle both."

"Chutzpah," Max said. "This little lady's got it."

I wouldn't argue with him on that point. Vikki was the kind of woman who got knocked down, then picked herself up and started over. A female version of Rocky Balboa.

Still, I didn't think the timing was right for the Thunderbird Casino. "I don't expect that you had the same distractions at St. Elmo's that you have here in Bob."

"Such as?"

"An insane paramilitary brigade. A paranoid reverend. Dozens of wildly erratic pregnant women." Actually, St. Elmo's might have been plagued by the two latter problems. "I'm pretty sure that St. Elmo's wasn't engaged in a discussion with the FBI, DEA, and Fish and Wildlife Service to explain why they shouldn't pay taxes because they're an Indian reservation."

Quietly, she said, "I really don't have much choice. I'm almost flat broke."

Max had left the table and was stalking around Buddy's house. "Phone? Where's your phone?"

Buddy pointed to a counter in the kitchen. "It's a mobile. The calling area is a little unpredictable."

"You haven't even got decent phone service," I pointed out. "No matter how you slice the facts, Bob is a long way from civilization."

"It's a new frontier," Max said. "Adam, you might try a more positive attitude about Bob. It's not so bad. How many *putzes* can start their own country?"

Max's newfound attitude as a supportive father was losing charm fast. Though I was happy that both Favermans were feeling all warm and fuzzy toward each other, I hadn't signed on as a psychotherapist. I was just the chauffeur, and I wanted an estimated departure time.

But I couldn't talk with Max right at the moment. He was on the phone, greeting a buddy in Queens and arranging an emergency airlift of bagels into Bob.

When he'd finished I claimed the telephone and punched in the number for Alison's condo in Portland. It rang four times before the answering machine picked up. "Alison?" I said, after the beep. "Are you there? Can you hear me? I'm talking on a mobile phone from the country of Bob. If you're there, pick up."

I waited for a moment, knowing that she was usually still in bed before eight if she wasn't out jogging or in the shower.

"Alison?" For some reason, it disturbed me not to be able to reach her. "I'll call you later."

I set down the phone and stepped outside with my coffee. The morning panorama from Buddy's front deck was peaceful. The backhoes on the hillside behind the house had not yet begun to churn, and I could hear birds in the forest. My studio at home was on the bank of the Willamette River and was, therefore, exceedingly moist. The dry air was a pleasant change.

The natural surroundings weren't too shabby. Left to the chipmunks and deer, it might have been an okay place to live. However, Bob was messed up as soon as humans imposed their reign. I'm not an environmentalist who bemoans every strip of asphalt, but I had the feeling that this land was headed for disaster.

About half a mile away on the graded dirt road, I saw a rising plume of dust, like a tornado. Even from that distance I recognized the red convertible, and my blood froze in my veins. "Margot."

Chapter
Seven

Margot, my evil sister, drove like a maniac. When she stopped in front of Buddy's house she managed to squeal her tires even without asphalt. She leapt from her shiny red chariot. The reflection of the morning sunlight off her gold belt, necklaces, and bracelets was blinding. Other than the jewelry, she wasn't wearing much, only a neck to mid-ankle spandex bodysuit in a print, patterned like snakeskin. Her buns were steel, and her abs were platinum. I had to give credit to the seven personal trainers she'd gone through in the past six months.

When she looked at me, her nostrils flared. I could have sworn she was breathing fire. When Margot the Maleficent stalked the earth she burned a swath twenty yards wide.

"Adam, you jackass," she started right in. "Did you

think you could keep this fabulous investment opportunity all to yourself?''

"Fabulous?"

"Yes-s-s," she hissed. Her outfit enhanced her she-dragon demeanor. "Don't play dumb. Or, should I say, dumber than you already are. Benjamin told me I could double my money."

"Benjamin?"

"Don't tell me you're still calling him Buddy? That is *so* high school. When are you going to grow up?"

"Everybody calls him Buddy."

"Everybody hasn't been to bed with him," she said. "How could I possibly, in the throes of passion, scream out the name Buddy? How? I'd feel like I was in a cartoon."

"I understand. What were you saying about money?"

She reached into the back of her car and pulled out an overnight bag. Margot almost always traveled with a suitcase. She liked to stop, spontaneously, and inflict herself upon unwary people. Also, she usually packed enough cosmetic supplies to paint a large bridge.

She placed the bag on the hood of her car, unfastened the catch and flipped up the lid. Inside, I saw several banded stacks of one hundred dollar bills.

"Fifty thousand," she said.

Though I could have told her that she would be exchanging her Ben Franklins for Monopoly money printed with the slogan, "In Bob We Trust," I have discovered over the years that it is virtually impossible to explain anything to my younger sister.

Buddy, the unsuspecting chump, emerged from the front door, and Margot's snarl modified to a facial expression that might have been similar to a python sighting in on a juicy vole.

"Margot," Buddy said.

"Darling!" Her eyelashes fluttered out a Morse code for: Run like hell. "Do you really own this whole country?"

"Not exactly, I've been selling off—"

"But you do own the bank, don't you?"

"That's right."

"Darling," she repeated as she sucked him into an embrace.

Max followed, and Margot treated him to an air kiss on either side of his face.

Then she saw Vikki. Margot's acrylic red fingernail pointed disdainfully. "Who's that?"

"Vikki Ramone," said the lady in question. Prudently, she kept her distance.

"Call me Margot," my sister said. After her fifth husband, she'd pretty much eliminated the long string of names. "Only one name. Like Cher. Or Madonna."

"Or Satan," I said.

"Shut up, Adam."

Vikki squared off. "What are you doing here?"

"I've come to invest, Sweetheart." Margot's tongue dripped with venom. "Something I'm sure you know nothing about."

"The hell I don't," Vikki said. Apparently, at St. Elmo's in Boise, they called a spade a spade. "I know everything about what happens here. I'm Buddy's chief administrative assistant."

"Really. You're his secretary."

"And I'm sure you're his—"

"Ladies!" Buddy broke in. "We really have to be going. It's almost eightish, time for the Jethro search."

I glanced up at the backhoes, bulldozers, and a giant earthmover on the partially terraced hill behind Buddy's house. There was zero activity. "I guess Jethro didn't make it to work."

"Van Glock called a few minutes ago," Buddy said. "Jethro is still missing. Shall we go?"

"Buddy and Max will ride with me," Margot said. "Adam, you take this other person."

Though I really hadn't counted on participating in the actual search, I didn't feel as if I had much of a choice. Besides, if I had my own vehicle at the jail, I could leave at any time.

During the drive through Bob, Vikki fumed. In colorful language that was certainly not accepted at St. Elmo's, she informed me of her derogatory opinion of my sister. I found no reason to object.

When we parked at the Silver Stream jailhouse, she turned to me. Her eyebrows wrinkled with concern. "Do you think she's after Buddy?"

There was no kind way to break this news. "When my sister is shopping for a new man, she generally requires that they be male, fairly wealthy, and breathing. Buddy qualifies."

"Damn," she said as she turned the car mirror toward herself and peered into it. "How old is she?"

"Margot is eternal." I remembered Max's hope that his son, the *putz,* might actually get himself hitched to Vikki. "Are you serious about Buddy?"

"I never joke," she said grimly. "I came here to make my fortune and set up a career as a lounge singer. Nobody, and I do mean nobody, is going to stop me."

I drew the conclusion. "So, you're just using Buddy."

"No." When she turned toward me, I saw a hint of the hopeful, innocent girl who had left Boise for the bright neon of Las Vegas. "I care about Buddy. He's a good, kindhearted person. But he'll never grow up, settle down, and get married. He's too busy chasing the next great deal."

"Do you love him?"

"Like the song says—'What's love got to do with it?'"

As she climbed out of my car and marched toward the crowd that had gathered outside the jailhouse, her tousled blond hair shone like a brass helmet in the sunlight. Vikki Ramone wasn't anybody's little pushover.

Apparently, the search for Jethro Kowalski fell under Van Glock's jurisdiction. He had a map of Bob spread out in front of him, and as people reported for duty he sent them out to cover various sectors.

In my position as reluctant sheriff, I decided to select my own venue. I looked down at the map. "Where was Roger Engersoll's cabin?"

Van Glock glared at me. "Why would you go there?"

"Have you got a problem with letting me see the remains?"

"I don't care what you do, McCleet. Just get out of my face."

The day was still young and I'd already irritated Van Glock and insulted Vikki. If the Reverend Petty had been within earshot I probably could have made the hat trick. "So, where's the burnt cabin?"

Bambi popped up beside me. "I'll show you where it is."

Could I ask for anything more?

We took my car, and she directed me down twisting roads that became little more than one-lane pathways. We stopped in a shady forest glen, and when I turned off the engine I could hear the rippling of fresh running water. There were no other trailers or houses in sight. "How much land did Engersoll own?"

"Seven acres on the creek," Bambi said. "He didn't want anybody getting too close. He was kind of a loner."

Through the trunks of conifers I could see the remains

of a small cabin. The setting had a secluded charm. "How come nobody else has bought the other land around here?"

Bambi explained the topography. "Engersoll's property butts right up against that mountain of rocks. Nobody can build on that. In the other direction, following the creek, it's all old growth forest. Clearing a space of land would be incredibly expensive."

"But this is a great setting," I said. I could live there, tucked away in a deep forest. I was beginning to have an empathy for Roger Engersoll. "How come Buddy hasn't developed this area?"

"I'd like to think it was because, deep in his heart of hearts, Buddy doesn't want to destroy the forest." Her lips pulled back in a smile, revealing her perfect white teeth. "But, I guess, Buddy has enough to sell with land in the valley that's already clear."

We strolled beside the creek toward the cabin. The rushing waters were only about six feet wide and fairly shallow. At this time of year, early autumn, there wouldn't be any runoff. The source had to be a natural spring.

There was something about the setting that bothered me as an investigative sheriff. "When the fire started, how did anybody know?"

"It was about ten o'clock at night," Bambi said. "A lot of the young couples come to this area because it's private."

"I thought most of the people here were married."

"Duh, Adam. Figure it out. Most of the flock are two or three wives and one husband. And they live in dinky little trailers. Do you really think the men are going to have sex with one wife while the other one is sitting in another room, five feet away?"

"A definite drawback to polygamy," I said.

"Most of them would rather drive out here and have sex in the back of their trucks. It's more private."

"So one of these couples noticed the fire. Do you remember who?"

"I think it was Jimmy and Tammy Light. They're really kind of cute, even if they are followers of that jerkface Petty. And I think they're really in love because, like, Jimmy's other wife left town."

"What happened after the Lights saw the fire?"

"They sent up an alarm. Everybody came crashing over here with axes and shovels and buckets. I mean, the volunteer fire brigade sucks, but they got here fast and put it out."

Not fast enough for Roger Engersoll. "Did anybody question the Light couple? Did they notice anything suspicious?"

"Like an arsonist throwing gasoline on Roger's cabin?" Bambi laughed. "Even the people in Bob aren't that dense, Adam. Nobody came forward with information that would prove this fire was set."

"Of course, most of the witnesses were in the back of their trucks, screwing like bunnies."

"You got it," she said.

The front wall of the log cabin was charred but still standing, as were portions of the walls on two sides. The roof had completely collapsed, and I noticed tar paper and shingles amid the debris. It was a small place, maybe thirty feet across and twenty feet deep. "Not a lot of space," I commented.

"I think Roger had plans to add on," she said. "I was only out here once. The cabin was two rooms. A kitchen and a combination living room bedroom."

We circled around the remains. It wasn't hard to imagine the simple floor plan. Two rooms with one wall dividing them. Though the furnishings had been reduced to rubble, I could see the metal frame of a bed, part of a table leg, and a partially burned desk. At the center of the house the heavy, iron Franklin stove was still identifiable.

Bambi pointed to it. "That's where the fire started. With the stove. Then it spread up the dividing wall. Roger's bed was right up against that wall."

Even a cursory investigation like this raised a lot of questions in my head. How could a fire jump from the stove to the wall? Without trekking through the ashes, I could see that the stove was on a stone foundation. People who live in log cabins are generally pretty careful about fire.

It also occurred to me that fires usually started with something easily flammable, like on a curtain or a piece of furniture. "Was there wallpaper on the dividing wall?"

"The whole interior was panelled in pine. Not the cheap stuff, either. Roger must've had money."

"Who inherited his money?"

"Nobody's figured it out, yet. He had some papers in a metal box that survived the fire. That was where we found the will."

"And what did the will say?"

"Something like, I leave my land and everything on it to Reverend Petty."

"But Roger didn't come here with Petty's flock, right?"

Bambi kicked at a charred piece of wood. "I didn't know Roger real well. We'd only talked about water use for irrigation, and he promised that he would never dam the creek. But, he was kind of a sympathizer with Petty's paranoid theories."

"Like the weather machine in Iceland? And the Ayatollah's submarine fleet lying at the bottom of the Columbia River?"

"That's the stuff. He had a lot of old newspapers in his house."

Ah ha! Finally, I had an idea of how the fire could have spread. "Did he keep the newspapers in the kitchen? Near the stove?"

"Not when I was here," she said. "He had them all boxed up and stored on the far side of the house. Away from the stove."

An experienced arson investigator could have sifted through the ashes and found out if the newspapers were still there, but I wasn't experienced. I assumed that newspapers would go up in flames. But I saw the spines of several books in the debris. There was nothing that resembled a box or newspapers.

I really couldn't believe that nobody had investigated. Roger's untimely death was an unlikely fire, and Petty had a big fat motive. "This looks like murder to me."

"I thought so," Bambi said. "What are you going to do about it?"

"We've got a whole mob of feds standing at the front gate, waiting for something to do. It might be a good plan to let one of them in here to have a look." I glanced at her. "That's kind of a problem for you hemp growers."

"Why?" she asked with a burst of naivety. "We're just farmers."

"Growing a field of marijuana? Bambi, we're talking about the DEA, Drug Enforcement Agency."

"In the first place, I'm growing hemp, not pot. Believe me, there's a big difference. You wouldn't want to smoke the stuff I've got growing in the fields. And, in the second place, I want it legalized. We've got a real nice operation here. There's even been a harvest, and we shipped it to my brother, who made paper."

"Wait a minute," I said. "If you think the DEA is going

to let you off because you've done a harvest, you're definitely smoking something."

"Maybe I am." She tossed her head. "But it's not something I've grown in the fields."

So, Bambi went for the imported grass. I sighed heavily. It had been a long time since I'd indulged in that particular vice, and I had warm memories of coming back from Vietnam, sitting with a circle of friends and passing a joint. To tell the truth, I kind of empathized with Bambi.

"I guess we should look for Jethro," I said.

"This way." She set out toward the pile of rocks at the far end of Roger's property. I allowed her to go first. The view of her firm buttocks in cutoff jeans was an inspiration.

We climbed until we came to a high ledge overlooking the treetops. From that vantage point I could see the several acres of Bambi's farmland, much of which was covered with camouflage netting. "Interesting farming technique," I said.

"Doesn't have anything to do with hemp growing," she said.

"Does it have to do with hiding the marijuana crop?" I guessed.

"Unfortunately, until people recognize the many uses of hemp, we need to be careful. Someday," she said, with her beautiful blue eyes glistening, "hemp will grow free across the land, like the buffalo."

I didn't point out that wild buffalo were pretty much extinct. Another thought rose to the forefront of my mind. "Last night, the FBI agent hinted that someone had been talking to the DEA. Do you have any idea who? Maybe Petty?"

"He doesn't take much interest in the crop." She shrugged. "Did you know it was possible to get permits to grow certain varieties of this noble weed? For medicinal purposes.''

She started toward higher ground before I had a chance to ask if she had been the one who applied for such a permit, thereby bringing down the attention of the feds. It would take an amazing degree of innocence to try something so naive, but I thought Bambi might qualify.

At our next stopping point Bambi wasn't even winded. I collapsed on a rock, panting like a dog. "Why are we going all the way up here?"

"You got a better plan?"

"No," I admitted.

When she started to climb again I called her back. "So, tell me, how'd a nice girl like you end up in the oldest profession?"

"Farming?" She skipped back down the rock and sat beside me. "It's in my blood. My parents are totally organic. That's how my brother and I grew up. Believing in the purity of the environment and saving the whales. I'm a second generation hippie."

Her pronouncement made me feel very old. Too easily I remembered when psychedelic was radically new. It was over twenty years ago that Sergeant Pepper brought the band to play. The idea that the hippie spawn were fully grown into creatures like Bambi was depressing.

She was sitting so close that I could smell the fresh scent that clung to her. If she was sweating, she'd found a way to turn that stink into the fragrance of wildflowers and honey.

"Here's what I think we should do," she said. "I think we should find Spanky. I think Jethro took off to join Spanky."

"The ninja in cowboy boots?"

"Nobody knows where he lives," Bambi said. "But I've

seen him headed in this direction, and there might be a cave up here."

I still didn't understand her attraction for the mysterious weirdo. Maybe it had something to do with the horse. "Isn't Spanky kind of old for you?" I asked.

"Age is in your head, Adam."

Not for a nano-second did I believe that. I might still have the urges of a husky eighteen-year-old, but certain body parts were definitely showing wear and tear. My guess was that the mysterious Spanky was close to my age. He had the look of a baby boomer, part of the post-hippie, post-Vietnam generation.

I might have enjoyed discussing this and other meaningless topics with the beauteous Bambi. However, she was rested and ready to hike.

With an athletic bounce she was on her feet. "Let's go, Adam. Make tracks."

I slogged along behind her, unenthusiastically climbing over boulders, looking for Spanky.

We found nothing but an itinerant family of tree squirrels that Bambi insisted upon cuddling even though I warned her about rabies. It was after eleven o'clock when we staggered down the rocky hillside and returned to Van Glock's clearing outside the Silver Stream jailhouse.

In the heat of the day the ranks of searchers had thinned. There was practically no one around, and Van Glock reported that the search was, thus far, uneventful.

I saw Max sitting in the shade near the militia bunkhouse, fanning himself with a folded map. Buddy, Margot, and Vikki were nowhere around.

I joined the old warrior. "How's it going?"

"Let me put it to you like this, Adam. This search is just about as successful as a fly fisherman in Death Valley."

"Jethro's gone?"

"On the plus side, nobody has found his dead body."
Max frowned at me. "So what's the deal? How come your
sister is acting like she has the hots for my son the *putz*?"

"She does have the hots for him," I said. "This is not
a good thing."

It was a very bad thing. Once Margot sank her fangs
into Buddy, he wouldn't have a chance. Before he knew
what had hit, he'd be humming the wedding march.

Max said, "She's not a bad looker, your sister. Maybe
a little skinny."

"It's hard to gain weight when your entire diet is the
still beating hearts of bachelors. Listen, Max, I warned
Buddy, and I'll warn you. Stand clear of Margot."

"She's with him right now." He sighed. "Margot went
with Buddy and Vikki to help at the money exchange."

Of course. If there was one thing Margot liked more
than acquiring husbands, it was the acquisition of cash. "I
guess that means that they're going forward with this Bank
of Buddy thing?"

Max slowly nodded. "Adam, I have to ask for another
favor. There's something about this place that makes me
very nervous. The *putz* might think he's king of Bob, but
he's up to his *tush* in enemies. Van Glock, for one."

I agreed. "And Reverend Petty."

"Even Vikki, that cute little number," Max said. "Sometimes, she looks like she wants to brain the *putz.*"

"Sometimes, so do I." I asked, "What's this favor?"

"Give me one more day in Bob," he said. "Tomorrow
morning, we can leave. But I want one more day for things
to settle down."

That meant another day of Margot and the rest of the
insane crew of Bobites, but I couldn't fault Max for his
fatherly concern. There did seem to be an undercurrent

of hostility in Bob, and much of it was directed at Buddy. "Do you think it's dangerous, Max?"

"You never know. Somebody got killed here, didn't they?"

"Roger Engersoll, victim of a suspicious fire."

As sheriff I had dozens of reasons to investigate Roger's death. But when it came right down to making a decision, I frankly didn't give a shit. Roger Engersoll was nothing to me, and Buddy had enough problems without adding a murder inquest. Sooner or later somebody was going to have to notify the authorities about Roger, but the damage had already been done. I doubted they would ever figure out who did it, and the murder would turn into a job for lawyers, who would eventually sort out the dead man's estate.

For the rest of the day I mostly stayed with Max, avoiding Margot, the bank, and Buddy. I talked weaponry and footwear with Fishman. After noticing Bambi's happy buzz in the afternoon, I was tempted to ask for a hemp sample.

Around sunset, Max and I returned to Buddy's house, where the backhoes and a giant yellow earthmover on the hillside above the house had almost completed their terracing work. Apparently, they'd found a way to keep working without Jethro's supervision. The heavy machinery ground to a halt just as we parked next to Buddy's Beamer.

He was alone, sitting on the porch swing with his snout buried in a snifter. He greeted us with one word. "Brandy?"

Max and I nodded.

Slowly, Buddy stood up and led the way inside. On the kitchen counter was a bottle, and he pointed to it before flinging his long, skinny body down on the sofa. "Help yourself."

Max sat opposite him. "Rough day?"

"From hell."

Though I didn't like to gloat and tell him that I knew people wouldn't want to exchange their real money for Bob bucks, I couldn't help a dig. "Trouble at the bank?"

"People brought in all kinds of shit they wanted to exchange for Bob bucks. I should've made it clear that this was a cash transaction only. One family brought in livestock that they wanted to sell. What am I going to do with a nanny goat and three chickens? Keep them in the safe?"

"Chickens aren't so bad," Max said.

"Then Vikki and Margot took over behind the counter," Buddy said. "Don't get me started on those two. They would have killed each other if they hadn't been so busy."

"Busy?"

"Customers all day long. We collected seven hundred fifty-nine thousand dollars in U.S. currency. Cash money. I'm going to need to print up more Bob bucks to handle the checks and certificates of deposit and bonds."

I couldn't believe they were busy. So much for the old I-told-you-so. "People actually turned in their real money for In Bob We Trust?"

"Everybody loves a deal." He shrugged. "I was offering two for one."

In the real world, ten thousand Bob bucks and ten quarters would get you a *latte*. But the fact that Buddy's scheme had worked created a whole new set of problems.

I didn't like the idea of consolidating all the cash in Bob into one flimsy building. "That's a lot of cash, Buddy. Are you sure the security is okay?"

"Van Glock's boys are standing outside guarding." He looked at me over the rims of his glasses. "I expect that's really the job of the local law enforcement. But, as a sheriff you're not exactly Wyatt Earp."

"Do you want me to go down there and check it out?"

"You don't think I can do security? You didn't see the computerized surveillance cameras?"

"I'd like to take a look around. Just in case."

"No problem," Buddy said. "I'll give you the key."

I moved on to another distasteful topic. "How'd your meeting with the feds go?"

"They are so fucking predictable," Buddy said. "They want us to cease and desist anything that we might be doing, but they're scared about storming in here. We made an agreement to disagree. They'll stay outside the borders of Bob. But they won't go away."

"Predictable," I agreed.

Max patted his son on the shoulder. "Maybe you need a vacation. Why don't you come back to Portland with us? For a week, maybe?"

"You still don't get it, Max. I'm making a fortune here. Two months and I can retire any place I want."

"Listen to me, *putz*. Money isn't everything."

"Right. It's the *only* thing."

We managed a dinner, thawing frozen stuff in the microwave, and finished off the bottle of brandy. It was dark, probably near ten o'clock, when Max went to bed, and I asked Buddy for the key to the bank.

He turned it over. "Be careful when you're around the Van Glocksters," he warned. "They might think you're a burglar and shoot your dick off."

"You going to bed?"

"I think I'll stop by Vikki's place," he said. "After a day with Margot, I've got some patching up to do."

That sounded like my life story. "Where is my dear sister?"

"The last time I saw her she was bonding with Van Glock. He's a millionaire, you know. His family owns oil land in Texas."

Immediately, I comprehended. There were two things in life I could always trust: The sun rose in the east, and Margot would always find the money. Her talent was uncanny, like a bloodhound to a trail.

I climbed behind the steering wheel of my Chevy and drove into Bob. Near the tavern, Main Street was hopping. The rest of the town was quiet. Too quiet, I thought.

At The Bank of Buddy I found no sign of Van Glock or any of his elite commando nutcases. Expecting them to leap from the shadows with weapons blazing, I circled the perimeter of the bank. Nobody was there.

Was it break time? Recess? I strolled down toward the bar. There were mostly men inside, and I didn't recognize any of them. I did, however, notice that several of them were wearing the desert fatigues that seemed to be the Van Glock uniform.

I returned to the front door of the bank and pulled out Buddy's set of keys.

Behind me, I heard the honking of a car horn. Reverend Petty slammed to a stop outside the bar. In his booming voice he announced, "Come quickly. There's been an accident."

Chapter
Eight

When I fitted Buddy's key into the slot on the front door of the bank, I was hit by a jolt of electrical current that fried my fingers, rattled my brain, and gave me a sudden erection. I flew backward fifteen feet in a single bound.

My ears rang as if a cheap rotary telephone had been installed inside my head. Above that noise, I heard an alarm that sounded like repeating blasts from a World War II air raid siren. Apparently, the alarm was a signal, because the Van Glockian commandos staggered from the rear of the tavern, hoisting their weapons and bellowing commands to each other.

At the same time, Reverend Petty continued to announce to the population in general that there had been an accident.

Never before in my life—not when I was a cop, not when I was in Vietnam—had I seen the true definition of pandemonium. Men with beer mugs in hand darted in zigzag patterns down the street. A truck and two cars collided while backing out of their parking spots in front of the tavern. Pregnant women waddled and gestured frantically with their stick-like arms. Randomly, the commandos fired their weapons into the air.

My erection went flaccid as all the energy and intelligence drained from my body. I was in a dazed state due to the electrical shock, and all I could do was stand and stare with jaw agape. When I rubbed my eyes to make the insanity go away my face felt numb, a fact that struck me as hysterically funny. I hooked my finger in the corner of my mouth and pulled it out so I could see that my lips were still there. I tried to touch my nose with my tongue, then locked my mouth shut. I must have looked like a complete moron. Or maybe playing with your face was acceptable behavior in Bob. Maybe on Saturday night, the citizens lined the street and made faces at each other. A huge guffaw crawled up my throat, but my lips stayed closed, and I began jerking spasmodically with the force of suppressed laughter.

"Enough!" Reverend Petty climbed onto the roof of one of the crashed vehicles. He thrust his arms heavenward, drawing down the power of the skies to his Ford pickup pulpit. His preaching voice resounded even louder than the air raid siren. "Enough I say. Stop and listen to me."

Everybody slowed down and turned toward him. Maybe the Bobites were, in fact, mindless sheep. Or, maybe, they were, like me, astounded by the reverend's incredible lung power.

"An accident!" he yelled.

"No," yelled back one of the commandos. "It's a bank robbery."

"Secure the bank," shouted another.

They all turned toward me. I spread my arms helplessly, unable to talk without laughing.

"Sheriff McCleet!" The reverend pointed directly at me. "There's been a terrible accident at Buddy's house."

I sobered up quickly. "What?"

"You must come," he ordered.

I grabbed one of the commandos. There was no way in hell that I was touching that electrical bank alarm again. I dragged him toward the door. "See that key in the lock?"

"Yes, sir."

"Get it for me."

"Sir. Yes, sir." Obediently, the little tin soldier ran to the door.

His response to the shock was even more cartoonish than mine. He bounced backward, landed on his butt, and skidded for five feet. Figuring that the bank was sufficiently protected, I left the booby trap key in the lock, jumped into my car, and headed back toward Buddy's.

My old pal was going to have some explaining to do about the rigged lock. He had just handed over the key as if I had nothing to worry about. If this was his idea of a joke, I wasn't laughing.

When I saw what had happened at Buddy's place, a cold fear replaced the last remnant of humor. Reverend Petty hadn't been exaggerating when he said this was terrible.

A freestanding light pole shone down on a churning cloud of dust, but otherwise the house was dark. The Beamer, parked in front, was untouched. Most of the porch was still standing. But the rear portion of the triple wide trailer house had been crushed by a giant yellow earth-mover, the largest piece of equipment that had been working on the hillside above the house. The shovel stuck up in the air like the bow of a sinking freighter. The cab and the giant tires had flattened the master bedroom and most of the rest of the house, including the guest room where Max had been sleeping.

I bolted from the car. The front door hung cockeyed in its frame, and I pushed my way inside. Every window was busted. The furniture was mangled debris. "Max!" I called out. "Buddy! Are you in here?"

The roof of the house slanted at a steep angle. I crouched down, heading toward the rear, listening to the creak of over-stressed support beams as the weight of the earthmover settled lower. The ceiling of the kitchen was smashed almost down to the countertops. Was that a propane stove? I heard a hissing and imagined bare electrical wires.

The fucking place could explode.

I hustled out to the front, where Petty had returned with several other men. I grabbed the reverend's sleeve. "Get somebody to turn off the power generator. If there's a tank, turn off the propane."

"Magnetic forces of the earth," he said. "Our very gravity is being manipulated by the—"

I shook him. "Did you fucking hear me?"

"The power," he said. "Propane."

"Do it," I said.

He nodded his head. His eyeballs were waving around, looking for a conspiracy. "Of course. Yes. What else should I do?"

I scanned the people arriving, hoping to see Bambi or Vikki. Even Van Glock would have been preferable to the reverend. Nobody else I recognized appeared, so I turned back to Petty. "Keep everybody else out of the way. The building could completely collapse."

"Very dangerous," he agreed. "But it is only a mote in
the dust storm that is headed in our direction. The Antichrist is coming."

I glanced at the flashlight he held in his hand. "I need
that."

"But why? Surely, you aren't going back inside there.
You could be crushed."

"I guess that's my choice." I grabbed the flashlight from
him. I had to go inside. Until I located their dead bodies,
there was a chance that Max and Buddy might still be alive.

Inside the house, I picked my way through the front
room to the kitchen. The door to the guest room was
crunched down to three feet, and a large section of wall
was rubble. On my hands and knees, I crawled into what
had once been a nice little room. Acoustic tile dangled
from an aluminum framework. Beams, metal and wood,
had buckled and broken. Pieces of wall and wallpaper had
split away. The carpet was wet, probably from broken pipes
in the bathroom, turning the swirling plaster dust to muck.
It was totally dark, impossible to see more than a few feet,
even with the flashlight.

Though it seemed unlikely that there were survivors, I
reminded myself of the amazing resilience of the human
body. As a cop I'd seen car accidents where people were
extracted from twisted hunks of metal and were still okay.

Overhead, the remaining skeleton of the house groaned
beneath the tonnage of the earthmover. I ducked lower,
inching ahead on my elbows. The floor was a mosaic of
broken glass and splintered wood that sliced through my
shirt.

I saw part of the bedframe. The mattress was on the
floor, and Max lay upon it, still and quiet in his striped
pajama bottoms. His lower body was pinned under a beam.

There was a bloody gash on his forehead, and his eyes were open, staring blankly.

I watched the gray hair on his chest, hoping for a sign that he was still breathing. But there was nothing. No movement.

Twisting myself in the tight space, I felt at his throat for a pulse. Again, nothing. His skin had already begun to cool.

"Goddammit, Max."

My mouth clogged with dust. There was a lump in my throat the size of a Ping Pong ball. He'd been like a father to me, offering rough advice and endless gentleness after my own dad died. I remembered Max's swagger, his incredibly fast hands when he taught me the rudiments of boxing.

I reached out and closed his eyelids.

Though I knew he was dead I wasn't going to leave him there to be completely crushed by the caterpillar equipment. It took all my arm strength to push down on the mattress and ease his body out from under the beams. Once I had a grip under his arms, I dragged him toward the door.

I was moving as fast as I could. There was still the master bedroom to search.

Struggling, I got Max into the hall, where there was more room.

The roof settled another foot.

In the front room, I could almost stand. I managed to lift Max into my arms and carry his limp body to the door.

When I emerged into the crowd, I was crying. I could feel the wet trail of tears on my face, and I didn't care. Max Faverman had been one of my heroes. One of the best men I ever knew.

I was about to set him down beside Buddy's small garden and go back into the house when I saw a little blue sedan plowing its way through the people who'd come too late to help. Vikki was driving, and Buddy leapt out from the passenger side. He ran toward me.

When he saw Max he tore the cigarette from the corner of his mouth. His face transformed into a mask of tragedy. Wordless, he approached me and held out his arms.

I gave Max to his son.

Buddy sank to the earth, holding his father. Though he knew in his heart that Max was dead, his head didn't yet believe it. He was whispering to his father, "I love you, Dad. You know that, don't you? I love you."

When the Reverend Petty came near, looking as if he might offer a benediction, I intercepted him. "You and all your people, get out of here."

"But we need to—"

"Give Buddy some privacy. His father is dead."

Petty raised two fingers and made a quick, wholly inappropriate Sign of the Cross. Then he pivoted and started issuing orders to his flock. "We've done all we can. A terrible accident. Everyone go home."

With a surprising amount of decorum, they quietly shuffled back toward their cars. A young couple separated from the others and came toward me. They were both blonde and looked to be no more than eighteen years old.

"Excuse me," the male half of the couple said. "We're Jimmy and Tammy Light."

Their name rang a bell with me, but I was too stunned to make coherent connections in my brain.

Jimmy said, "Do you think Buddy will be needing us?"

"What for?"

"We made the coffin for old Mister Engersoll and took care of the burial."

"You're undertakers?"

"It didn't start out like that," Jimmy said. "But I guess we are. Should we come back in a little while?"

"Prepare a coffin," I said. "A simple pine box for transporting the body of Max Faverman."

"Then he won't be buried here in Bob?"

"No," I said.

Max was going home to the plot beside Selma. His marker would stand beside hers, reunited with the seagull, the cat, the dog, and the stone flowers. I knew there were people to contact, arrangements to be made. Buddy had an older sister who lived in Portland. Most likely, she'd be in charge.

In the meantime, the logistical planning wasn't something I was familiar with. From Selma's death, I knew that their tradition was a quick burial followed by a period of mourning, sitting *shiva.*

I turned to Vikki, who was standing beside me. "We need to get Max back to Portland."

"I'll take care of it." She pulled Jimmy and Tammy aside and explained about needing a box for transport and clothing for Max to wear. "Soon," she told them. "And would you please ask Commander Van Glock to contact us here?"

"Van Glock?" I questioned.

"We'll need the helicopter," she said. Turning back to the cherubic Light couple, she listed a number of details that never would have occurred to me.

I faded away from their little group and stood apart, staring into the dark night, not seeing anything but my memories. Sorrow hung around my shoulders like a heavy yoke. It would take a while to realize that Max was really dead. He was in his seventies and he'd led a long life, a good life. Still, I wasn't ready to accept his death.

The youthful undertakers left, and Vikki joined me. Her

voice was soft. "This never should have happened. It was pure carelessness."

I didn't agree. Max's death was the second fatal accident within a week, which immediately led me to the conclusion that these two incidents weren't coincidence. The earthmover didn't accidentally fall down the hill. Somebody started the motor. A murderer drove the heavy equipment over the edge. Most likely, they were hoping to kill Buddy. His bedroom was squashed flat. Max had just been in the wrong place at the wrong time.

Even as my sadness pressed down upon me, I felt the stirrings of rage. The death of Max Faverman would not go unanswered, not while I was sheriff of Bob.

As I glanced back at the house, the earthmover settled for the last time, completing the demolition with a grating thud.

Buddy hadn't moved. He was still holding Max in his arms, talking urgently in a low voice, saying all the words that he never had time to tell his father. That was the worst thing for survivors of a sudden death. They never had the chance to say their final words.

Vikki shuddered. "We could have been in there. Me and Buddy."

"He said he was going to your place," I recalled. "Why didn't he drive the Beamer?"

"I came up here," she said. "After spending the day at the bank with your sister, I needed to talk." Her eyes widened. "Oh, my God! If we had been here, we could have saved Max."

"I doubt it." They might have heard the earthmover being started up. There might have been a minute's warning. "This happened fast."

"How? How could it happen?"

"I don't know." What I did know was that the lot above

Buddy's house belonged to Bambi Stokes, and I hadn't seen her. "Who's in charge of that construction crew?"

"I'm really not sure," Vikki said. "You know those were Jethro Kowalski's men."

"Right." If the accident that killed Max was actually a murder attempt on Buddy, it made sense to have the crew foreman out of the way. I wondered if Jethro's vanishing act was part of a complicated plan. But why? What was the point in making a murder so complex? It wasn't as if there were any law enforcement people in Bob to pursue an investigation.

Not until I'd been appointed sheriff. Probably, whoever did this crime didn't expect me to stick around, which was a big mistake on their part. I was staying here, right here in fucking Bob, until I had the answers.

I looked toward Buddy again. He was silent, standing sentinel over his father's body. His long, skinny arms hung limp at his sides. His shoulders stooped even more than usual.

Vikki and I joined him. She stretched her arm around him. "I'm so sorry, Buddy."

He turned his head toward me. The tortured expression in his eyes spoke volumes, and there was no need for long-winded explanations. We had both loved and respected his father. The death of Max Faverman diminished our world.

"This was murder," Buddy said.

"Yes."

"Find the killer, Adam."

"I will."

That was my solemn vow. Undertaking an investigation would be my mourning for Max. For the final time, I beheld the old warrior who had taught me to be a man. I wouldn't fail him or Buddy.

Through the trees I saw the flash of headlights. In an instant, I recognized Margot's red convertible rocketing up the hill, and I steeled myself to deal with my sister. She wasn't a sensitive woman.

I separated myself from Vikki and Buddy to meet her. Slamming on the brakes, she screeched to a halt.

"Adam," she snapped before I could tell her about Max, "come quick."

"Margot, there's something—"

"I said now, you jackass! Somebody's robbed the bank."

The plot was thickening too fast for me to understand what was going on. A bank robbery? On top of two murders and a disappearing Seahawk? It was too much for me to grasp.

"Don't just stand there," Margot said. "Get in."

Though I could have taken my own car, I waved good-bye to Buddy and Vikki and climbed into the passenger seat beside my sister. As soon as she whipped in a U-turn that brought us perilously close to the edge of the road, I knew I'd made a giant mistake. Every time I rode in a vehicle with Margot behind the wheel, my life passed before my eyes at ninety miles an hour.

I fastened my seatbelt. "Did you hear about Max?"

"I feel just terrible about it," she said.

I thought I saw a slight gleam at the corner of her eye, perhaps a tear. She'd liked Max Faverman. But Margot's emotions were difficult to gauge. On occasion, I'd seen her weep profusely about a wine spill on the wall-to-wall white carpeting in her palatial home. When our own father died, she was stoic. Giving her the benefit of the doubt, I decided that she truly was unhappy about Max's death.

"He was a genuinely kind person," she said. "Did you know that he paid for my prom dress in high school? The red strapless one?"

"I didn't know that." Because I'd had a prior engagement in Vietnam, I hadn't been around for Margot's prom.

"You know, Adam, it really isn't fair. Why Max? There are so many people, especially ex-husbands, who deserve to die. I'm really sorry about his death."

"His murder," I corrected.

Margot slammed on the brakes, skidding to a stop on the curving gravel road. "No!"

I didn't know if her emphatic denial was a knee-jerk reaction to the basic indecency of murder or based on experience. Margot and I had somehow managed to get ourselves mixed up in a couple of other untimely deaths over the past few years, when I should have been working on my sculptures.

I tried to explain. "It had to be murder. The earthmover didn't jump off the hill by itself. I mean, I'll have to wait until tomorrow to try and figure out how it happened, but I think it's safe to assume murder."

"But who would want to kill Max? Nobody here even knew him."

Prior acquaintance with the victim didn't necessarily negate a murderer's motivation. Otherwise, there would be no assassinations. But I didn't think that was what happened here. "The killer was after Buddy. Max just got in the way."

She drummed her long acrylic fingernails on the steering wheel before she started up the car again. "You're wrong, Adam."

"According to you, I'm always wrong." Why should tonight be any different?

"That's only because I'm always right," she snapped. "Don't argue with me."

I didn't. I likened disagreeing with Margot to arguing religion with Reverend Petty.

She turned to me and snarled through her lipstick, "Can't you see that I'm upset by Max's death?"

"Seems to me that you're coping."

"Just because I'm not weeping and wailing doesn't mean I don't feel anything. I have so many emotions inside me that I can't even begin to express them all." She glared at me. "By the way, you're a mess."

"Crawling through rubble will do that."

"You're not bleeding, are you? I don't want these leather seats ruined. The color is so hard to match."

I didn't even try to fathom the obscure psychological machinery that made my sister tick. It would've been easier to launch a space probe to Saturn. "Why do you think I'm wrong about Max's death being murder?"

"Somebody drove the earth mover off the cliff and smashed the house. That's so obvious."

"Uh huh."

"But I don't think the plan was for anybody to die."

"Buddy's bedroom was completely flattened," I pointed out. "It seems likely that dropping an earthmover on somebody would cause extreme death."

"It was manslaughter," she said. "You know, like when somebody crashes into a car and the person in the other car dies."

"I know the definition of manslaughter."

"So, here's what happened," she said smugly. "Pay attention, Adam."

"All ears," I said.

"The murderer dropped the earthmover on Buddy's house. But it was only meant as a diversion. They arranged an accident to draw everybody out of town. That way, they wouldn't run into any interference when they robbed the bank."

I couldn't believe that Margot was actually making sense. "That's not a bad theory."

"Of course it isn't. Crime solving is my forte. Don't you remember when I was going to turn my life story into a made for television movie? Margot—The mini-series?"

"How could I forget?"

"Then all those stupid cinema people got involved, and it was turning into a money hole. Well, screw them. I've been considering becoming a private eye." She tried out the idea in a breathless voice. "Margot, Private Eye."

Much as I hated to dissuade my sister from a course that might involve danger, I said, "That's really not a safe plan."

"I think it's very cool. I could be the only private eye in Bob. I can have my own adventures."

"This isn't an adventure, it's—"

"Shut up, Adam. We've got a bank robbery to solve." Her waxed eyebrows arched. "Some asshole made off with fifty thousand of my money."

"Real money or Bob bucks?"

"Real money. Greenbacks. U.S. issue. E Pluribus Unum."

From the murky depths of my brain, I recalled a figure of somewhere around seven hundred and fifty thousand dollars. The Bank of Buddy had collected that much today. Three-quarters of a million dollars.

"You know, Adam," she said, "the killer might not have been after Buddy. You were supposed to be sleeping at the house. When the earthmover fell, you could have been killed. It could have been you."

Somehow, that might have been easier.

Chapter
Nine

The Bank of Buddy looked nothing like the site of a careful investigation in progress. The interior was lit up like an open house. The front door stood wide open. Several of Van Glock's armed men circled haphazardly, peering into shadows, while the curious Bobites strolled right up to the bank building like tourists visiting Disney's Delusionary Land, three rides beyond Fantasy Land.

The sloppy attitude might have been forgivable except that a major crime had been committed, a robbery which might be related to the death of Max Faverman.

Even Margot noticed the irregularity. "They're not supposed to walk inside, are they? How are we going to get fingerprints?"

"Fingerprints are irrelevant," I said. "Practically every person in this country went through the bank today."

"What a bunch of morons!" She flung open her car door. "Stand back, Adam. I'm going to kick some Bobite butt."

"No butt kicking."

She drew herself up like a queen cobra preparing to strike with her orthodontically perfect fangs. "Excuse me, Adam? Are you telling me what to do?"

"That's right, Margot. I'm telling." I had no patience with her attitude. "Somebody I cared about was murdered."

"I care, too." Her nostrils still flared, but her voice was a hair less strident. "What should we do?"

The smart thing would probably be to report Max's death to Special FBI Agent Richard Gosinia. No doubt the feds could pursue an efficient investigation. Unfortunately, they would probably also close down Bob, which would hurt Buddy, and I didn't want that to happen. Buddy had been through enough.

Plus, I suspected the feds wouldn't have the same priorities as I did. They'd be happy to write off Max's death as an accident while they confiscated weapons from Van Glock, closed down Bambi's hemp farm, and locked the doors on Vikki's casino before it even had a chance to open.

"Well?" Margot demanded. "I'm waiting."

"I think we should do as much as possible to figure out who killed Max, and why."

Though I was strong on motivation, I was short on manpower. There were over two hundred people in this country, and I had no idea which among them were trustworthy. Against my better judgment, I was going to have to depend upon my sister. "Margot, I need your help."

A grin of pure evil stretched her lips. "It's about time you realized that."

The last time I'd trusted her to help me, I ended up being chased by a naked volleyball team across the plateaus and mesas of New Mexico.

"I'll be the sheriff," I said. "You be deputy."

"Deputy? It sounds like somebody who's second in command."

I humored her. "Then you can be Special Investigator."

"How about Supreme Investigator?"

"Fine," I said. "Your job is to take statements from all the witnesses. And alibis. Check the alibis for everybody, especially Van Glock."

"You're an idiot, Adam. He's rich. His family is in oil. Why the hell are you picking on Mauser Van Glock?"

Van Glock's first name was Mauser? Of course, that was the sort of thing that Margot would know about. She'd insisted upon calling Buddy by his given name of Benjamin during sex. I forced myself not to imagine Van Glock and Margot in bed together. There were some things better left uncontemplated.

"Besides," she continued, "he has an alibi. He was with me."

"While the bank was being robbed?"

"I'm not sure exactly what time the bank was robbed, but I think so. He was showing me his helicopter."

Before I got sidetracked into a discussion of the eligibility of Mauser Van Glock as a potential future brother-in-law, which was also something I didn't care to seriously consider, I pressed her for action. "You've lost some serious money here, Margot. Take the statements. Write them down."

"My memory is exceptional. I don't need to—"

"Please write them down."

"I'll think about it." She lifted her chin and peered down her nose at me. "Don't I get a badge?"

"You're a plainclothes Supreme."

"Hah! Nobody has ever accused me of wearing plain clothes."

Though she was now dressed in designer jeans of simple denim, her blouse was gold lamé and her stud earrings were two-carat diamonds. My sister resembled a plainclothes cop less than anyone I could imagine.

When we left her car I headed directly toward Sergeant Fishman. Back when he'd been a hotel security guard, he was stammering, nervous, and borderline incompetent. However, his video surveillance of the hotel in Seattle worked on a high level of sophistication. Hopefully, Fishman could put his knowledge to use in downloading the bank's computerized cameras.

"Fishman," I said.

He elevated two feet off the ground, whirled, and stared at me. "Oh, it's you. Why don't you go bother somebody else for a change?"

"Because I like you. Has anybody started investigating this mess?"

"Listen, McCleet, I'm going to get in trouble with Van Glock if I start taking orders from you. This isn't any of your business."

"I'm the sheriff," I reminded him. "I want you to come inside with me and download the video computers."

"No way. I'm waiting for a direct order from Commander Van Glock."

The commander himself came blustering over to us. I noticed that when he looked at Margot there was a gleam in his piggy little eyeballs. "Back off, McCleet," he said. "This is my jurisdiction."

A few hours ago I would have been happy to let him

dig his own grave. But not now. Not with Max's murder unresolved.

"We're working together on this," I said. "Order your men to secure these premises. Get everybody out. I'm taking Fishman, and we're going to check out the video surveillance."

He dithered, recognizing the validity of my orders and yet struggling to maintain his aura of authority.

Quietly, I said to him, "This isn't about strategic maneuvers and uniforms and saluting. Max Faverman was killed when somebody drove the earthmover off the cliff and onto Buddy's house. We're not playing games anymore, Van Glock."

Peevishly, he asked, "What does the accident at Buddy's have to do with the bank robbery?"

Margot stepped in. "My theory," she announced in less than dulcet tones, "is that the two crimes are related. The accident at Buddy's house was a diversion so the bank could be robbed."

"Huh?" He looked from Margot to me.

"Get your men to secure the bank," I repeated. "Do it."

"Now," Margot said.

Van Glock was predictably responsive to Margot's terseness.

He ordered his men to clear the bank of all bystanders and to guard the entrances. Because he was working with idiots, this simple directive took several specific instructions along the lines of take two steps forward and don't shoot yourselves.

While Margot set out to gather her statements, I snagged Fishman and dragged him inside the bank. "Do you have any idea what happened here?"

"I wasn't here," he said.

The interior of the bank was cluttered with overturned desks, trashed computers, and a chaos of paper from ledgers, flyers and stationary. The steel door of the walk-in safe hung open on its heavy hinges. The rear entrance had been demolished, apparently in an explosion that seared the wooden jamb.

When I checked at the front door, the keys Buddy had given me were still in the lock. "Fishman?"

"What is it?" Fussy as a maiden aunt, he planted his fists on his skinny hips. "Now, what's the problem?"

I pointed to the dangling set of keys. "Earlier tonight, Buddy asked me to come down here. I didn't see anybody guarding the bank, and when I tried his keys in the lock I got an electric shock and set off some kind of alarm."

He grinned. "That was my idea."

"The air raid siren or the shock?"

"Both. I'm pretty good with electronics, and I set up a couple of booby traps so we wouldn't have to waste our time standing around watching the bank."

"Oh, yeah," I said, "wouldn't want to waste time."

He got all huffy. "What's that supposed to mean?"

"I don't know what the hell keeps you guys so fucking busy."

"We have lots of important stuff to do. I mean, there's the guard duty at the perimeter. And maintenance at the heliport. And weapons control. And, for your information, we do some heavy duty physical conditioning."

I thought of my long ago experience with marine infantry training, with twenty-mile forced marches, thousands of push-ups and chin-ups, survival training, and obstacle courses. Van Glock's volunteer commandos didn't have a clue about physical conditioning.

But why should they? They were a pretend militia who'd never see actual combat. None of Van Glock's men expected to die in action. None of them would be sent home in a body bag with only a toe tag for identification.

I didn't say any of this stuff out loud. I never did. Nobody who hadn't been there could understand, and there wasn't much point in indulging my own bitterness. Not anymore. Vietnam had been a long time ago.

Why was I even thinking about the past, dwelling on the dark side? Because of Max? The uselessness and irony of his death had brought back other deaths, futile ends.

I wanted him back. I wanted to know that I'd hear Max's voice, ordering up another monument for his beloved Selma. I wanted revenge for his death.

I looked back at Fishman. "What kind of booby traps did you set around the bank?"

"The main one was a motion detector, like a car alarm but louder. If anybody touched either of the doors or any of the windows, there was an air raid siren. And the key-holes were electrified, in case anybody tried to pick the locks."

I eyed the keys, still hanging in the front door. "Are the booby traps deactivated?"

Fishman nodded. "I had to shut everything down when the alarms got set off."

"Did you reactivate before the robbery?"

"It's complicated wiring, and I didn't have time. One of the other alarms at the jailhouse went off, and I had to go see what was happening there."

"So, it's off?"

"That's right."

Without fear of electric shock I plucked Buddy's keys from the lock and stuck them into my pocket. "Let me see if I have this straight? You and a bunch of commandos deactivated the alarms and went racing back to the jail-house."

"Right," he said. "And some other people went up to Buddy's place to see if they could help."

"Leaving the bank pretty much unguarded."

Two diversions had been set in motion, sending the people of Bob off in two different directions and insuring that the area at the bank would be relatively deserted. It was a simple but effective plan which probably required at least three people. I wondered who, among the denizens of Bob, had been capable of enacting this strategy.

Van Glock had, supposedly, been with Margot.

Vikki and Buddy were together.

Reverend Petty had been the person who announced the accident at Buddy's place. Why? How had he happened to witness the accident? It seemed likely that he was involved in at least that part of the bank robbery.

"McCleet," Fishman said, "what do you want me to do?"

"See if you can get the computer on the desk near the rear exit working. Then try to access the camera surveillance, and we'll see if there are any home videos of the robbery."

"Shouldn't be any problem," Fishman said confidently. "When I was at the hotel I had a pretty doggoned nifty computer system."

"I remember."

Hitching up his baggy camouflage pants, he swaggered toward the rear of the bank. In spite of his supposed physical conditioning, he groaned when he lifted the computer from the floor to a desktop.

I went to the walk-in safe and checked the locking mechanism. The impressively heavy door worked on a fairly simple system of combination lock, probably a tumbler, and an additional key. It hadn't been blown open, which meant specialized safecracking equipment and a steady hand.

Again, I mentally reviewed suspects. Who would know about this kind of equipment? Other than Fishman, I was drawing a blank.

At the rear door, I guessed that the lock was blown with a small explosive charge. It would have made a loud pop, but not too much more than that. With all the other commotion, blowing the back door wouldn't have caused a stir.

The picture developing in my mind indicated a tidy operation. First, the citizenry was distracted. Then, the rear door was blasted open. There must have been a truck pulled up to haul away the money after they cracked the safe and emptied it.

Earlier, when Buddy and I watched the armored truck guards unload the Bob bucks, their part of the operation, hauling heavy canvas bags, had only taken about fifteen minutes.

I went to look over Fishman's shoulder. He had the computer booted up and was scanning for the video surveillance.

"Stop watching me," he snapped. "I'll tell you when I have something."

"I'll give the genius some room," I said, stepping back.

"There's no need to be a smartass, McCleet."

"But there is." If I didn't let off some steam, it was a sure bet that I was going to explode. Like it or not, my chosen form of release was smartass comments. Many times, this tendency had gotten me into deep shit.

Near the front door, I recognized the hapless commando I'd conned into trying Buddy's key in the booby trapped front lock. It occurred to me that he might have been stunned enough to hang around rather than chasing either diversion.

When I tapped his shoulder he turned in slow motion. "Huh?" he said cleverly.

"What's your name?" I asked.

"Franklin." His eyes bulged, and the pupils rolled around the whites like dice in a cup. "Hey, aren't you the guy who—"

"I'm the sheriff. Did you see what happened here?"

When his head bobbed up and down, his eyeballs *boinged*.

"Tell me about it, Franklin." He looked confused, so I clarified, "I want you to tell me about the bank robbery. Start from when you tried to turn the key in the lock."

"Whooee, that was some shock." Franklin was one of those compact, stocky, no-neck men. I guessed he was somewhere in his thirties with an IQ in about the same range.

"And then?"

"Well, I just sat there," he said. "Everybody was running all over the place."

"But you just sat there," I said.

"I was real dizzy, and I think somebody pulled me out of the street so's I wouldn't get runned over by none of the cars."

"This side of the street? The bank side?"

"Nope. I was across the street, just a-sitting and a-staring. And it seemed like I heard a gun going off. There was all kind of people running around, but I didn't see no guns."

"Uh huh."

"There was a woman on her knees near the bank, and she was praying. One of Reverend Petty's people, I guess."

"You didn't recognize her?"

His eyebrows knotted in concentration. "She might be one of Jethro's wives."

It sounded like Lois, the insane Yugo driver who thought she'd prayed up Spanky to deliver the baby. This was actually good news. Lois was weird but fairly intelligent. "Then what?"

"She looked at the bank and stood up and said, 'Halleluiah.' And she ran off."

"What else?"

"I saw a van with tinted windows. It drove out from behind the bank and then went toward the jailhouse."

Which was also the general direction out of Bob. No doubt, Franklin had seen the getaway vehicle. "License plate?" I asked hopefully.

"Yup. It had a license plate."

"Did you see any numbers? Did you notice what state it was from?"

"Maybe Oregon."

"Great," I said as I patted him on the head.

When I thought of vans with tinted windows, the feds came to mind. Special Agent Richard Gosinia and his acronym cronies probably had such vehicles at their disposal. Several pieces of this operation had the earmarks of government planning. For one thing, it required coordinated effort, the kind of planning that FBI guys, who were usually former accountants or lawyers, enjoyed playing around with, giving code names and synchronizing their watches. For another, the break-in involved explosives that the SWAT guys used with frequency and expertise. Also, the feds would have no problem obtaining the right equipment to open the walk-in safe.

But why?

It wouldn't have been hard for the feds to gain access to Bob. Though the border was heavily guarded at the front gate, there were secluded wooded areas. Gosinia said they'd been keeping this country under surveillance for some time. He'd talked to Buddy this afternoon, and Buddy must have blabbed about the bank being open for business.

Again, I asked myself: Why would designated agents of the United States government be concerned with The Bank of Buddy?

And I answered myself: Taking over a small country and robbing it blind was one of the things the feds did best.

Though I might be as crazy as Reverend Petty to imagine this was a conspiracy, I decided to have a chat with Special Agent Gosinia as soon as possible.

Dismissing Franklin, I went back to Fishman. "Any luck?"

"There's a surveillance image in here, but I can't access it. The computer doesn't want to make the connection. Probably got screwed up after it fell on the floor."

"What about the cameras themselves?"

"Possible, but not likely," he said. "These aren't like mini-cams, McCleet."

"Maybe you can get the images off one of the other computers."

"Maybe." Sighing, he glared across the bank to another computer which had been upended. "But don't get your hopes up."

I'd about had it with whining and reluctance. When I'd been a cop, we were all on the same page. "A murder has taken place," I said to Fishman. "We're investigating. We leave no stone, or computer, unturned. Take nothing for granted."

"Adam!" I heard a female voice calling and turned. Vikki Ramone stood at the front door, waving her arms on either side of Franklin like a point guard. "Adam, we need your help."

I went out the front door. Rather than trying to explain to Franklin that it was okay to let Vikki inside, I joined her outside the bank. "What is it?"

"I managed to contact Buddy's sister in Portland. Of course, she's terribly upset, and she wants to get everything taken care of immediately."

"That seems like a rational response."

"Everything," Vikki repeated emphatically.

Was I being slow on the uptake, or was she being unnecessarily obscure? "What's the problem?"

"Everything as in a death certificate," she said. "I don't need to tell you that we don't have a doctor in Bob. As soon as Max's death is reported, we're going to have problems."

I agreed. "Did you tell Buddy about this?"

"Adam, I'm worried about him. He's sitting beside Max, holding his hand and talking to him. A couple of times I heard him laugh."

Like most sons, Buddy probably had a lifetime of guilt to apologize for. I said, "Let him grieve."

"But what are we going to do about the death certificate? The police are going to want to investigate. And as soon as we let them into Bob, it's all over. All of it." She dragged her fingers through her shiny tuft of gold hair. "Oh God, this never should have happened."

"I have a friend on the police force," I said. "His name is Nick Gabreski. When you get to Portland, contact him, mention my name, and ask him to help."

"Will he cover up for us?" she asked.

The idea of Nick engaging in a cover-up was absurd. My friend Nick had been a cop all his life. Unlike a lot of others, he'd chosen that career path for all the right reasons, like justice, honor, and truth. There was no way Nick would do a cover-up, but he trusted me enough to stretch the boundaries. "Tell him I'll be in touch before Max's funeral. And I will be bringing the murderer in."

"All right," she said. "But you know that the funeral is going to be real soon. Buddy's sister wanted to know when Max's body would be delivered to Portland, so she could start making immediate arrangements."

"You've got that part figured out," I recalled. "Van Glock could take him on the helicopter."

"Which brings up another problem. The takeoff. I think we might want to notify the FBI so they don't get all worried about what we're doing and shoot us out of the sky."

"Good point."

"I'm not a fool," she said.

I acknowledged her intelligence. In spite of her infatuation with Wayne Newton, Vikki was a sharp thinker, as ready to turn a profit as Buddy. Vaguely, I wondered if she was capable of plotting a bank robbery.

"I'll talk to the FBI," I said. This made a perfect opportunity to question Gosinia. "Have you got a cell phone so I can contact you when it's clear for takeoff?"

She reached into her shoulder bag, retrieved a mobile telephone, and gave me the number.

At that moment, Margot sauntered over to us. Pointedly ignoring Vikki, she said to me, "I've got most of my interrogating done. Basically, nobody saw much of anything."

"What about a vehicle?"

"The getaway car?" She grinned smugly. "It was either a black van or a Land Rover or Wagoneer."

"An off the road vehicle with tinted windows," I said. "I don't suppose anybody got the license plate number?"

"Of course not," she said snappishly. "Anybody who lives here is an idiot."

"Bitch," Vikki said.

Margot cupped her hand around her ear. "Did I hear something? The squeaking of a tree shrew?"

"Do you mind?" Vikki shouldered her way into the conversation. "Adam, I have another problem. The radio station."

"K-BOB," I remembered. "What about it?"

"I've been running it. In addition to music, I usually provide local news, and everybody is expecting some comment on the bank robbery. But I can't handle the transmission if I'm going with Buddy to Portland."

The radio station seemed to me like the least of our problems when we had bank robberies, murders, and the disappearance of Jethro to keep us busy. "Forget the radio station."

"It's important," she said. "K-BOB is virtually the only promotion for the casino opening. It's important that we keep it open so people will know when we're ready for business."

I really couldn't imagine a vast radio audience waiting with baited breath for this news. "How far does your signal transmit?"

"A long way," she said. "There's not much else out here. We're beyond the fringe of the Portland stations."

"I'll do it," Margot said.

"You?" Vikki sneered. "What the hell do you know about broadcasting?"

"One of my former hubbies was in show biz," she said. "What's to learn? You turn on the machines and talk into the microphone."

Vikki made a growling sound in the back of her throat.

The similarity between the two women did not escape me. Both were avaricious, ambitious, and self-involved.

I made the decision. "Vikki, you have to go home with Buddy. He needs you."

"But what about K-BOB?"

"Margot can handle the radio station." I turned to her. "Don't mention Max's death, okay?"

"What about the bank robbery?"

"No details," I said.

Before Vikki could lodge further objection, I turned to her. "Now, do you have any other problems?"

"Logistics," she said, pouting. "I should check with Tammy and Jimmy about the coffin."

Tammy and Jimmy Light. I remembered the unusual name. Bambi had mentioned them in connection with the fire at Roger Engersoll's cabin. "I'll come with you," I said.

"Why?"

I glanced over my shoulder at the bank. "Until we get the information from the video cameras, there's not much else I can do around here."

Riding with Vikki in her car was a treat. After Margot and Lois the Yugo Queen, I had almost despaired of finding a female who wasn't intent on vehicular homicide. Not that I have anything against women drivers. Alison was one of the best, darting around in her Mustang.

As soon as her name flashed in my brain, I missed her. Alison Brooks. She'd know exactly the right words to help me come to grips with Max's death. We'd been through tragedies before, and she was of that rare breed who understood when silence could be the best comfort and when words were needed to stir the cold night air.

Something tightened inside me. I wanted to feel her warmth in my bed and to touch her skin, soft and fragrant as rose petals.

Vikki pulled up outside a small trailer that was set apart from two others. This was a pack rat home. Though they couldn't have been living here for more than a couple of months, they'd accumulated a junker truck, several tires, a stack of firewood, a threadbare sofa with springs sticking out, and a rusting refrigerator. A canvas tarp had been pulled back to reveal another varied wood supply of two-by-fours and sheets of plywood.

Using the light from their windows, Jimmy and Tammy Light were hammering together another coffin. With nothing resembling craftsmanship to slow their progress, the crude box was nearly finished.

When we got out of the car, they both looked up.

Again, I was struck by the innocent faces of the young couple. Jimmy was tall and skinny. His hair was an angelic mass of blond curls. Equally blond, Tammy's hair hung past her shoulders. In the headlights of our car I could see her freckles.

"Are you almost done?" Vikki asked.

"About another half hour," Jimmy said. "Buddy's really in a hurry, isn't he?"

"We're so sorry about his father," Tammy said. "He seemed like a nice old man."

I wasn't sure if Max fell into that category. Nice was too bland an adjective. He'd been tough, brave, and honorable.

I introduced myself again to the two and added, "I'm acting as sheriff."

"Oh, good," Tammy said. "We need a sheriff."

"That depends," her husband said. "We don't need a bunch of stupid rules."

"No stupid rules," Tammy said, hasty to agree with whatever he said. "You're right."

I got right to the point. "You were the people who found Roger Engersoll's body."

"Not exactly," Jimmy said. "We noticed the fire."

"Tell me about it," I said.

"We'd gone out for a drive," he explained. "Then we got tired of driving and we parked the truck. After we'd been, kind of, um, sitting there . . ."

Tammy giggled and said, "Sitting there."

I remembered what Bambi had said about that secluded part of the forest being the chosen make-out spot in Bob. It was the place where husbands with too many wives took their favorite breeder for procreating.

"I smelled the smoke," Jimmy said. "And I asked Tammy if she smelled it, too."

"And I did." Her blue eyes were so wide and agreeable that I couldn't imagine her ever saying no to anyone.

"I got out of the car," Jimmy said, "and I could see the orange blazes through the trees. Scared the piss out of me, and I started yelling."

"Fire! Fire! Fire!" Tammy illustrated, waving her slender arms in the air. "There were a couple of other people around and they came running over. And you know what was really funny? Not that a fire is anything to laugh about, but it was comical when some of them—"

"Honey," Jimmy said in the tone of a reprimand. "This is my story."

"Sorry." She literally clapped her hand over her mouth. "Go ahead, sweetheart."

He shuffled his feet. "There's nothing else to say. We all got together and put out the fire with water from the creek and using hatchets to tear the place apart. It was a blessing that the fire didn't spread."

"A blessing," Tammy repeated.

Their statement was almost completely worthless. They saw a fire and put it out. I asked, "Before the fire started, did you notice anything unusual?"

In unison, they shook their blond heads.

"Who else was there in the forest?"

Jimmy said, "We were too busy putting out the fire to take much notice. There were four or five couples. I remember Jethro Kowalski because he's such a strong guy. Knocked down the front door of the cabin with one whack of his axe."

I turned to Tammy. "And what was it that you found so comical?"

Her eyes sparkled. "Everybody there was married, so there wasn't any sinning going on."

"Of course not," I said.

"But they were doing some kissing and hugging. When people came running up, they were halfway undressed. Two of the men tripped over their own trousers. The Reverend Petty really gave them what for. On account of how we always need to be ready for attack from parachuters or sneaky troops coming across the country."

"The Reverend Petty was there?"

"Johnny on the spot," Tammy said.

And he'd also been the first person at Buddy's house when the earthmover fell. Either Petty was really good at anticipating fatal disaster or he had some explaining to do.

Chapter
Ten

──

Half an hour later I drove my Chevy to the front perimeter of Bob. Two of Van Glock's uniformed drones sat side by side outside the sentryhouse playing an extended game of Rock, Scissors, Paper, and discussing the eternal question of whether the scissors could really cut through paper that was as thick as a hand.

When I parked and approached I kind of expected a Who-Goes-There routine. Or a demand for the secret Bobite password. Or, at the very least, a threat. But these two barely looked up. As opposed to the gung ho attitude of many of Van Glock's militiamen, these younger guys had already perfected the lazy malingering attitude of forced draftees.

I doubted that they recognized me. I didn't look too suspicious. Once again, I'd managed to find a change of clothing, so I wasn't running around in a torn and bloodstained shirt. "All quiet?" I asked.

"Dead, as usual," one of them said.

"Wish we were in town," his partner said wistfully. "There's some stuff going down, and I'm not talking about the pregnant women."

Beside them was a boom box. The music was Elvis during his "hunka-hunka" years. Then, from the radio, came an all too familiar voice. "Listen up, people. It's me, Margot the Supreme. Here's the late breaking Bob news. Somebody robbed The Bank of Buddy, and when I find out who you are, Mister Buddy Bank Robber, I'm going to take a weed whacker to your private parts."

The two Van Glocksters on guard duty giggled.

Margot continued, "Okay, our next song is Frank Sinatra's 'Luck be a Lady.' God, who picked this ancient stuff? I'm running out to my car to get some Beastie Boys."

"Righteous," said one of the guards.

Shock jock radio host was probably a natural career for Margot. My sister had always been a megalomaniac.

I peered into the darkness beyond the chain link fence. "Have you seen the feds around?"

"They're out there."

Unless Agent Gosinia had cleverly disguised himself as a big rock, I didn't think so. "Where?"

"Dunno."

I unlatched the gate and pulled it open. Neither of the churlish young dolts moved a muscle. Apparently, their job was to make sure nobody got inside, but departures weren't a problem.

Just for yuks I asked, "Did either of you happen to notice a van or a Land Rover with tinted windows leaving here about three hours ago?"

"Nope."

"But we've only been on duty for an hour."

Was stupidity a major requirement for wearing the camouflage uniform of Bob? I glanced at my wristwatch, noting that it was a little past midnight. "Where were you stationed before that?"

"That would've been in the bed station. Barrack."

I asked, "Were you in the barrack when the jail alarm went off?"

Together, they chortled. "Man, that was some crazy wake up call. I about jumped out of my shorts."

I asked, "Do you have any idea who set it off?"

"Somebody playing a practical joke."

The other said, "Or else Fishman's dumbass motion sensor is too delicate. You know, like those car alarms that go off 'cause somebody a block away flushed the toilet."

As they returned to their game of Rock, Scissors, Paper, I drove through the gate, returned to lock it, and got back in my car. Being free from Bob felt damned good. I was sorely tempted to keep on driving. Within ten miles I'd be back to main roads, then onward to Portland and Alison. On the road ahead lay the sanity option, wherein I would forget about vengeance and attend the funeral of my friend Max, pay my respects like a regular person.

Unconsciously, my foot pushed heavier on the accelerator, and I forced myself to ease up. Whether I liked it or not, I couldn't leave until I answered the questions surrounding Max's murder. I owed it to the man who'd bought Margot's red strapless prom dress, the elegant gentleman who showed me how to defend myself against bullies. I had to know who killed him and why.

Of course, this was the kind of thinking that had gotten me sent to Vietnam and kept me on the streets as a cop. It didn't make sense, but I knew myself well enough to understand that I couldn't turn my back on a dragon and expect that somebody else would slay the beast.

I found the feds encamped less than a mile away. In a forest clearing, they'd set up in a parking lot a hi-tech jungle of radio antennae and satellite dishes surrounding two trailers, none of which could be seen from the front gate of Bob because of a curve in the road and a rise in the terrain. When I stopped my car, Agent Gosinia was waiting for me. He aimed a high beam flashlight directly in my eyes.

"I've been expecting a communication," he said.

"From me?"

"What's going on in there, McCleet?"

In order to avoid the glaring beam I stepped up beside him. There wasn't a lot of light in their encampment, and I suspected they were on some kind of black out, stake out, or some such spook nonsense.

Beyond my overriding mission to inform the feds about the helicopter, I had been considering whether or not I should turn the whole mess over to Gosinia and the other people who were trained and equipped to do the job that I was only winging. If I hadn't suspected that they were somehow involved in the strategic planning of the bank robbery, I would have happily passed the ball. But I had my doubts. Also, I didn't figure that Max's murder would take top priority on their agenda.

"Well?" Gosinia stared at me through the night. "What's up, McCleet?"

All other thoughts fled my mind as I caught a whiff of a wondrous fragrance. "Is that coffee?"

"Fresh brewed." Agent Richard Gosinia leered as if he were offering me a bribe. "Want some?"

"You're on, Dick."

"Don't call me Dick."

He directed me toward one of the trailers. We climbed inside and he poured a large mug of coffee. I sat at a tiny table and took a swallow. Like most loyal citizens of the great northwestern United States, home of Starbucks, I love my coffee. I could feel the caffeine taking the edge off my mood and sharpening my thinking. Thank you, Juan Valdez. The noble beverage was truly the nectar of the gods.

Gosinia slipped off his FBI windbreaker and sat opposite me. He appeared to be a rational, even pleasant, guy. He waited for me to speak.

"Here's the deal," I said. "I wanted to inform you and your men that a helicopter will be taking off from Bob within the hour. They're on their way to Portland."

"And I suppose these people think that sending you out here to tell me is equivalent to filing a flight plan. The FAA might have something to say about that."

I sucked down another sip of coffee. "I would've expected the FAA to be here."

"Don't think they wouldn't like to shut down those assholes and their black helicopter. We've had four sightings of UFO's that I'm presuming are Van Glock, flying low."

"Okay. So, will you inform your men? I don't want anybody trying to blast ET out of the skies with a disposable rocket launcher."

"How about if I make you a deal?"

It always surprised me when the FBI was as eager to deal as Max Faverman had been when he was selling shoes. Basically, the feds had all the marbles—their resources and the support of the most powerful military industrial complex on the planet. "Why?"

"Waco. Ruby Ridge. We don't want another incident."

"Bob really isn't that kind of place."

"That's what your friend, Buddy, said."

"He wasn't lying," I informed Gosinia. "There are a couple of nutcases in Bob, but most of the people are just interested in pursuing their basic freedom as capitalists."

I held out my mug for another cup of coffee, and Gosinia responded to my unspoken request with the speed of a drug dealer taking care of his best customer.

"You're talking about this casino," he said. "It's going to take weeks to verify this supposed Indian treaty and shut them down. Frankly, we couldn't care less about the gambling angle."

"Which angle bothers you?"

He took a deep breath. "The DEA wants to burn the marijuana."

"Don't we all? But it's hemp," I corrected. "They'd just git a mild buzz and a headache."

"You know what I mean."

"It's just hemp, for paper and rope."

"Yeah, sure. And the FCC is pissed about the pirate radio station. Plus, I can tell you right now, nobody likes that Petty character or any of the conspiracy bullshit he's spouting."

"I don't like him, either," I said. "But there are those nasty First Amendment rights."

"If we were in fucking Iran, we'd cut out his tongue and serve it with a loaf of bread and Grey Poupon."

"Colorful," I said. He still hadn't said anything that would merit the kind of attention that had been focused outside the gates of Bob. "What else?"

"Alcohol, Tobacco, and Firearms is concerned about Van Glock and his weaponry. We have reason to believe he is negotiating for the purchase of even more powerful and highly illegal firepower."

"Like what?"

"I'm not at liberty to—"

"Yeah, yeah," I interrupted. "What about The Bank of Buddy?"

I purposely left my comment open-ended. Perhaps I was hoping Gosinia would burst forth with a confession about how he and his men had stolen the cash. But his gaze didn't waver. His expression didn't betray the slightest hint of a cover-up. Deliberately, he lifted his own coffee mug to his lips and took a sip. "What about it?"

Since I could safely assume they'd been monitoring Margot's radio broadcasts, there was no need to pretend he didn't know about the robbery. "Somebody just stole three-quarters of a million dollars from the safe."

Without changing expression on his bland FBI face, Agent Gosinia offered a nod. "Do you want us to investigate?"

Bingo! I'd hit the jackpot! All of a sudden, the robbery made sense to me. It was an FBI operation, and they'd done it so they could gain access to Bob. "Is that the deal you wanted to offer me?"

"You're the sheriff," he said. "It would make sense for you to request our assistance in solving a big crime."

Unless, of course, they had been instrumental in committing said crime. "Then you guys would be seen as a benevolent intervention. No fireworks, no objections. Once inside, you could gradually dismantle Bob."

"Our concerns are only for the safety of the people," Gosinia said.

Except that Max Faverman was dead. If the feds had set up that diversion with the earthmover so they could rob the bank, they'd been careless. They hadn't taken the time or energy to check the premises and make sure Buddy's home was vacant. They'd ignored the white-haired gentleman snoring in the guest room. And now, he was dead.

I wasn't ready to forgive and forget. "I'm investigating the bank robbery. I don't need any help."

Finally, Gosinia cracked a smile. "You're a sculptor. Not a cop. Not anymore. We know all about you, McCleet."

"Yeah? How?"

"We're the FBI."

Which meant they knew everything and understood nothing, least of all my dedication to solving the murder of Max Faverman and avenging his death. "You also know a lot about what's going on in Bob."

He shrugged. "We have an agent inside."

Whoa, Nellie, that was a new piece of the puzzle. One of the wackos in Bob was an FBI agent? Certainly not Van Glock or Petty. I doubted it was Vikki, because she was too focused on opening her casino, and she struck me as the sort of female who would have someone else do her dirty work. But what about Bambi? I hadn't seen her since the bank robbery. Was she out there? Conferring with Gosinia?

Also, if they actually had a spy in Bob why hadn't they demanded an investigation into the death of Roger Engersoll? "Does this person keep you posted on everything that's going on in Bob?"

"Anything we'd need to know."

Which, apparently, didn't include bloody murder. I thought of the burn pattern which focused on the one wall beside the bed and the unlikely spark from a Franklin stove and the body which was certainly burned beyond recognition. No matter how you sliced it, this was a highly suspicious demise. Why wouldn't an FBI agent have reported it that way? "And you trust this agent?"

"Hell, yes. This is a well-trained, very special agent, extensively trained in covert operations," Gosinia said. "Sends out daily transmissions in Morse code."

"Isn't that a little antiquated?"

"Makes me nostalgic," Gosinia said.

I studied him carefully. Richard Gosinia was a well-tanned, pleasant looking man in fairly decent physical condition, the type of guy I'd expect to see all over a golf course on the weekend. I would have placed his age at no older than his mid-thirties. "Nostalgic for what?"

"I was born too late to be an Untouchable, or to work Black-Op's in Nam. Maybe that's why I'm willing to humor this guy. The Morse code is like the old days when there were real spies. You know, like the French resistance in World War II. It's cool."

Oh yeah, Vietnam was real cool. Too bad there was too much fiery death, mayhem, and horror for me to remember the essential coolness. "I bet you miss the KGB."

"Damn right."

I finished my coffee and stood. "I don't suppose you'd give me the name of this agent."

"You bet your ass I won't."

This was all a game to him. Gosinia had lost all the sympathy points I was willing to grant. No way would I be sharing information with the FBI. "Can you make it safe for the helicopter to take off?"

"No problem."

He flipped open a mobile phone and notified all the armed government employees hiding in the shrubs outside Bob.

Likewise, I called on the mobile phone to Vikki, informing her that the chopper might not get shot down.

Gosinia and I stepped outside.

He said, "Know this, McCleet. We're not the enemy."

That remained to be seen. If the fibbies had organized the robbery that accidentally killed Max, I intended to do everything in my power to bring them down. Waco and Ruby Ridge would look like parking violations when I got through with accusations of governmental terrorism that had affected a herd of pregnant women and had killed an innocent old man.

We heard the chopper overhead, and I looked up. To Max Faverman, I made a farewell vow. His death would not go unnoticed, covered up, and forgotten. *You deserve better.*

"Buddy is going to be gone for a while," I informed Gosinia. "Meanwhile, I'll be the spokesperson for Bob."

"How do I contact you?"

"You don't," I said. "I'll be in touch."

That was sufficiently cryptic, and a good exit line. I headed back toward my car.

"Hey, McCleet."

I looked over my shoulder at Gosinia. "Yeah?"

"Don't fuck with me."

For a moment, I vacillated between "Oh, yeah?" and "You're not the boss of me." Then I opted for silence. Obviously, an FBI agent had more experience with terse, threatening farewells than I did.

I got in my car and headed back to Bob, passing the supposed security loons at the front gate and going directly to The Bank of Buddy.

Outside, talking to Franklin the guard, I saw Bambi. Was it possible that the gorgeous granola-head was really an FBI agent? She'd seemed more concerned than most people about the probable murder of Roger Engersoll, and she had a thing about finding Spanky. Gosinia had referred to a very special agent. Bambi could fit that description with looks and personality alone.

When I came up beside her, she gave me a greeting hug, and her braless breasts crushed against my chest. I couldn't help but notice the firmness or the hard nipples on the aforementioned breasts. No way was this woman older than twenty-five.

"Adam," she said, "I heard about the accident with Max. I feel so responsible."

"Why?"

"That's my property above Buddy's house. If I hadn't been terracing the hillside, there wouldn't have been an earthmover, and it never would have happened. This is such bad karma."

I was sure Max would agree.

She frowned attractively. "A terrible accident."

It wasn't an accident. On this point, I was one hundred percent sure. The earthmover hadn't accidentally fallen over the edge. It was started up and driven.

After the rubble settled I intended to return to the site and climb all over the big yellow machine, where I would probably find a key in the ignition.

Apparently, Bambi had been saying something to me, because she looked at me with a question in her eyes.

"I'm sorry," I said. "My mind wandered. What did you say?"

"I usually don't have to ask twice." Her eyebrows lifted, and a sultry smile played around the corners of her lips. "You don't have anywhere to sleep tonight. Would you like to spend the night with me?"

Did that mean what I thought it meant? Was it just my crude, primordial logic? How could I think about sex when I was hot on the trail of the crime spree in Bob? "Oh, yes," I said. "Yes, I would."

"Shall we go?"

"First, I wanted to check something with Fishman," I said. "Then, we're on our way."

Together, Bambi and I went into the bank. We weren't holding hands, but we might have been. There was a connection between us that I interpreted as willingness. She was subtly communicating the message that she might be interested in sex tonight. I might have been imagining things, but I enjoyed considering the possibility.

Fishman hunched over one of the computers. His skinny fingers flew across the keyboard, and he was concentrating so hard that he was sweating.

He looked up as we approached.

"Did you access the video cameras?" I asked.

"This was a pretty goddamned serious effort," he said. "The hardware was damaged, and I basically had to reconfigure the program from scratch. I hope you appreciate this, McCleet. There are probably only three or four people in the entire country who could have done this."

Though I really didn't know enough about computers to be impressed, I said, "Excellent work, Fishman."

Bambi draped herself over his shoulder, offering a fine view of healthy, young cleavage. "Wow, can we play games on these machines?"

"Of course," he said, "if you have the software. I myself have the advanced Quake."

"And surf the net?" she asked.

"Oh, you betcha," he said with the burgeoning enthusiasm of a serious hacker. "Recently, I set up a Bob website for Vikki to publicize the casino."

Much as I hated to bring an end to this computer love-in, I said, "The video images, Fishman."

"Okay." He tapped on the keys. "I've already looked at it, but I think you should see for yourself."

On the computer screen a video image came in sharp and clear. This was from the outside camera focused on the rear, and it showed the top of a black vehicle backing up to the door. It was an off the road vehicle, something like a Land Rover. Unfortunately, the camera didn't show license plates.

A dark figure, wearing a nylon stocking over his head, emerged from the driver's side, aimed directly into the lens of the camera, and fired. The screen faded to static.

"Can you freeze those images?" I asked. If we went through the brief scene frame by frame, we might find a clue to the identity of the shooter.

"Already done and printed," Fishman said. He pointed to a stack of paper beside the computer. "The pictures are pretty much a blur, but that's not important."

"It's not?"

"Let me show you what came up on the inside camera."

He punched a couple more keys and another image appeared. Two men dressed all in black scurried around inside the bank. Because the interior lights weren't lit, it was hard to see anything more than shadows.

One of them carried a satchel which he took to the walk-in safe.

The other came toward the camera. He was a big guy, muscular, and he had a nylon stocking pulled over his face, distorting his features beyond recognition. He squinted directly into the camera lens, raised his handgun, and fired. Apparently, he missed, because he fired again.

And missed again.

This time, he yanked the stocking off his face to aim the gun.

Fishman froze the image. A clear picture of the bank robber.

"Oh my God," Bambi whispered. "It's Jethro Kowalski."

At least now we knew he wasn't dead.

Chapter
Eleven

"**W**hat a *putz!*"

I heard Max Faverman's words reincarnated and coming out of my mouth. I couldn't help it; the description was accurate. Jethro Kowalski defined the essence of *putz*. He made the strategic diversions and planning of this operation look like Forrest Gump Robs a Bank.

"Replay it," I told Fishman.

When the program backed up and started again on the computer screen, I was mesmerized by the former Seahawk's stupidity. Jethro was one of those huge guys who reminded me that a brontosaurus, though weighing several tons, had a brain the size of a walnut.

I asked Bambi, "Why did you hire this guy to work on your house?"

"He looked big enough to run a backhoe," she said.

"Hell, he's big enough to *be* a backhoe."

On the second viewing I noticed even more evidence of outright stupidity. Jethro ran into the door on his way inside. He tripped over a desk. Jethro, with a stocking over his face, went to the camera, aimed, and missed twice. His frustration was apparent. He pulled off the stocking for a better view and looked directly into the lens. His tongue stuck out of the corner of his mouth when he shot the camera dead.

Unfortunately, the other person on the screen was unclear in the shadows.

"Fishman, is there any way to get a better picture of the other robber?"

"Sorry," he said. "We'll never get any resolution of those images. The pixels are too large. I can't even tell if it's a man or a woman."

Which made me think of Lois, the insane Yugo driver who was one of Jethro's brides. Earlier, when I'd questioned Franklin, the electrocuted guard, he'd said he'd seen a woman praying. That sounded like Lois. Then, according to Franklin, she'd leapt to her feet and run off. Maybe she recognized her darling hubby, the father of her darling unborn child, carrying bags of money to the darling getaway vehicle.

This whole routine would've been really amusing if Max hadn't been killed. This man who'd lived his life with purpose and strength died because of stupidity. He would have appreciated the irony. If his ghost was anywhere around, Max was probably laughing his ass off.

I turned to Bambi. "Do you know where to find Lois Kowalski?"

"She lives with Jethro's other wives in a trailer near Reverend Petty's house."

"Let's go."

Fishman whined, "What about me?"

I patted his skinny shoulder. "You did a good job on these computers. You're a genius, Fishman. Make a printout of this scene and put it someplace safe."

"I've already done that." His lower lip stuck out in a pout. "I wanna come with you."

This sounded like a shift in allegiance from Van Glock to me, and I wasn't altogether sure whether I was ready to start recruiting a posse. On the other hand, since I already had deputized Margot as Supreme Investigator, there was nowhere to go but up.

Fishman said, "Commander Van Glock doesn't appreciate me. I'm a darn good detective, and I want to work with you."

"A vote of confidence? Thanks." I shook his hand. "Welcome aboard, Deputy Fishman."

He was beaming. "What should I do?"

"Right now, stick with Van Glock," I said. "Kind of as an undercover deputy. I've heard that he's negotiating for some kind of extreme firepower, and I want to know what it is. Also, your alarm was set off at the militia bunkhouse. See if anybody witnessed anything, and report back to me."

"Where will I find you?"

Bambi replied, "Tonight, Adam is staying with me."

"Oh?" Fishman's bass-like mouth curled in an adolescent leer. "What happened to your other girlfriend, McCleet? The redhead I saw in Seattle?"

"Alison Brooks," I said. "She's—"

But there wasn't any explanation. Alison was in Portland, not answering her phone. And I was here in Bob without a place to sleep.

I told Fishman, "Keep me informed."

"Roger that."

Bambi and I left the bank. We took my car because
Bambi had walked to town, and I followed her directions
through another clump of trailers behind the fat-steepled
church to the Kowalski residence. It was a double wide
trailer with white siding and plastic geraniums planted in
a half-barrel tub near the front door. Loud, high-pitched
voices echoed from within.

Bambi pointed through a nearby stand of conifers.
"That's Petty's house."

The vicarage was a narrow two-story with a steep roof
and fancy gingerbread trim. A single light shone from the
upstairs window, reminding me of something gothic from
the TV Addams Family. Given the reverend's penchant
for conspiracy theories, I surmised that the interior was
honeycombed with trapdoors and secret hiding places.

I turned my attention back to Casa del Kowalski.

When I hammered on the front door the argument
faded to whispers. Then a trembling voice called out,
"Who's there?"

"The sheriff," I said.

The door opened immediately. One of the women was
just starting to show. The other appeared to be well into
her third trimester. Neither of them looked glowing and
serene.

"I'm looking for Lois," I said.

"I told you!" the larger one yelled. "Lois is no good.
Now she's in trouble with the law."

"She's gone and left us here," the other Mrs. Kowalski
wailed. "Now who's going to take care of us?"

If Lois's main job was caring for the other wives, I didn't
blame her for disappearing. "Do you ladies have any idea
where she might have gone?"

"No."

"Have you heard anything from Jethro?"

"No, but he must have come back here while we were out searching, because some of his clothes are gone."

That made sense. Since he'd robbed a bank, Jethro probably wasn't planning to return home in the near future. At the very least, he'd need a change of underwear.

"Did he take food?" I asked.

The two women shook their heads "no."

The fact that Jethro returned home for a change of clothing but took no food told me that he might be hiding somewhere nearby. He was not the kind of man who'd put appearance before food. Someone around here was feeding him. If the trail got cold, I could hang around for a few days and follow the most emaciated person in the region home to Jethro.

A more immediate problem confronted me in the form of a duet from Mrs. Kowalski and Mrs. Kowalski. "What are we supposed to do?"

Though I was, of course, concerned about their delicate condition, I had no intention of delivering more babies or offering the logical counseling that they ought to go find themselves an experienced midwife. I pointed through the trees. "Why don't you ask the reverend?"

They argued with each other about not wanting to be a bother to the reverend and yet being in dire need of guidance. Both agreed on one thing. They were hungry, and it seemed to fall within Reverend Petty's duties to tend to the sick, the downtrodden, and the voracious.

As the Kowalski twosome set out for Petty's gothic manse, Bambi and I followed in their wake.

"Wow," she said, "they make a real good argument for birth control."

Normally, I would have agreed with her. But I'd recently witnessed childbirth for the first time, and I was still under the miraculous spell. "Infants are pretty wonderful."

"It's too bad women have to be pregnant to get them."

"A baby store would be convenient," I said. "A baby store with a return policy for the teen years."

"What do you know about teenagers, Adam?"

"I'm an uncle," I said in my defense. "And I remember being an adolescent male. It's safe to say that I was your typical rotten little shit."

She laughed. "Did you give your parents hell?"

"Drove my mother crazy. My dad died when I was a kid, but Max helped to fill the void. He gave the patriarchal lectures about not stealing motorcycles, not shooting holes in road signs, not getting the girls pregnant. Max bought me my first condom."

The Kowalski women were at the reverend's door, banging the knocker and sobbing.

When Petty answered he was wearing a green brocade robe with black satin trim on the lapels, similar to the smoking jackets that the British wore in Noel Coward plays, except that Petty's robe went all the way to the floor. It was the first time I'd seen him without his clerical collar, and he looked strangely vulnerable, with a skinny, hairless throat. No hair at all. Maybe he just looked strange.

"What?" he demanded.

Talking at the same time, the Kowalski women ranted through their explanations, finally making clear to the reverend that they were suffering from very specific hungers. One of them wanted blue Jell-O. The other asked if he had a steak bone she could gnaw at.

Petty threw open the door. "You ladies know where to find the refrigerator."

As they bustled into the house, Bambi and I followed. I said, "I need to ask a few questions, Petty."

"My condolences," he said, putting on his funeral face. "I understand you were close to the deceased."

It gave me the creeps to hear Max being described as "the deceased." I really hated the way Petty talked. "I need to know as much about Max's death as possible. You were the person who ran into town, warning us about the accident. Tell me what you saw."

"Though I did not actually witness the giant yellow machine plummeting from the hilltop, I must have arrived shortly thereafter. The swirling cloud of dust was apocalyptic."

"Did you hear the crash?"

"I was in my car," he said, "and I always listen to tapes."

"Must have had the volume pretty damned high," I said.

He glared at my obscenity but didn't bitch about it. "When I arrived at Buddy's house I recognized his car parked in front, and I suspected the worst possible outcome from the accident."

"Are you sure it was an accident?" At the very least, I'd expected a conspiracy theory.

"Nothing is really accidental," he mused. "Those events which are not part of the satanic plot to take over the world are predetermined by God's will."

"Is that G.O.D., or God?"

"Perhaps . . ." Beneath his dark red hair his eyes darted. "Perhaps the heavy machinery was drawn by the magnetic pull which the forces of the Antichrist have directed through the earth's magma to cause volcanic eruptions in Tibet."

"Right," I said. "I was thinking more along the lines of seeing someone running from the site or a car driving away."

"Can you imagine the explosion when Everest erupts? Part of the second coming, the rapture."

"Did you see anyone else?"

"No other human," he said.

Not wanting to hear about zombies or other creatures of his imagination, I quickly asked, "Why did you go to Buddy's?"

"I was responding to a telephone summons. Someone called and said I should go to Buddy's to discuss the implications of the FBI surveillance."

"Someone? You don't know who called?"

He shrugged. "It was a woman."

"And you didn't recognize the voice?"

"I work with a lot of women." He nodded toward the hallway, where the Kowalski wives were exclaiming with delight over foodstuffs. "They are the most blessed of the creatures on spaceship earth."

"Creatures?" Bambi questioned.

"Most blessed," Petty said. "Females are entrusted with the sacred reproductive function for our species, and it is their prime directive to nurture their young. We must always protect our women."

"Protect this!" Bambi raised her middle finger, thrust it in his face and pivoted. "I'll wait in the car, Adam."

Prudently, Petty waited until she'd gone before saying, "Someday, she'll understand. With wide hips like that, she's a woman made for bearing."

"Too bad she has a brain," I said.

His chuckle was condescending. "I see that you've been poisoned in your thinking by the radical feminists and lesbians, pawns of the Antichrist. Someday, women will realize that we hold them in highest esteem. They give the gift of life. In that way, they are superior to men."

"As long as they're pregnant," I said.

"Exactly."

"Speaking of women," I dragged him back. "Have you

seen Lois Kowalski? Did you see her after the bank robbery?"

"I can't say that I did." He cinched the sash on his
green silk bathrobe more tightly. "You don't think you
agree with me, Adam McCleet. But you do. For example,
do you like women?"

"As a gender, I like women a lot."

"Then you're one of us." He clapped his hands together
in proselytizing fervor. "We like women. We respect them.
Did not the spirit of the Lord come to Mary? Was she not
elevated among women, with immaculate conception?"

"I don't discuss religion," I said.

"Ah, but you should. As the ancient Hebrews studied
the Torah, we should all seek the truth through the ultimate Geo-political Omni Doctrine."

"I'll say one thing."

"Yes?" Reverend Petty looked at me, all bright-eyed and
expectant.

"You are full of shit."

I returned to the car where Bambi was waiting. She was
steaming. Also, she was smoking, and I caught a drift of
sweet marijuana on the breeze.

"He's such an asshole," she said. Her pupils were
dilated.

"Sampling the product from your fields?" I asked.

"It's a dirty job, but somebody's got to do it."

I don't know why I should have been surprised by this
revelation, but I was. All along, Bambi had insisted that
she was growing hemp, not marijuana. Now, she turned
out to be a midnight toker.

I started the car. "Where's your house?"

"Down the hill, other end of Main Street, and turn left.
It's only a temporary home. But I think you'll know it when
you see it."

Her head lolled back on the seat, arching her slender neck. Her eyes closed, and a slight smile touched the corners of her mouth.

We drove in silence. It had taken me a while to get over my initial reaction to her, which was *hubba hubba*, and I started to put together what I knew about Bambi's character.

Though she was six feet tall and incredibly beautiful, she had the attitude of someone who didn't much care about appearances. As far as I could tell, she wasn't paired up with anybody in Bob, but she had a crush on the mysterious Spanky. Her coyness when she invited me to spend the night was intriguing but not a direct promise of sex. Was she one of the lesbian pawns?

Somehow, I didn't think so. Not that my radar was infallible, but Buddy hadn't slipped her into the don't bother category, and he was an expert. So what else did I know about this easygoing vegetarian who was into herbal remedies and never wore leather?

If I considered her a suspect, I had to take the earthmover into account. It was on her property. And I didn't think she had an alibi for the time of the bank robbery.

But why would she rob the bank? She didn't seem to care about money.

I took the left turn at the far end of Main Street, and glanced toward her. Again, I was struck by her natural beauty. "Bambi? Where should I—"

"You'll see it."

After a few turns, I noticed a porchlight on a cute little cabin that looked as if it had been constructed from Lincoln logs. The adorable-ness carried over to the lawn ornaments. Matching Disney-style fawns.

I parked at the front door.

She opened her eyes and grinned. "Those are my Bambis."

"Is it your real name? Bambi Stokes?"

"Nope."

She left the car and drifted toward the front door, which was, of course, unlocked. Without looking back, she went inside.

The interior of the cabin was only two rooms, similar to the design of Roger Engersoll's place, and I wondered if this was some kind of prefab design.

Bambi tossed me a comforter and pointed to the sofa. "Good night, Adam."

As I stretched out, the question of sex was the furthest thing from my mind. It had been a hell of a night, and I was tired. Even in the presence of a marijuana smoking nymphet, I was limp. With a low grunt, I rolled onto my belly. A pillow might have made sleeping more comfortable, but before I could ask I was asleep.

I'd been too wiped out to dream until right before I woke up the next morning. Sunshine warmed my eyelids, and my brain went through sluggish calisthenics as I struggled toward wakefulness. There seemed to be elongated shapes dancing in my head, like distorted shadows in front of a bonfire. A steady tom-tom beat accompanied this leaping dance. The shapes were dressed in masks and loincloths. So was I. Like Tarzan. I heard a voice say, *"Ongowah."*

I responded, *"Bass ay, simba."*

A noble lion posed at my side.

"The natives are restless."

I opened my eyes.

Last night, I hadn't comprehended the intimate layout of the cabin. There was only a kitchen and one other room, which meant that Bambi had been sleeping maybe fifteen feet away from me. She was the first thing I saw in the morning, lying on her side, staring at me with her brilliant blue eyes. Her shoulders were bare, but a sheet covered all the important parts.

I woke up, as I usually did, with a woody.

"Hi, Adam." She inhaled and exhaled slowly. Her nipples creased the sheet. "You look cute in the morning. Kind of rumpled."

What would happen if I asked her to join me on the sofa? Would she get out of her bed, naked, and walk over there? Or maybe I should scamper across the room and hop into the sack with her.

What about Alison? I told my conscience to shut the hell up. Alison would never find out if I slept with Bambi. Alison was a woman of class and distinction. It wasn't as if she had a burning desire to visit Bob.

I glanced at Bambi again. I could smell the pheromones from here. She was straight out of the *Victoria's Secret* catalog. My woody was telling me to jump her bones, and to do it now.

Staring into Bambi's eyes, I said, "Phone?"

She pointed to the table beside the sofa.

I groped, grabbed the receiver, and punched out the long distance number for Alison. If there's one thing I've learned in life, it's to ignore any plan of action suggested by organs below the waist.

Once again, I got the answering machine.

"Alison," I said, "if you're there, pick up."

I didn't want to tell her about Max's death over the phone. She'd liked the elegant old man a lot. I was, however, assuming that the funeral was tomorrow, and I wanted to be there.

"Alison," I repeated with a sigh. "I'll be back in Portland tomorrow. I need to see you. I miss you."

When I hung up, Bambi smiled at me. "Is that the redhaired girlfriend?"

"Auburn," I said.

"She's a lucky girl."

Then, totally unself-conscious, Bambi got out of bed. She was stark nude, and beautiful enough to elevate my blood pressure to the point of cardiac arrest.

Being a sculptor, I saw a lot of nude women. I spent months crafting their naked bodies from smooth marble and pliant clay. But this was different, unexpected, strangely intimate.

She went to a dresser, pulled open a drawer, and took out a pair of jeans which she slipped into. No underwear, I noted with great approval. None on the bottom. She pulled on a sleeveless T-shirt. None on the top.

She tossed her head, sending ripples through her long black hair, then looked at me. "Aren't you going to get up?"

Not with a granite erection, I wasn't. "Oh, I just think I'll lie here for a minute."

She disappeared through a doorway that I assumed led to the kitchen. "Want some granola for breakfast?"

"Sure." I never ate granola. It hurt my teeth.

By the time Bambi returned with a bowl of granola and a cup of coffee, I'd managed to sit up.

"Bathroom?" I asked.

"Outhouse. It's up the hill. I didn't sink a well because this is only a temporary house, but I have running spring water in the kitchen sink if you want to clean up."

After the outhouse, the wash up, the coffee, and two bites of granola which was probably going to do disgusting, cleansing things to my colon, I was ready for action.

"I guess I'll be going," I said to Bambi.

"If you want, you can stay here tonight," she offered.

"Not necessary," I said quickly. "I want to head back to Portland for Max's funeral, and I should leave this afternoon."

"Adam," she said softly. "There's something I need to tell you about."

There was the tone of confession in her voice, so I sat back down on the sofa. It would break my heart if she informed me that she'd been responsible for Max's murder. I wanted vengeance, and my baser instincts would not be appeased by dragging Bambi off in handcuffs. "Go ahead."

"The guys at the front gate," she said, "all those feds."

"What about them?"

"It's my fault that they're here. About a week ago, I contacted the DEA so I could apply for a contract to grow legal marijuana for medicinal purposes."

"Legal?"

"In California, they've okayed the use of cannabis in treating certain conditions, like glaucoma. So they need people to grow it, under controlled circumstances. You know, with quality control."

"And you thought you'd compete with Eli Lilly?"

"They'll need farmers," she said defensively. "I've heard that they're going to give licenses."

The idea that the federal government would hand out permits to every pothead who wanted to plant a stash was insanely innocent. "You're joking, right?"

Her blue eyes snapped wide. "Why shouldn't they support small business people like me? I could raise top grade, organic marijuana, and I'm a good person at heart. I mean, it's not like I'm some kind of drug cartel or something."

Unfortunately, the feds were far more likely to play *Let's Make A Deal* with third world slimebag drug dealers than to negotiate with a lovely pothead who wanted to raise a few prime acres.

"Okay," I said, "you contacted the DEA. And then what happened?"

"I asked them to send information about their legalized marijuana growing project, and they were real nice about it."

"You gave them your name and address?"

"It sounds so dumb." She flung herself down on the sofa beside me. "I mean, I didn't call up and say, 'Like, hi, I'm Bambi, and I've got a couple of acres of prime cannabis delicious to unload.' I was careful."

"But you told them where you were, and you mentioned that you're interested in growing an illegal substance."

"They were so friendly on the phone, and then they turn up at the front gate with machine guns. The bastards!"

I could've lessened her guilt by telling her that the FBI had been keeping a watch on Bob for months and even had an agent inside. But why should I? "Bambi, is there anything else you haven't told me about?"

"Like what?"

"Like your real name?"

"Clarice," she mumbled. "And Stokes is my married name. And my brother with the paper processing plant isn't my brother. He's my husband, but we're—what do you call it?—we're estranged. Living apart."

"Anything else?"

"I'm really sorry, Adam, about the DEA. Please don't tell Buddy about it."

I slowly stood. "Where were you last night when the bank was being robbed?"

"I was here at home all night until I walked into town, heard what was going on, and ran into you at the bank."

"Home alone?"

"Yes, of course." Her pretty head bobbed up and down. "You don't think I had anything to do with the bank robbery, do you?"

I hadn't drawn any specific conclusions, but she'd lied to me more than once. If Bambi had been the mastermind who planned the bank robbery, she could have recruited Jethro easily. I'd seen his other wives.

"Bambi, where did you get the money for all this? The cabin and the acreage?" Supposedly, she was a free spirit, a hippie spawn. "How do you afford it?"

"I'm a trust fund baby. When I turned twenty-one, my grandpa arranged for me to get a lot of cash."

And she'd used it to plant a field of hemp. Grandpa must be real proud.

Chapter
Twelve

On my drive from Bambi's to the murder scene, otherwise known as Buddy's house, I tuned to K-BOB, where I was somewhat surprised to hear Margot the Supreme. It was early for my sister, only a little after nine o'clock.

"Before we get back to the music," she said, "I want to tell you yokels something. Bob needs an espresso stand. I mean, really. Every wretched little hole in this state has a Starbucks. What's wrong with you idiots? I had to brew my own this morning."

Margot's coffee was nothing to smirk at. I'd always assumed that she made it in a cauldron with eye of newt and toe of frog.

"Could I just tell you," Margot continued, "that I would kill for a latte? Oh, and speaking of capital crimes, I'm still awfully peeved about that bank robbery. If you ask me, we ought to hire some real hotshot detectives to get in here and solve it.''

Thanks, Margot.

She droned on, ''Somebody like Tom Selleck on *Magnum.* Remember that? What a stud. Anyway, why don't some of you Boboons call in with your ideas? Now we're going to hear the demo tape for the Margot-ettes with Rob Crusoe, my recent ex-husband, who should be sliced, diced, and fed to a shark.''

Discordant noise from the Margot-ettes vibrated through the speakers, and I turned off the radio while I speculated on the nature of crime in Bob. To the best of my knowledge, it started with the murder of Roger Engersoll. Then Max. Then the bank robbery.

These were disparate acts of violence, involving arson and an earthmover, but it seemed to me that one individual was responsible for them all. There was a weird similarity to the crimes. Both murders looked like accidents. None of the crimes were witnessed, but there were people nearby, and all were discovered shortly after they'd happened. It was almost as if the murderer liked the risk of almost being caught. All took place under cover of darkness.

And the murderer didn't always act alone. In the case of the bank robbery, the mastermind had Jethro along to screw things up. And there had been the phone call to Petty. Could this be a band of criminals?

I didn't think so. I was going to stick with a single killer theory. The same person killed Engersoll and Max, and robbed the bank. One psycho. But lunacy wasn't a complete explanation. And I had to ask why.

The most obvious motive was, of course, the three-quarters of a million dollars which had been collected in The Bank of Buddy. That was a hearty chunk of change, enough to keep most people in Fruit Loops for the rest of their lives.

But if the motive was greed, why was Engersoll killed? He'd left his property to G.O.D., which moved the reverend to the head of my list of suspicious persons.

But why would Petty drop an earthmover on Buddy's house? The obvious answer was: Because he wanted to kill Buddy. When he saw Buddy's car parked in front, Petty said he could only assume that the owner was inside, sleeping.

I parked in front of the rubble that had once been Buddy's house. When I got out of the car I looked down at the trampled flowers in the garden, and last night's tragedy replayed in sharp, quick images that ended with Buddy kneeling beside Max's body and whispering words that his father would never acknowledge. I couldn't accept that Max was really gone, that I'd never hear his voice again, that he'd never call with another request for sculptures on Selma's grave.

I indulged myself with a few tears before I took a mental step back, distancing myself. I'd had considerable experience with setting aside my emotions. There would be enough time for mourning later. If I allowed myself to dwell in that empty place too long, Max's murder would never be solved.

Today, I was the sheriff of Bob, investigating a suspicious death, and I was ready to get on with it. In the morning light, the destruction was uglier and more grotesque than at night when the scene had been obscured by shadows.

The yellow earthmover was rusted-out in several places, definitely not a state-of-the-art piece of equipment. It looked like something that had been sitting neglected in a farmer's field for the past ten years. Beneath the giant rubber tires, the house was a muddy mess of splintered boards and beams. Warm sunlight glittered on bits of broken glass and metal.

I climbed over the wreckage to the cab and hoisted myself aboard. As I had suspected, the key was in the ignition, turned to the "on" position. This was no accident. Someone had fitted the key in the ignition, started up the engine, and driven the earthmover to the brink of the cliff.

Fingerprinting might be useful. When I went back to Portland tomorrow, I could get a forensics kit from Nick Gabreski. There were a lot of things I needed from Nick, mainly background checks on Bambi, Engersoll, Vikki, Van Glock, and Petty—especially Petty, because he'd looked familiar to me from the first time I laid eyes on him.

It was a lot of asking, and Nick was going to want a good reason not to notify the Oregon Criminal Investigation Department about the crime wave in Bob. Nick played by the book, and the rules dictated official inquiry into major crimes.

I climbed off the machine and picked my way across the ruins. Hoping to find something resembling a clue, I hiked up the road to the terraced area where Bambi's land was being cleared. From the top of the hill, the three hundred and sixty degree panoramic view of the valley was remarkable. Enough trees had been left for landscaping, but the land was mostly cleared and leveled. Up here, there would be sunlight all day.

An excellent choice of site. When Bambi finished her house she could probably share well water and generator power with Buddy. Maybe she'd known that Buddy wasn't planning to stay in Bob, and had expected to purchase his property after he left.

Two backhoes rested side by side, about twenty yards from the edge. If I'd been lucky in my search for evidence, I would have found neat earthmover tire tracks leading to the edge, where it crashed. But there was no sign of what had happened the night before, nothing but well-packed earth.

I looked down on the scene of destruction. The earth-mover looked as if it had been held over the house and dropped straight down instead of rolling down the hill and shoving against the back wall of the house. If the driver of the earthmover had taken a running start to pick up speed, then jumped out at the last minute, the big machine would have leapt off the cliff. Maybe the accelerator pedal was jammed down and the brake released to send it flying.

It was a damned shame that there were no witnesses.

But maybe there had been a watcher. There was at least one person in Bob who spent much of his time creeping around and spying. The mysterious stranger. Spanky.

It was too much to hope that he'd been there last night, but I didn't have any other possibilities. So, who was this unmasked man, the ninja in cowboy boots? It seemed likely that Spanky was FBI Agent Gosinia's man inside Bob, the senior agent who sent out his daily messages in Morse code.

And, maybe, he was a witness.

For lack of any other leads, I decided my next order of business should be to locate Spanky. Which was a hell of a job. The guy was a ninja shadow who'd hidden himself somewhere in the twelve square miles of Bob or in the neighboring Wallowa National Forest. I had a bad feeling that if Spanky didn't want to be found, I couldn't locate him.

Pacing back and forth on the future site of Bambi's home, which had to be one of the best lookouts in Bob, I scanned the area. To the west, on the side of the hill furthest from Main Street, I spied a ribbon of gray smoke, curling skyward, from an opposite hillside. The transient

vapor was so faint that it might have been an illusion. Or
it might have been Spanky.

And I didn't have another clue.

Since there were no roads in that direction, I hoofed
it—down into a slight valley, then up another incline.
I'm not in the world's best physical condition for a man
approaching fifty, and I'm not planning to participate in
any Senior Iron Man competitions.

This wasn't a bad walk and the weather was cooperating.
The early autumn was crisp, not too hot, and without a
sign of rain. There were only high puffy clouds overhead.

I wondered what it was like in Portland, where Buddy
and his sisters planned their father's funeral, and Nick
Gabreski sat behind his desk in Missing Persons eating a
donut, and Alison wasn't answering her phone. Though
I'd only been away from her a couple of days, I missed her
in the purely carnal sense that I wanted her body, and also
because talking to her helped me think more clearly. I
couldn't wait to tell her about delivering the baby, the
moment when that tiny human had squeezed free. Alison
had a terrific artistic sense. She'd appreciate the amazing
wonder of perfect little fingers and toes.

As I hiked up and over a small ridge, I smelled the
smoke I'd seen from a distance. It gave a pungent edge
to the musty stink of the old growth forest. And I heard a
low murmuring noise, rhythmic and steady, not unlike in
the Tarzan dream I'd had this morning before Bambi gave
me the free peep show.

I walked more carefully, trying to be light on my feet,
but my approach was just about as subtle as Sasquatch. I
thrashed through the low-hanging branches and shrubs.
Twigs snapped loudly beneath my sneakers.

Through the forest of tree trunks, I caught sight of a
man sitting Buddha-like in the middle of a clearing. His

eyes were closed, as if meditating. He was naked from the waist up, chanting unintelligible words like a mantra.

As I got closer I saw that he'd tied a red and black strip of cloth across his forehead. His chest was painted with white cross-hatching that looked like a tic-tac-toe board, and he had on several necklaces with beads and colored rocks. The pendant on one of them looked like a bird with outstretched wings. Another held dogtags.

Behind him was a dome-shaped tent made of army green tarps. That was where the smoke was coming from.

I stepped into the clearing.

"Welcome, pilgrim," he said.

Spanky's eyelids lifted. Half of his face was smeared with the same chalky substance he'd used on his chest. The other half was black. "I knew you'd find me, McCleet, and I knew you'd come alone."

I'd taken just about as much weirdness as I could stand. "You don't know anything about me."

"We're two sides of the same coin, pilgrim."

His tone was a low, compelling whisper. Two sides of the same coin might mean he was a federal agent and I'd been a cop. Or he might have been referring to Vietnam. From the gray flecks in his close-cropped hair and ragged beard, I guessed that we were close to the same age. The scrap of material he'd tied around his forehead was Asian in design.

He was staring hard at me, trying to communicate a secret understanding, but I've never been psychic and I don't pick up on vibes from other people. I didn't know what the hell he was talking about. "Which coin is that?"

With a lithe movement, he stood up. In his bare feet, Spanky was a little shorter than I was. His body was lean, no gut, and I guessed that he was in better physical condition, one of the benefits of living in the wild, eating berries and roots.

I pointed to the dome-shaped tent. "Your place?"

"My sweat lodge," he said. "Once a week, I build a fire, heat stones, and go inside to sweat out the impurities in my body and my soul. When I come out, I look to the four directions of the wind for wisdom. I become one with the earth."

"Which would explain the body paint," I said.

"The meaning of life becomes clear to me in images of the great bear and the wolf. The secret journey of the curious mouse enlightens me, and I fly as the hawk above the earth. Have you ever heard of the vision quest?"

"A computer game?"

"Your cynicism doesn't fool me, McCleet. You can't hide yourself from me."

"My disguise?" He was the one dressed for Halloween.

"You wear the clothing of a civilized man."

"This isn't mine." I pulled at the T-shirt and windbreaker I'd borrowed last night to replace my clothes, which were destroyed when I failed to rescue Max. "Usually, I wear a cat suit with sequins."

"I see your heart. You're like me. Untamed."

"But housebroken," I said.

He went to a large earthenware pitcher that rested upon a flat rock beside a conifer. Spanky lifted the pitcher above his head and poured out water. The liquid streaked the markings on his face and body, and he shook himself like a dog.

Then he stepped into a shaft of sunlight and raised his arms above his head as if he were preparing to dive into an invisible swimming pool.

"Is this part of the ritual?" I asked.

He lowered his hands, hooked his thumbs in the belt

loops of his jeans. "Why didn't you do as I said? Why didn't you look out for Buddy?"

"How did you know Buddy was in danger?"

"I know everything that happens in Bob. These are my people, lost in the wilderness, and they must be cared for, protected. I am their father."

This guy had more than a screw loose. The whole front end of his brain was out of alignment. "Okay," I said. "So, you skulk around in the forest, watching and protecting. Where were you last night? Did you see what happened at Buddy's house?"

"You ask too many questions." He shrugged into a green Army fatigue jacket. There was a name stencilled over the pocket, but it was so faded that I could barely make out the letters. "Look inside yourself for the answers. If you really dare to know the truth."

He whipped the tarp off his makeshift sweat lodge, revealing a fragile skeleton of bent branches and a charred circle of round smooth rocks. There was a subtle mist of smoke, faintly tinged with the scent of marijuana. Apparently, Spanky was taking advantage of Bambi's crop to aid in his vision quest.

Though I had nothing against the occasional recreational use of pot, it pissed me off when people justify their habit by claiming special insights to a mystical world. I didn't buy it. Getting loaded wasn't like buying a ticket for the bus ride to grand enlightenment.

All of Spanky's cryptic posturing and posing and phoney ritual were the actions of a guy who was bored, playing games with himself in the woods while he got stoned.

He held out his hand, palm up. "Join with me, McCleet."

I declined his offer to circle jerk. "Who the hell are you?"

"No more questions," he said.

I was willing to play this game. No questions, only statements.

"You're a federal agent," I said. "You were sent here to keep surveillance on Bob, and you send out your messages every day via Morse code. You're spying on these people, and you're sure as hell not their father."

Silently, he folded his tarp and checked to make sure the fire in his sweat lodge was completely out.

I continued, "You know who murdered Roger Engersoll. You also know who drove the earthmover off the cliff, killing Max Faverman."

He gave a low whistle and his magnificent white stallion surged through the trees. I was startled. I hadn't seen the animal earlier. It was as if the horse materialized from nothing.

Spanky placed the tarps into his saddlebags.

The jerk was pulling up camp, getting ready to ride off into the sunset, and I'd be damned if this son of a bitch took off without talking to me. I moved closer to him. If necessary, I'd throw him on the ground and hog-tie him with my belt.

"You know exactly what's going on here in Bob," I said, "but you haven't reported your information back to Agent Gosinia. If you told him about Engersoll, you called it an accident. The same with Max. Am I right?"

"No questions."

"What you're doing isn't right," I said. This guy was a clear case of burnout. He'd been in the field, undercover, too long. "It's time to come in from the cold. You're losing track of your mission, and people are getting killed."

He whirled around and sprang at me so fast that I barely had time to sidestep his charge. In his right hand he held

an eight-inch blade with serrated edges. Spanky was trying
to kill me.

In a crouch, I circled away from him. I kept my eyes on
the knife. "Don't do this. I'm on your side."

"Gosinia sent you."

"No," I said. "I'm here on my own. I want to know
who killed Max Faverman."

"There's only one truth. Everybody else is the enemy."

"Whatever you say." I was trying to placate him.

"Once, I was like you. I was on the side of napalm
and agent orange and burning, twisted death. I held the
children in my arms, babies too weak to cry. That was my
team. We're number one."

"Vietnam was a long time ago."

He feinted with the knife and I dodged, keeping a safe
distance. I needed a weapon.

"Not so long for me," he said. "I thought I was right,
that we were right, protecting our borders. I stood at the
Texas river and watched them fight the current. A mother
was separated from her little boy. I tried to reach him, but
I was too late."

Jesus Christ, didn't the FBI have psychological counseling for their agents?

"My team," he said, "hunted in the city streets for a
man who was called a crime lord. I fingered him. He was
my friend. He told me his secrets and his dreams."

"You were working undercover," I said. Now he seemed
to be talking about a sting operation with a mob boss. "It
was your job."

"They tracked him down, hunted him like an animal.
They were only supposed to arrest him, but he fought
back. I couldn't pull my gun. It didn't matter. My team-
mates were quick shots, and I brought his six children the

news that their papa was murdered. The youngest brother, only seventeen years old, slit his wrists and bled to death.''

I slipped behind the skeleton of the former sweat lodge, using the flimsy structure as a barrier.

"We've both seen a lot of shit," I said. "You can't blame yourself.''

"Because I was following orders. Don't start, McCleet. I've heard it all before, and I give the orders now.''

"Why not make a career change?" I said.

"What?"

"You don't have to stay in the FBI." What was I? A fucking job counselor? "You could retire. Get yourself a little cabin in the woods. And a dog. Dogs are nice.''

He grabbed one of the branches of the sweat lodge frame. It looked like he meant to throw the whole structure aside and charge at me again.

I held the opposite side.

We wrestled with the frame. It hadn't been built to withstand struggle. It was only slender branches tied with twine. It collapsed.

My only weapon was one of those smooth rocks. I knew it was going to be hot, but I didn't have anything else to use against him, and he had a knife that was capable of gutting me like a downed elk.

I ducked down and grabbed a rock. It seared my hand, and I flung it quickly at him.

Though caught off guard, Spanky dodged.

I took another stone and pitched it underhanded, making a direct hit in his solar plexus.

With a grunt, he doubled over.

I was reaching for my third stone, trying to ignore the intense, burning pain in my hand, when he made his move.

Spanky caught my chin with a hard uppercut. When I

arched back, he head-butted my midsection, knocking me off my feet.

I was flat on the ground. He was on top of me. His knife was at my throat.

"My team wins," he said. "I guess that means I'm right."

This wasn't right. This wasn't the right time for me to die. I hadn't even made out a last will and testament. There were too many things left to do. I'd always wanted to design my own gravestone and sculpt it with my own hands. I hadn't said good-bye to Alison.

"You won't join me," he said. "I respect your decision, but know this. I am truth. I know what's right for these people, and I won't let them destroy themselves."

The edge of the knife cut into my flesh.

He stuck his face close to mine. "Hear this, McCleet. This is my last chance at redemption, and I'm going to take it."

The weight of his body on my chest constricted my lungs. I sucked down air like a drowning man, hoping that each breath wouldn't be my last. My time was measured in seconds, in each gasp.

My brain searched for a final statement, and my eyes rested on his necklaces, dangling in my face. One of them was a thunderbird. I saw the name stencilled above the pocket on his fatigue jacket.

I read it out loud. "Brand."

He smiled. "Branded with the mark of Cain."

In a burst of energy, he leapt off me and darted toward his horse. He mounted fast and rode through the trees.

I wasn't about to give chase.

I lay on my back in the forest, my eyes wide open and staring through the branches at the blue sky. I had never been so glad to be alive.

Chapter
Thirteen

After I got my act together and staggered back across the countryside to my car, I couldn't think of anything else to do in Bob. I decided to head back to Portland, where I could find a doctor to treat the burns on my palm. The skin was angry red and painful, but I was still alive and grateful.

On Main Street I made a stop at the store named Sprouts, which was the closest thing to a druggist's I could find. I purchased herbal aspirin, herbal ointment, and gauze. The lady behind the counter helped me wrap my wounds. It actually felt better when she was done.

Though I wanted to drive alone to Portland, I figured I should tell Margot my plans. She hadn't bitched at me for over twelve hours, and was probably going through withdrawal.

At the casino where the radio station was housed I was surprised to find several people working in the warehouse-size building. Much of the concrete floor was carpeted in a garish design of swirling red and orange. There were a lot of lights, a horseshoe of hundred watt bulbs, some neon, and several glowing beer advertisements that I assumed Vikki had gotten for free. The only evidence of future gambling was two green felt poker tables, two black-jack tables, and twenty slot machines along two walls. Construction workers in steel-toed boots and hardhats plugged quarters into the slots.

K-BOB broadcast loudly over speakers. Margot was play-ing a gentle Billy Joel ballad. However, as I approached the glassed-in broadcast booth I could see that the atmo-sphere at K-BOB was anything but serene.

Vikki had returned. She stood toe-to-toe with Margot. Both women gestured angrily. Though I couldn't hear what they were saying behind the soundproof glass, I assumed that it wasn't a pretty noise. If I'd been a prudent man, I would have turned tail and run out the door. But I was the same idiot who got into a Yugo full of pregnant women, mouthed off to Van Glock, and confronted a burned-out fed in his lair.

Using my uninjured left hand, I twisted the knob and opened the door. Neither Margot nor Vikki paid me the least bit of attention as they snarled.

"You don't have any idea how to run a radio station," Vikki yelled. "You're a fucking witch, and you haven't mentioned the casino opening once."

"As if this cheap, tawdry, little place of yours will ever open," Margot snapped back.

"I've got twenty more slot machines being delivered tomorrow. The day after that, we open."

"And who the hell do you think is going to drive all the way out here to play?"

"They'll be here," Vikki said with confidence.

"Bimbo! Your plans are as phoney as your hair color."

"If I build it," Vikki said, "they will come."

I stepped into the line of fire. "Excuse me."

Both women turned on me. "What?"

"I'm taking off for Portland, Margot. I just wanted to tell you."

"You can't leave now, Adam. You have to stay here and tell this bimbo that she should sell the radio station to me. I'm so good at this, I can't even tell you. Who would have thought it?"

Not me.

She continued exultantly. "I always thought I was better in person because, let's face it, I'm a babe. But radio was made for me."

"Whatever," I said.

"Is that all you can say?"

"I have to leave now. I want to go to Max's funeral." I looked toward Vikki. "It's scheduled for tomorrow, isn't it?"

"Eleven o'clock in the morning. And everything went smoothly with the death certificate, thanks to your friend Nick."

"Okay. I'm gone."

Margot grabbed my right arm. "Wait a minute. I wanna go to the funeral, too. You have to take me."

"Actually, I don't."

Vikki latched onto my left arm. "Please, Adam. Get her out of here. She's fucking up everything. I have a continuous tape of Wayne Newton and announcements about the casino, and she refuses to play it."

"I work live," Margot said.

I'd done my duty by my sister, informing her of my plans. Yanking both arms, I detached the two women. "I'm gone," I said.

"Oh, all right," Margot said. "I'll drive."

Riding all the way back to Portland with Margot driving? Just shoot me now. "I'll need my car when I get to town."

"Don't be an ass, Adam. You can use one of my other cars." She spun past me. "Come on, let's blow this pop stand."

"Bye, bye, bitch," Vikki said.

"I'll be back, bimbo."

After another brief argument, I decided to go along with Margot's plan. My hand was killing me, and a prolonged stint behind the wheel would only exacerbate the pain.

At the road to Van Glock's militia headquarters and jail, she made a sudden left turn. "I have to stop by here and say good-bye to Mauser," she said.

That was fine with me. I could check in with Fishman. While my sister flung herself into Van Glock's beefy arms, I found the bug-eyed sergeant.

Warily, Fishman whispered, "I've got some big info."

"Spill it."

"Van Glock picked up something big when he went back to Portland. He keeps saying that the feds are going to have to take us seriously, that we're really a nation."

Visions of a nuclear device exploded in my brain. "What is it?"

"I don't know. But it's big."

"Big in importance. Or big in size."

"Both," he said cryptically. "Maybe a hand-held bazooka that launches ground to air missiles. Van Glock says it quadruples our fire power."

"See if you can find out what it is," I said.

"He's got it hidden away."

"Good. Make sure it stays hidden. I'll be back day after tomorrow."

"Opening day for the casino," he said.

Could this get any more idiotic?

As Margot and I drove through the gateway to Bob, I mentally debated talking to Gosinia about his wacked out senior agent and decided against it. I doubted that the feds would pay any attention to me, and it wasn't worth the frustration.

If I closed my eyes, riding with Margot wasn't too bad. Long ago, I'd learned the trick of turning off the sound of her voice. Most of the way, I slept. It wasn't until we reached the outskirts of Portland that I woke up.

"You're a fun companion," Margot accused. "I could have been riding with a zombie. Did you hear anything I said?"

"Every word," I lied.

"Then you agree with me. I should buy my own radio station here in Portland and start my new career as the female shock jock of the Pacific Northwest."

Blandly, I nodded. It really didn't matter what I said; Margot never took my advice, anyway.

I stretched my injured hand, surprised at the lack of pain. When I unwrapped the gauze I saw the skin was pink, already on the way toward healing. I might have to give a bit more credit to alternative medicine.

At Margot's house I selected her least flamboyant car, a cherry red Mercedes sedan, and drove downtown to the cop house. It was almost five, and I hoped to catch Nick before he left. Though I wanted to see Alison, I had to take care of business.

I found Nick Gabreski behind his desk, munching disgustedly on a rice cake which was probably one of his wife's latest attempts to bring Nick's cholesterol count down. He glowered when I approached.

Since most of the other guys were going off shift, I didn't have to put up with too much antagonism, which was the usual response to anybody who quit being a cop and found another livelihood.

I sat in the straight-back chair beside Nick's desk. "Thanks for helping," I said.

"Too bad about Mister Faverman. I liked the old guy." His voice was low and gravelly from an old throat wound. "It's really too bad he had to die in that idiot place. Bob?"

"He was murdered, Nick."

"I was afraid you were going to say that. Buddy was doing a lot of fast talking about an accident, but it didn't ring true. A murder has got to be investigated, Adam."

"Trust me when I say that's the least of the problems in Buddy's magical little kingdom. The murder, however, is the only reason I'm interested. I want to find out who did it. Give me three days before you report the murder to the CID."

He considered for a minute. "Two."

"I'm not even going to get back there until the day after tomorrow," I said. "I came back for the funeral."

"Two days. That's all."

It was better than nothing, and I didn't want to push. "Okay. I need something else."

"Why me?"

"Because you're my oldest and most trusted friend who has access to the police computers."

He leaned back in his chair and pulled in his jaw, creating a threefold chin. Nick had always been bulky. Now age and gravity had loosened his muscle tone and shifted his weight. He frowned at me. "What do you need?"

"Background checks on these people." I slipped him a list of my main suspects. "I need it by tomorrow."

"Anything else?" he asked drily. "You don't, maybe, want me to slip into a pair of tap shoes and do a time step around the block?"

"Save next weekend," I said. "We'll go sailing."

"It's going to take more than a weekend on *The Raptor* to call it even." But he took the list. "Where can I reach you?"

"If I'm not at home I'll be at Alison's." I rose from the chair. "Thanks, again."

"Hell, us old farts gotta stick together." Clumsily, he patted my arm. "I'm really sorry about your friend's death."

"He was more than a friend." I felt like I was burying my own father for the second time. "I'm going to find out who did this."

"I know it doesn't do any good to say this to you, but try not to get yourself killed. And if you can't be careful, Adam, make sure you leave *The Raptor* to me in your will."

"Done."

I really was going to need that will, but a lot of other stuff came first. Rather than telephoning, I drove to Brooks Gallery in the Pearl district of Portland.

The first thing I saw when I walked in the door was my most recent work, a bronze casting. No matter what else I tried, I generally returned to a seafaring theme. This was a statue of a fisherman at the helm and a mermaid rising toward him from the waves. There was an aura of mystery in the woman and solid strength in the man. I liked it.

Alison must have liked it, too. She'd placed this three-foot-tall sculpture where it would have maximum exposure. The lighting was great, very dramatic.

"The poor little mermaid," said a warm feminine voice. "Forever trapped in the dark, lonely sea."

"She won't be lonely for long," I said, turning to face my own sea siren.

Alison's thick, lustrous auburn hair was pulled back in a knot at the nape of her slender neck. The green of her eyes was mysterious, enchanting. As always, her clothing was elegant and graceful, a clinging sheath that was slit to mid-thigh. I took her in my arms and held her close, inhaling the fragrance of her expensive perfume.

Though she usually scolded me about professional decorum while we were in the gallery, she said nothing. I sensed a hesitance in her embrace as if she were holding back slightly.

"Adam," she whispered near my ear. "What's wrong? You seem serious."

Some things I couldn't joke about. "Max Faverman was killed yesterday. The funeral is tomorrow."

"Oh no." She pulled back and stared into my face. "I'll miss him."

"Me, too."

When she took my hand, she noticed the gauze wrapped bandage. "How did you hurt yourself?"

I couldn't tell her that I'd been in a life and death struggle with a burned-out fed named Spanky. Because Alison cared about me, she tended to be irritated when I got into mortal combat. "I burned it. But I've been using an herbal balm, and it's a lot better."

Her eyes were suspicious as she led me toward her office. "We should call Buddy and ask if there's anything we can do to help. We should take food."

It was nice to sit back and allow her to take care of the practical things. Alison was efficient, never made mistakes, always knew the right thing to say.

Using her desk phone, she contacted Buddy's sister, Marcia, and ascertained that the family would, in fact, be receiving visitors at home for the next three days. The eleven o'clock in the morning graveside ceremony would be simple, no flowers, donations to one of Max's favorite charities. There would be a service tomorrow night with a cantor.

When Alison got off the phone she folded her arms on her desktop and lowered her head. "Oh, Adam. I feel so awful."

When she looked up, her eyes were damp. She bolted toward the bathroom adjoining her office. In a moment, she came out, fresh, lovely, and efficient again. "There's something you're not telling me about Max's death. Marcia said he was killed in an accident. But that's not exactly right, is it?"

"No, it's not."

"Damn it, Adam." Her voice trembled. "Why would anybody want to murder Max Faverman?"

"I don't think he was the intended victim. They might have been after Buddy. Or it might have been part of the bank robbery that went wrong."

"Bank robbery?" She sat behind her desk again. "Tell me everything."

I gave her an abbreviated version of the events in Bob, leaving out the parts about mortal combat and naked Bambi. I also reserved the story about delivering the baby, which I figured I could tell her later.

When I'd finished she leveled a stern gaze at me and said, "You're not going back there, are you?"

"I have to. I promised Buddy I'd find his father's killer."

"Buddy will understand, he's—" She waved her hand in front of her face, interrupting herself. "Come home with me. I have fresh salmon to throw on the grill."

"Do we need wine?" I asked.

"Not for me."

"I'll meet you there," I said. "I brought Margot's car."

"Adam, I have something very important to discuss with you."

I waited for her to continue. Tiny worry lines appeared between her eyebrows. Her full lips twisted as if she couldn't quite find the words. Alison was usually unflappable. This must be something very important.

"It'll wait until after we eat," she said.

As I drove to her house I was distracted. Something important? As if I needed more complications in my life.

I wondered if her important topic had anything to do with the fact that she hadn't been answering her phone. Maybe she hadn't been home. Maybe she'd been with another man. Well, shit, I'd only been gone three days.

When I got to her place, I'd worked myself into a state of high anxiety which Alison easily defused with a kiss, a glass of wine, and instructions that I should take a steamy hot shower while she made dinner.

I balked. "What did you want to talk about?"

"Later, Adam."

As I trudged up the stairs to her bedroom with the adjoining master bathroom, I decided that this was major news, big enough that she had to soften me up before springing it. She was a sneaky one, that Alison. The shower relaxed me. I treated the burn on my hand with more herbal goop, amazed at how quickly it was healing. When I dressed in a pair of sweats I kept at her house, my contentment was complete.

Downstairs, she'd set the table with flowers and waxy tapers of primrose yellow that matched her dress. When I came down the stairs she was placing the salmon on the table.

Refilling my wineglass, she said, "Tell me more about Bob. What on earth is G.O.D.?"

"Geo-political Omni Doctrine, and that's just one of Reverend Petty's conspiracy theories. Did you know there were submarines surrounding Portland, like the Huns at the gate? And the weather is controlled by a big machine in Iceland."

While we ate I regaled her with more Bob stories, ending with my midnight ride in the Yugo with the pregnant ladies. "We bounced off the road, and one of them went into labor."

She took a sip of milk. Strange, I'd never seen Alison drink milk before. "Then what?"

"The baby was coming fast, but I was faster." I went through the whole story. "I've never seen anything like it. Here was this infant, all red and slippery. It had perfect little fingers with fingernails, and its feet weren't any bigger than my thumb."

In the candlelight, her eyes were shining.

"Beautiful," I said. "It was the most inspiring thing I've ever seen. I thought about life, death, age, and renewal."

She reached across the table and took my hand.

"Adam," she said softly, "I'm pregnant."

The sky crashed down and hit me on the head. I was stunned.

We'd talked about babies before, and we were pretty much agreed that Alison loved her career and didn't want to take time out for children. I'd always taken the position of an enlightened nineties kind of guy who would be supportive of whatever the woman wanted to do. It was her body. Her decision. Her life.

Yeah, right. I forgot all about that. I didn't ask her how she felt, what she wanted to do, if she was ready. An amazing, unadulterated joy smacked me up side the head.

I leapt to my feet and yelled, "We're going to have a baby!"

"Adam, we need to talk about—"

I rounded the table, pulled her into my arms and swung her around. "A baby! You're sure about this?"

"I did the home pregnancy test two weeks ago and it was positive. I went to the doctor day before yesterday, and he confirmed it."

"I'm going to be a daddy. This is incredible."

"Settle down."

"That's why you're drinking milk. That's why you got sick to your stomach earlier. That's why you weren't answering your phone, right?"

"I didn't want to tell you over the phone. I've been kind of upset."

"Upset?" I went back to the table, poured another glass of wine, and drained it in one gulp. If she was thinking about an abortion, I didn't want to hear it. "Why upset?"

"It's a big change in my life. The gallery is doing well, and I could adjust my schedule so I'd have time to—"

"Me, too. I can adjust. I'll watch the nipper while you're at work." I dropped to one knee in front of her. "Marry me, Alison. Let me be the father of our child."

"Well, you are the father of our child. I really didn't think you'd be so excited."

I repeated, "Will you marry me?"

"Yes."

I carried her upstairs to the bedroom and set her down on the bed. I eased her out of the sheath dress and kissed her belly. This might have been the happiest moment of my life. I guess I'd really wanted a child. Who knew?

Chapter Fourteen

T he next morning, while Alison puked daintily, I lay on her bed, staring up at the ceiling and thinking about my impending fatherhood. I was going to have an heir to the McCleet throne, an actual offspring to write into my will. I'd also have the reassurance that my genes would survive my demise, which seemed like a bleak, pathetic grasp at immortality, since I already knew that my sculptures would outlive me and be found by whatever aliens took over the planet in two thousand years. My brain wandered off on that track. After all of us native earthlings were gone, the aliens with oversized almond shaped eyes would land. They'd jabber in staccato as they found my mermaid sculpture and presume that earth women had fishtails.

"Adam?" Alison called to me from the bathroom.

"Yes, my love."

"This sucks."

Back to the concept of fatherhood. It hadn't really sunk into my brain. How would I treat the kid? I wanted to be a role model, to be loving and wise, to follow the example of Max Faverman. However, as far as I could tell I hadn't changed at all since yesterday when I was knife fighting with Spanky and checking out suspects with Nick.

Alison wouldn't think those were the actions of a role model, but I did. I had to do what came naturally, and my kid would understand. He or she would think I was a cool dad.

Alison staggered back to the bedroom and collapsed face down on the bed. She muttered, "This sucks."

I knew she'd be a cool mom.

The telephone on the bedside table rang, and I picked it up. "Hello?"

"It's Nick. I've got background checks on the list you gave me."

"Hey, Nick," I said, beaming and preparing to hand out my very first prenatal cigar. "Guess what?"

Alison lurched to her knees and grabbed me by the ears. "Not yet," she snarled. "Don't tell anyone yet."

"Huh?"

"Not until I've talked to my mother."

On the other end of the phone Nick rumbled, "So what, already?"

"Nothing," I said.

Apparently, Alison's hormone-induced insanity had already kicked in. She again bounded from the bed and raced to the bathroom.

"Okay, Nick. What have you got?"

"Not much. The only criminal record is on Vikki Ramone, who's been picked up twice for shoplifting. Mauser Van Glock and Clarice 'Bambi' Stokes have Oregon driver's licenses and a couple of traffic violations. Apparently, Van Glock is a gun collector, because he's got a couple of dozen permits.''

"What about Petty?" I asked.

"He was a victim, not a perp. He owned a warehouse that burned down, probable arson. That was eight years ago, when you were still on the force."

"I knew I'd seen him before." I wouldn't have been working an arson, but Petty's warehouse was probably on my beat. Since I'd never made good as a cop due to my smartass mouth, I always got assigned the crappy beats. "Why do you say he was a victim?"

"Petty was investigated for running a possible scam on the insurance company, but he wasn't charged or arrested."

Still, Petty's involvement with arson was a good clue. It tied in with the first murder. "What about Roger Engersoll?"

"I've got nothing on him," Nick said. "According to my computer, he doesn't exist. No driver's license, and I checked nationally. He's got no criminal record. Nothing."

"That's weird." From what Bambi had said about him, Roger Engersoll was in his late fifties or early sixties. Even if the guy was a hermit, it was almost impossible to go through life without leaving a paper trail. "Nothing at all?"

"Zilch point shit," Nick said. "If I had fingerprints or a social security number, I could be more thorough."

Fingerprinting Roger Engersoll would be a problem. Not only had he been badly burned, but he was buried behind the fat-steepled church in Bob.

"Spanky Brand," I said. "Anything on him?"

"Are you sure that's his first name?"

"No." He was Brand X.

"There's other people named Brand, but no Spanky."

"He was in the military, probably Army. Vietnam."

"You could try tracking him through the VA military records," Nick suggested. "But it'll take some clearances, and they probably won't know where he is now, anyway. Not unless he comes in for regular treatment."

Spanky should have been seeing a shrink, two or three times a week, but he obviously wasn't. "What if he was a fed? An FBI special agent?"

"Working undercover?"

"Yep," I said.

"Then I won't find any more than they want me to find. For special ops, the feds can cloak identity. I don't have the password to break into those files."

Something else occurred to me. Spanky had been wearing a thunderbird necklace. Maybe it wasn't just for decoration. "Nick, do you remember any group in Vietnam who called themselves the Thunderbirds?"

"Nope, but it sounds like an Air Force thing," he said. "I was a grunt like you, Adam. I didn't know shit about code names and special troops. All I thought about in Vietnam was getting my ass out of there in one piece and going home."

"That's the truth." Spanky had his truth. Nick and I had ours. Neither of us liked war. We'd put in our time and done our duty, but Vietnam wasn't the high point of our lives.

"Okay, Adam, I've done my part," Nick said. "I'm turning Max Faverman in as a homicide to the CID in forty-eight hours. You've got until then to figure this out."

I wanted to beg for more time, but I was already pushing the envelope with Nick. "I'll be in touch."

"Would you tell Buddy I'm sorry about his dad? I only met Mister Faverman a couple of times, but I liked him."

"Thanks, Nick."

I hung up the phone. Max Faverman was another old warrior, vintage World War II. I didn't really think there was any connection between him, Spanky, and Roger Engersoll. It was possible that they were all three veterans, but that wasn't an elite group. At one time or another, half the male population had been in the armed forces.

Alison appeared from the bathroom. She seemed to have regained some of her usual equilibrium.

"Honey," she said, "I'm sorry I grabbed you by the ears."

"No problem, Sweetpea."

"It's just that I'm barely pregnant, and I don't want to start telling everybody."

"Why not? Is there a chance you'd lose the baby?"

"From what I understand, the first trimester is always a little tricky. Especially for somebody as old as me."

She was thirty-seven, not exactly ancient. "But you've talked to the doctor, right? And he says everything's okay."

"I'm healthy as a horse, and I have a ton of prenatal pills to take." She snuggled into the bed beside me. "I really should tell my mother first. Mom and I have a wedding to plan."

"That's right. Whatever kind of wedding you want. I'll even wear a pastel blue tux if you so desire."

She laughed, and her warm body vibrated against me. "I'm amazed, Adam. Your usual response to the idea of marriage is a gurgling noise in the back of your throat."

"Urk," I said.

"That's the sound. Is it possible that you've actually grown up?"

Doubtful. "Maybe."

"You seem happy about this."

"I love you, Alison." My hand strayed to her belly.

"And I love you." She craned her neck to look into my eyes. "That's why I don't want you to go back to Bob. You're almost a father, and you have to start behaving more responsibly. It's not safe for you to go back there."

"Ah ha," I said. "Here I was, musing about how fatherhood would change me."

"And I've made it clear. You shouldn't take unnecessary risks. Agreed?"

I definitely didn't want to argue with her, not while she still had a lethal glimmer of hormonal unpredictability in her lovely green eyes. But I didn't equate fatherhood with emasculation. I still needed revenge for Max's murder.

Alison's jaw twitched. "You do agree with me, don't you?"

"What if I don't?"

"I'll have to kill you."

It seemed prudent to say, "Agreed."

"Good." She kissed me quick. "I have to get ready for the funeral, and so do you. Why don't you run home, get changed, and pick me up back here at ten thirty?"

"You got it, little momma."

I did exactly as she said—went home and got dressed in my black funeral suit and tried to find an appropriate necktie. It occurred to me that I was being lame, nodding my head and saying "Yes, dear." According to Alison, I was supposed to put the needs of somebody else ahead of my own. That's what fatherhood is all about.

I wasn't comfortable with the new program.

After finding a dark necktie with little sailboats that was probably too narrow for the current fashion, I checked the messages on my answering machine. One of them was from Fishman.

He was talking fast in a hushed voice, "Adam, you've got to get back here right away. I know what Van Glock picked up in Portland. I mean, I haven't seen it, but he asked me about the computerization of, um, something I shouldn't talk about over the phone. It's big. And I don't think Van Glock is afraid to use it."

"Shit," I said.

Van Glock had been able to lay his greedy paws on enough machine guns to outfit his whole lunatic army. There was no telling what else he'd come up with. Something computerized. Not a bomb, I hoped. The thought of Van Glock with a bomb, pretending to be a superpower, was scary.

I had to return to Bob. Even if Alison didn't like the program, I was possibly the only rational human being who already had access to the weirdos inside the chain link fence. I was their fucking sheriff. All I had to do was convince Alison.

At the cemetery Alison and I joined the crowd, who had arranged themselves around the grave. We were ten minutes early, and more people were arriving by the minute.

"There's Margot," Alison said.

My sister's funeral chic was fairly sedate except for the raven plumes on her huge, round hat. She stalked toward us.

"Don't tell her," Alison muttered through clenched teeth.

"No problem."

The two women chatted in low voices while I scanned the swelling crowd. There must have been over two hundred souls. Most of the men in the crowd wore *yarmulkes*. There was a contingent of old veterans, standing stiffly at attention. People from Max's shoe manufacturing plant.

And some well-dressed folks who represented Portland's high society. In spite of his honest grass roots attitudes, Max had been a very wealthy man.

Members of the Faverman family sat nearest to the coffin. Buddy's two older sisters wept silently. Buddy was pacing. He was tense as a tiger in a cage—maybe not a tiger, but at least a very aggressive anteater. His nose seemed to droop even more than usual. Behind his glasses his eyes were glazed, as if he'd been smoking some of Bambi's finest.

When he saw me Buddy came through the crowd, ignoring condolences, and stood very close. He shook my hand and held on. His fingers were ice cold.

"Good turnout," I said.

"This isn't what Max wanted." Buddy spoke in a hoarse whisper. "He wanted no fuss, but my sisters, would they listen to me? I had to veto the hundred voice choir in the synagogue. In fact, I vetoed the synagogue. Simple. Max wanted it simple. Pine box. Dust to dust." A little grin touched his mouth. "Asses to asses."

"I'll do the gravestone," I said. "Max talked to me about it. He also wanted the birthdate on Selma."

"Whatever." Buddy squeezed my hand tightly. "Find the murderer, Adam. I need to know who did this to Max. Go back to Bob. Find him."

I had promised Alison that I would do no such thing. "I want him as bad as you do."

"I'll be back in Bob as soon as I can get away. I've got to sit *shiva* for a couple of days. Promise me you'll find my father's killer."

"I will."

Not more than three feet away was Alison, my future wife and the mother of my unborn child. She didn't want me to go to Bob. She wanted me to be settled down and rational. Risking my ass to find a killer wasn't a positive sample of my future fatherhood behavior. Yeah? And why not? I didn't want Baby McCleet to have a coward for a daddy.

The service, with a cantor and a rabbi, was simple. A few people got up and talked about Max. There were a few laughs and a lot of tears. The weather was clear, and the sunshine felt hot on the back of my light wool funeral suit.

Alison squeezed my hand. "Are you all right?"

I nodded. Actually, I hadn't been paying much attention. I wasn't ready to let go of Max, not even with his body being lowered into the grave. Max wouldn't rest in peace, and neither would I, until I knew who was responsible for his death. Goddamn it, a man's got to do what a man's got to do, whatever the hell that means.

Margot was standing beside me. In a hissing whisper, she pointed out important people in the crowd, which was a string of names worth dropping, including the mayor and two state senators.

I wasn't really listening to her, either. I was thinking about Bob, wondering why Roger Engersoll had no easily accessible record, dreading the possible firepower that Van Glock had recently acquired, trying to figure a good way to tell Agent Gosinia that Spanky had gone over the edge.

"Look over there, Adam," Margot murmured, "right next to Liz Fitzgerald in that horrendous hat with the spotty veil, is that Wayne Newton?"

I followed her gaze toward a tall, husky man with slick, black hair combed off a high forehead. He kind of resembled the world's most famous Wayne after the immortal Duke. "It's not him," I said.

"What do you know?" Low-voiced, she continued,

"That's Abel and Sissy Brand. I heard their daughter ran off with—"

"Brand?"

"It was shortened from something else, I'm sure. Some long, immigrant name. They're from Chicago. And there's DeeDee Kovak. She used to date Buddy. And there's . . ."

I wondered if Abel Brand had a brother who was an FBI undercover agent. Peering through a row of shoulders in front of me, I studied his features, hoping to find a family resemblance to Spanky. Abel was of average height and build, my age or a little older, with thinning dark brown hair. He could have belonged to anybody's family, even mine. His wife, on the other hand, was dark and dramatic, like Sophia Loren.

The service concluded, and the mourners started back toward their cars. Alison's slender arm linked with mine, and when I looked down at her, she smiled with inexpressible beauty and serenity. How could I lie to that face?

And yet I said, "Excuse me for a minute. I thought I saw an old friend I've lost touch with."

I took one step in the direction of Abel Brand when I realized that she hadn't let go. Her delicate fingernails clenched my arm. "I'll come with you," she said. "You can introduce me."

That would make things difficult, since I didn't really know the Brands, but I couldn't refuse. "Sure. Great."

We caught up with the Brand couple near their car, a silver Caddy. I tapped him on the arm. "Aren't you Abel Brand?"

"That's right." His expression was defensive, as if I'd just announced I was an encyclopedia salesman. "I'm sorry, but I don't—"

"You have a brother who was in Vietnam," I said. "We used to call him Spanky."

He glanced at his handsome wife, then back at me. "Spanky? I don't think so."

"Sure," I said, "he became an FBI agent or something like that."

"Not in my family," he said, turning away.

He was covering up, stonewalling. I grabbed his arm. "You know what I'm talking about."

"I had two brothers. They're both dead."

Before I could stop him, he and his wife were inside the Caddy. This wasn't the proper occasion for me to beat on the windows and demand answers which he probably wouldn't give me, and Alison would've broken my arm if I made a scene.

As the Caddy pulled away she said, "What was that about, Adam?"

"I just thought I recognized—"

"Spanky? Wasn't that one of the people in Bob?"

Here was a good example of what happened when I wasn't completely honest. I hadn't remembered telling Alison all about Spanky, and she was way too intelligent to forget a name. I was spared from digging myself into an even deeper hole with more ridiculous subterfuge when she made the complete connection.

"You're still investigating," she accused.

"I have to do this for Max," I said. "And I promise to be careful. I'm not going to get myself seriously injured."

"You promised not to go back to Bob."

"I have to."

Her ability to be tolerant was one of the traits I loved best about her. "All right," she said. "I understand."

I kissed her gently. "Thank you."

"Of course, I'll be coming with you, Adam. That way I can be sure you're not in any danger. We're in this together. For better or worse."

We spent much of the afternoon discussing all the reasons why Alison should stay in Portland, away from Bob. We also picked up a quiche from a gourmet food-to-go shop, then delivered the quiche to the home of Buddy's sister, Marcia, where we paid our respects to the family. Then we stopped by Brooks Gallery.

By late afternoon we were back at my studio, where I was in the bedroom, trying to subtly pack for my departure to Bob, and Alison was in the front room watching television.

"Adam!" she shouted. "Come here. Quick."

The scene on the television was the front entry gate at Bob, where Van Glock and his two lax guards were standing at attention. The camera panned, showing a line of RV vehicles lined up on the road. The people from the RV's waved at the camera and mouthed the immortal words: Hi, Mom.

I caught the TV reporter's commentary mid-sentence. ". . . an Indian reservation named Bob. FBI sources claim this is an illegal country, but are unable to refute the current treaty of this independent nation near the Wallowa National Forest."

The camera showed the reporter and Vikki. In the light of media attention, she was bubbly as a cheap champagne.

"I'm speaking with the manager of K-BOB radio," the reporter said. "Tell me, Vikki Ramone, what brings all these people to Bob?"

"Tomorrow morning, at ten o'clock, the newest casino in the state of Oregon is set to open. I guarantee we'll have the best payback ratio ever. Within a couple of weeks we'll open a performing lounge with Wayne Newton."

"Have you, in fact, spoken to Wayne Newton?"

"Well, no. Not yet. But we love him here in Bob. And I'll be performing, too. Come to Bob and make your fortune."

"I understand that the FCC is trying to shut down your radio station."

"Here in Bob, the airwaves are free. Every time they block our signal, we find a new one." She waved toward the RV's. "As you can see, people are interested enough to flip around the dial, looking for K-BOB."

"I've heard a number of charges, Ms. Ramone, ranging from drug trafficking to a defense system against a weather machine in Iceland. Is there any illegal activity in Bob?"

"Heck, no. We're capitalists, just like the USA."

With that blithe, perky, and completely untrue statement, the television returned to the standard fare about the weather in Portland.

I closed my eyes and groaned. Nothing illegal? Nothing except murder, arson, bank robbery, and polygamy. The opening of the casino did not bode well for my investigation into Max's murder. If all those additional people rampaged uncontrolled through the looking glass into the wonderland of Bob, the situation would reach critical mass in no time.

I confronted Alison. "I'm leaving right now. And you're not coming with me."

"Because it's dangerous," she said. "Those guys at the gate look as if they mean business."

"I don't care about the gate, or the casino or making a fortune in Bob. I want Max Faverman's killer."

"But the FBI is there, Adam."

"Also the DEA, ATF, FCC, and park rangers. I guarantee they're all going to have their hands full." I grasped her hands in mine. "Max was like a father to me, and I can't let his death go unanswered. If I'm any kind of man at all, I'll do the decent thing and find the murderer."

She searched my face, then sighed. "I don't understand

this weird set of ethics that you use to run your life. There isn't any way I can stop you, is there?''

I shook my head. "Here's what I need from you. Stay here and stay healthy. For me. For yourself. And for our baby. Trust me. I'm trying to do the right thing.''

She trailed her hand along the side of my face, and I thought she was going to grab my ears again. "When you put it like that, it sounds almost noble.''

"I love you, Alison. And I love the child we're going to have. I love the life we're going to share.''

She sighed. "If we have a son—''

"Yeah?''

"I hope he's just like you.''

She kissed my lips and sent me off into battle. Alison Brooks was the finest woman I'd ever known. It was a mystery to me why I hadn't married her long ago.

She followed me out to the garage, fussing about the proper clothing I'd need, and was I sure my injured hand was all right, and did I have a change of underwear. She needed a baby to mother.

I'd already decided against aiming my assault on Bob with Margot's Mercedes. I needed more mobility, and I had recently acquired the means. I whipped a tarp off my highly polished, totally cherry Harley hugger.

"Not the Harley,'' Alison said.

"It's not a dirt bike, but it'll be better off the road than a car.''

I put on my boots, my leathers, my gloves, and my helmet. I was b-b-bad to the bone.

"Be careful, Adam.''

"I'll be back before you know it.'' And I would do my best to return in one piece.

I headed east, up the Columbia gorge. The last time I'd done this journey it had been in my car with Max, and

I'd been contemplating my own mortality. Now Max was dead. And I had everything to live for.

It was after nightfall when I took the turnoff marked, Bob. A few days ago, the sign had been amusing. Now, I felt as if I'd passed the last marker before hell.

The stream of parked RV's extended for over a mile. These people had set up camp. Many of them were out of their vans socializing. I spotted at least five different television mobile units for on-site broadcasting. When I rode my Harley into the FBI encampment, two of the SWAT team guys stopped me.

I yanked off my helmet and said, "I need to see Agent Gosinia."

Though the situation in Bob had gone from wacky to worse, Gosinia maintained his FBI cool. The only hint of elevated stress level was a rash on his throat, which I thought might be easily cured by the herbal ointment available in Bob. "Hi, Dick."

"Don't call me Dick. What are you doing back here, McCleet?"

I dismounted my Harley with a creaking of joints, and approached him. "I need to talk to you about your agent inside. Does he call himself Spanky?"

"Could be. He likes to use code names."

"What's he saying in his transmissions?"

"All clear. Under control." The rash on Gosinia's neck crept higher. "That's the signal, and he hasn't changed it."

"With everything that's going on, don't you think that's a little bizarre?"

"Fuck, yes," Gosinia said. "Everything that's happening in this place is bizarre."

"Before I left I had a talk with your agent. This guy is burned-out big time. He's been undercover too long. Let me put it to you straight, Gosinia. Your agent inside is crazy."

"Are you sure you were talking to the right guy?" Gosinia's left eyelid twitched nervously. "This agent did three tours in Vietnam. He's amazing."

"He told me a story about a sting that he was part of. Something to do with organized crime."

Gosinia nodded. "I heard about that. The hit brought down some of the most powerful families in Chicago. That sounds like our man."

"Signal him to come out," I said. I didn't think Spanky would respond, but it was worth a shot. "Right now, he's another loose cannon in there."

"I'll try," Gosinia said.

"You're not going to let them open the casino, are you?"

"How am I going to stop them? With guns? They're heavily armed. Van Glock has made it pretty clear that if we open fire, he'll shoot back."

"What about negotiation?"

"I've got no chips," he said. "I can't threaten them with arrest because they don't acknowledge my authority. Believe me, if there weren't pregnant women and children involved I'd send in the SWAT team in a blink."

Never before in my life had I been so sympathetic to the feds. There were two hundred people in Bob who were, essentially, hostages. Gosinia was hamstrung.

"Tomorrow morning," he said, "they're going to open the gates and invite all these moron gamblers inside. This is the opposite of Ruby Ridge and Waco. Those people had a siege mentality, keeping everybody out. Here in Bob, they want everybody to come on down. Have fun. Spend your money. Don't forget to have a great time."

I made an offer. "I might be able to talk to them."

"Give it a shot," he said. "I can't authorize you to speak for the federal government, and I can't protect you."

"I'll try to set up a meet with the four principals—Vikki, Bambi, Van Glock, and Petty."

He slapped a cell phone into my hand. "Dial any number. It connects direct to me."

I stuck the small phone into the inside pocket of my windbreaker under the leather jacket.

"Hey, McCleet," he said. "Why are you doing this? For your friend, Buddy?"

"Justice," I said.

Chapter
Fifteen

The helmet saved my life.

    People who are waiting in line, even when the line isn't supposed to be moving, tend to get impatient, and the crowd outside Bob was no exception. They might have been gambling fools, but they were still Americans, and they weren't about to put up with me going off the road with my cycle to sneak in front of them.

I was seven RV's away from the entry gate when a sweet little old lady with curly blue hair started up the cry. "He's cutting in! Hey, wait your turn, asshole."

I wasn't about to stop and explain. There were greater nuts to fry inside the chain link fence that defined the boundaries of the oddest land in the country.

A TV cameraman darted in front of me. I swerved around him and accelerated. Then they started throwing things. I felt the shock of something solid like a medium sized rock bouncing off the side of my helmet as I raced up to the gate, spraying gravel. I yelled, "It's Sheriff McCleet. Open up."

The two goons who had been playing Rock, Scissors, Paper, had found protocol. One of them demanded, "What's the password?"

"I'll kill you if you don't open this gate."

"Nope. That's not it."

Behind me, the mob of gamblers was approaching. I had my little Weber automatic in my pocket, but I'd promised Alison I'd avoid violence, which probably meant I shouldn't pick off a couple of tourists on my way in. "Open up, you moron."

Fortunately, Van Glock recognized my voice and unfastened the lock.

I zipped inside, dismounted, pulled off my helmet which was cracked, and waved to Van Glock. "Thanks."

"Don't think I let you in because I'm glad you're back," he said.

"Thanks for clearing that up."

"The only reason I didn't leave you to the mob is that you're Margot's brother. When's she coming back?"

"Soon," I promised. She'd probably seen the television coverage of Bob, and Margot loved the cameras. To Van Glock, I said, "We need to talk."

"Don't think you're going to set up any jurisdictional boundaries," he said. "This is my show."

"How are you planning to handle this crowd tomorrow?"

He shrugged. "Open the gates and let them in. If there's trouble, we arrest them."

"Like you arrested Jethro Kowalski?" That had been a stellar maneuver. "Your men couldn't even keep one idiot like Jethro in custody. What happens if you have ten people in that jail?"

"The troops could use seasoning," he admitted. "But there isn't time. They'll have to learn on the job."

"How about the feds? What if they want to come in?"

"Not acceptable," he said.

His face was reddening up. It was nice to know that I still had that effect on Van Glock.

"How'll you keep them out?" I asked. "If the feds start through the gates, how are you going to stop them? There isn't even a good way to recognize them."

He smirked. "I've got something that'll keep them back. Bob is a superpower. Nobody's gonna mess with us. Nobody."

This must be the secret weapon which, according to Fishman, was really big and computerized. I wanted to know what it was. Trying to look completely innocent, I asked, "What's this something you have?"

He chuckled. "That's for me to know, and the feds to find out."

"Is it illegal to have this object in your possession?"

"Not in Bob."

What I didn't need right now was a guessing game. Is it bigger than a bread box? Does it start with B? Does it rhyme with boom? "You've got a bomb," I said.

His piggy eyes ricochetted around in his head. Van Glock was possibly the worst liar on the face of the earth. "Maybe."

He did. He had a bomb. Well, shit. "Listen, Van Glock, playtime is over. You've got real great uniforms, and it's been a lot of fun for you to march around with your guns shooting the indigenous wildlife. But you're endangering a lot of innocent people, and I can't let you do that."

"Fuck you."

"Where's the bomb?"

"You'll never find it."

The situation had escalated beyond the capabilities of his penny ante militia, but there was no way he'd hear it from me. I needed backup. "Town meeting," I said. "In one hour. At the casino."

"Tell them to come out here. Why the casino?"

"Because it's time to lay our cards on the table."

Discarding my mangled helmet, I rode the rest of the way into town. Lights were lit in all the shops, and the western style saloon overflowed with patrons. The citizens of Bob were getting ready for their visitors. I went directly to the casino.

Inside, the place had been upgraded from Bingo Night at St. Elmo's to something vaguely reminiscent of a gambling palace. Though it was still relatively incomplete, with a large space left uncarpeted, the four gaming tables had multiplied to twelve. There were probably fifty slot machines in neat rows. Carpenters were putting the finishing touches on a serving bar and a cashier's cage. There were lights all over the place. The Thunderbird logo, spelled out in lights, hung over the bar. Where the hell had Vikki gotten the money to furnish this place?

The lady herself, dressed in a sequin vest that showed off her remarkable breasts, strode back and forth, energized by her new habitat. She was instructing several dull-witted Bobites who were wearing Thunderbird T-shirts and sitting around three poker tables.

"No, no," she said, "four aces beat four kings."

"But I thought aces were ones."

"We're not playing Old Maid, okay? If you aren't sure what wins, check your cheat sheet."

If these were the dealers, I figured the house would lose big. "Vikki," I called to her.

"Deal another game," she said to her students. Then she bounced over and gave me a hug. "Isn't this great! I've finally got my very own place."

"Great," I said.

She handed me matches, a coaster, and an ashtray, all printed with the trademark Thunderbird. "I've never been so happy."

"Yeah, yeah. Real nice."

"Adam, do you know how to play poker? It would be really super if you'd take a table. I'll split the profit with you. Straight fifty-fifty. And that's a good deal."

"Speaking of profit," I said, "where'd you get the money to pay for all this?"

"A surprise investor came through for me. And it's a good thing. I'd had all the printing done, and the slot machines were already on the way."

"Lucky for you," I said. "Otherwise, you'd have to rob a bank."

"Very lucky." Unlike Van Glock, Vikki Ramone was accomplished at deception and half-truth. I couldn't trust a single word that fell from her ruby lips.

"What's his name?" I asked. "Your investor."

"You're going to think this is wacky and wild," she said, "but I don't know his name. Really."

"Were you sleeping with him?"

She rolled her eyes. "Don't you think I'd know his name if I was sleeping with him?"

"I don't know, Vikki. Would you?"

"Don't be such an asshole. I'm not ashamed of my sex life. Why should I be? Men sleep around all the time, and they brag about it. Do you remember every woman you've slept with?"

"Yeah, I do." But this wasn't about me. "Who's your investor, Vikki? Who put up the money for this place?"

"I already told you that I don't know his name, and I don't have anything else to say to you."

She whirled and started to walk away.

"Have you got a phone? I need to call Petty."

Inexplicably, her shoulders tensed, and she stood riveted to the spot. When she turned and faced me I tried to look as if I knew why that question had affected her. But I didn't have a clue, and Vikki saw it. She regained her composure in two seconds. "Why do you need to call Petty?"

"Town meeting. Here at the casino in forty-five minutes. We need to talk about the logistics for tomorrow."

"God, what a waste of time! There's a phone in the radio booth."

In the booth I found a sound engineer who was replaying endless blurbs announcing the casino opening. With him was Fishman, who was hunched over the board looking as if he'd lost his last friend. The little man seemed to have shrunk inside his camouflage fatigues. I tapped on the glass booth.

As soon as he saw me Fishman transformed into a live wire. His head jerked. His arms twitched. He looked like one of those Claymation figures coming to life. He took a step toward the glass, then remembered that he couldn't walk through it. With his AK-47 slung over his shoulder, he ran through the exit door and almost jumped into my arms.

"I thought you were never coming back," he said.

"I'm here." At least, somebody appreciated me.

"We've got to get out of here. We're all going to die."

I'd never actually heard a real person say those words before, but by the look in Fishman's eyes I had no doubt that he believed it. "It's okay, Fishman."

"These people are crazy, and Van Glock is the craziest of them all. He thinks he's going to take over the world."

"Calm down. First, I want you to contact Bambi and Petty."

Fishman whipped a mobile phone from his belt. "Right."

"Tell them there's a town meeting here in half an hour."

While Fishman made the calls I wandered around the casino. A couple of electricians worked on the lights. I noticed the two blond undertakers, Jimmy and Tammy Light, hammering away at the long wooden counter. This was probably the closest thing to employment they had in Bob. The casino might even make some real money, not Bob bucks, which again made me wonder exactly how Vikki had resolved the money question. As far as I knew, Buddy hadn't produced any Bob coins. These slot machines had to be using real quarters and nickels. They had to be stocked for payoffs. Where had she gotten the cash?

Fishman finished the calls and joined me. He saluted.

"Don't do that," I said.

"Right." He fidgeted like somebody who'd sat in poison sumac.

"Okay," I said, "tell me what you know about Van Glock's secret weapon."

"I haven't seen it. He's got it stashed away somewhere. But, from what he asked me about programming, I assume that it's a Chemalmeister Seven thirty-one."

"A what?"

"It's a state-of-the-art nitrogen bomb, activated on a fail-safe computer system. The components are mainly organic."

"An organic bomb?" I'd had experience with black

powder, plastique, and TNT, but this was outside my range of comprehension. "In layman's terms, Fishman."

"If this thing goes off, it'll vaporize everything in a one mile radius. Within five miles, it's pretty severe destruction. The good thing about the Chemalmeister Seven thirty-one is there's virtually no poisonous fallout, unlike the plutonium based weaponry."

"A clean bomb." Which had to be the brand preferred by herbal, vegetarian terrorists. Bambi would approve. "Do you think Van Glock knows how to set the thing off?"

"I don't know. Usually, you'd place the bomb and set the timer for however long it would take to get far enough away to not be exploded." He heaved a ragged sigh. "I don't think Van Glock understands the instructions. He could accidentally set it off."

"Do you know how big this thing is?"

"Big," he said, gesturing wildly with his arms. Fishman had been under some serious stress; he was about to snap.

"Calm down." I patted his scrawny shoulders. "How big?"

"About the size of a torpedo. I guess you could carry it around in the back of a van."

And it was hidden somewhere in Bob, in the middle of acres and acres of semi-wilderness. There was no way I could find it. I'd barely managed to locate Spanky, and he'd been sending up smoke signals. Spanky, on the other hand, might have a chance because he'd spent the last several months skulking around the countryside on his white stallion. He'd be useful in a search. Altogether, life would have been a lot easier if Agent Spanky hadn't gotten abeam of himself.

As the powers-that-be in Bob began to gather in response to my summons, I commandeered a poker table from Vikki. We took our places around the green felt. Petty arrived first, then Van Glock.

"Let's get this over with," the commander said. "I've got a lot to do."

"We'll wait for Bambi," I said. I wanted them all there.

Reverend Petty smiled benevolently at Vikki. "You've done an exceptional job here, my dear. Your casino will provide employment for many of my people."

"Thanks, Reverend."

"A truly free enterprise is a rare thing in the current geo-capitalist world. I can think of few other businesses that are not touched and corrupted by the satanists."

If I'd had to pick right then, I'd have said that Petty was my villain. Since he'd received Engersoll's property and possessions, Petty was the only one with a good motive for wanting the hermit-like Engersoll dead. Plus, the method of murder was arson, which Petty was familiar with from his warehouse fire six years ago.

I wasn't sure how he did the bank robbery. Petty had an airtight alibi for the time of the robbery because he was at Buddy's house with the rest of us, but he could have left the actual robbery to his underlings. It made sense that he'd recruit Jethro Kowalski, who was one of his followers, anyway.

If he then gave the money from the bank robbery to Vikki, it had to be because he was sleeping with her. Ah ha! Maybe that was why Vikki had gone all pale and panicky when I mentioned his name. Giving the cash to her had the additional benefit that the casino would provide income for his flock, who would then tithe their money to G.O.D. As a money laundering scheme, it was crude but effective.

This was all conjecture, of course, and I needed something resembling proof or witnesses before I started making wild accusations.

Bambi came rushing over to the table and sat. She was the only one with no alibi for the time of the bank robbery. She could have done it.

And what about Vikki? Maybe she'd hired a pro from Vegas to grab the money and help her open the casino.

The strategy of the bank robbery would have appealed to Van Glock, and his alibi was Margot, who had about as much sense of time as of charity.

All of them looked at me.

"Well?" Vikki said.

"When Max Faverman was killed," I said, "my friend, Nick Gabreski, arranged for his body to be given a death certificate and to be released to the family. As a favor to me, he agreed not to notify the Oregon Criminal Investigation Department for two days."

"Why would he do that?" Vikki asked.

"Because it was a murder," I said. "Unless we have a killer to turn over to the authorities by sunset tomorrow, we'll be hosting a murder investigation right here in Bob."

Van Glock squawked. "I'd like to see them try to come in here."

"They have no right," Vikki said.

"No satanists," Petty concluded. "We can't allow them to take even a small toehold."

I slammed my fist down on the table, quieting the rampant stupidity that was the way of Bob.

"If we catch the murderer ourselves," I said, "along with sufficient proof, we don't need anyone from the outside to investigate. But we can't ignore this, can't refuse to cooperate. There's been a murder."

"I thought it was an accident," Van Glock said.

"Not an accident," I informed him. "When I went back

to Buddy's house to look for evidence, I found the key in the ignition of the earthmover. It was turned to on. The machine was running when it went off the cliff."

"Not a genius criminal," Vikki said. "Who could forget a detail like that?"

"You tell me," I said.

"I don't have enough men to screw around with an investigation," Van Glock complained. "Can't we have more time?"

"It does seem unreasonable," Vikki agreed.

"No," Bambi said. "It's not at all unreasonable."

She was looking outstanding tonight in a tight red T-shirt that complemented her long, curling black hair. She was an amazingly attractive woman, but I was grateful I hadn't slept with her. Messing around while Alison was pregnant, even though I hadn't known at the time she was pregnant, would have been hard to live with.

Bambi continued. "Adam is right. We can't ignore a murder. If we do, what kind of country is Bob?"

"In the search for a greater truth," Petty said, "there must be sacrifices."

"You'd know about that," I said, snatching the opening he'd offered. "You had to sacrifice a warehouse. For the insurance money?"

"Blasphemer! I was never even accused of that crime."

"But you know a little bit about arson," I said. "Did you happen to take a look at the fire that killed Roger Engersoll?"

"You dare accuse me?"

His voice rose impressively, shaking the rafters and the neon lights over the slot machines. All the dealers Vikki had been training and the carpenters turned in our direction. Behind Van Glock, I saw Fishman making nudging motions. He wanted to talk about the bomb.

I focused on Petty. "Why did Engersoll leave his money to you?"

"He was a sad and lonely man, an outsider for most of his life. I visited him several times, and we discussed G.O.D. in great depth. Roger Engersoll had an outstanding grasp of the many governmental conspiracies. He wanted to belong."

"If we're looking for motives," Van Glock said, "there's a big fat one right here in this fancy casino."

Behind him, Fishman hopped back and forth, barely stifling his need to blurt.

Van Glock turned toward Vikki. "Last week, you were scraping the bottom of the barrel. Where did you get the money to finance this place?"

"An investor," she said. "Don't you people know anything about business?"

"Who?" Van Glock demanded.

"I don't know his name."

There were mutters of disbelief.

"Really!" Vikki protested. "He never told me. Not his real name, anyway."

Across the table from her, Bambi gasped. Her hands flew up to cover her mouth.

Because I knew about Bambi and her secret crush, I knew what she was thinking. There was only one man in Bob who refused to give his name. Spanky.

"You slept with him," Bambi said.

"What if I did? Why are you all so concerned about my sex life?"

I had the connection. It was right in front of my nose, printed on the matchbooks, spelled out in lights above the bar. The Thunderbird Casino. My only other association with thunderbirds was the necklace Spanky wore.

"Shit," I said.

It all made sense. From the start, I'd thought the complicated diversions and execution of the bank robbery looked
like the work of a fed. Spanky had robbed the bank and
given the money to Vikki, his lover, to open the casino.
Spanky was the shadowy figure in the video. Spanky had
killed Max Faverman.

Chapter
Sixteen

I stood up and stepped away from the green felt poker table. My work here was done. I'd found Max's killer, and I intended to track down Spanky and turn him in to the feds for prosecution.

"Wait a minute," Vikki said. "What are you doing?"

"I'm going to pick up your lover and turn him in."

She jumped in front of me, blocking my way. "Please let me open the casino."

I couldn't believe what she was saying. I'd just caught this woman in the middle of a conspiracy to rob a bank. A man had been murdered. And she was worried about her damned casino. "I'm taking him in," I said. "You're a witness, if not an accessory."

"But I didn't know what he was going to do," she said.

"He told me he'd get me four hundred thousand dollars in cash."

"And you didn't think he'd rob the bank to do it?"

Her face trembled as she tried to squeeze out the tears that had been building under the surface. "You've got to believe me, Adam. My part was to get Buddy out of his house and to call Reverend Petty fifteen minutes later. I didn't know he was going to smash the house."

I remembered the phone call to Petty, summoning him to witness the supposed accident at Buddy's house. Earlier when I told Vikki I needed to call Petty, she must have assumed that I'd known this connection.

Finally, a tear slipped down her cheek. "Max wasn't supposed to be there. He shouldn't have died. It shouldn't have happened."

Her words echoed in my head. She'd said exactly the same thing after the murder. Shouldn't have happened. "But it did happen."

"I really liked Max." Her shoulders were quaking, and it looked as if an honest emotion had shaken through her tough act. "He knew all the words to every song in *South Pacific.*"

She tried to lean on me so she could cry on my shoulder, but I held her back. I wasn't sympathetic to Vikki's sudden remorse. There was only one thing on my mind. Get Spanky.

The others were also standing, brimming with questions which I could have answered. But why bother? They wouldn't understand.

There was a loud, strangled noise from Fishman, who apparently couldn't take the pressure any longer. He shouted, "Van Glock has a bomb. We've got to stop him. We're all going to die."

Everyone went silent. It was so quiet in the casino that you could have heard a nickel drop.

Van Glock cleared his throat and hitched up his camouflage pants. "If we want Bob to be taken seriously as a super power, we need advanced weaponry."

"Are you crazy?" Bambi demanded.

"What sort of bomb?" Petty asked. "I hope you know that devices purchased from government surplus can be duds. Better let me inspect it."

"Like hell I will."

Fishman screamed, "The Chemalmeister Seven thirty-one!"

"Oooh," Petty said. "The herbal bomb. That's a nice one. But a little bit unstable. We might want to set up evacuation procedures."

"Disarm it!" Fishman shrieked. "We're all going to—"

"Shut up," Van Glock said. "I'm a team player. I'm willing to discuss."

Bambi appealed to me. "Adam, what should we do?"

For a change, they looked toward me for guidance. Finally, I had attained a level of respect, which was going to come in handy because I could use the help in searching for Spanky. "Here's the plan," I said.

It was then that the special phone Gosinia had given to me began to ring inside my pocket. I pulled it out and answered. "What?"

"It's me, Margot. I want you to come out here and pick me up. I can't get past these RV's without scratching the finish on my car."

How did she get through? I'd thought this was a closed line. "I'm busy."

"You? You're never that busy. Should I have Agent Gosinia order you to come out here and get me?"

"Forget it, Margot."

Van Glock reacted to her name like a grizzly to honey. "Margot? Let me talk to her. Gimme that phone."

I handed it over.

He murmured a few sentences, then I heard him ask, "Where are you?"

Silently, I prayed my sister wouldn't be dumb enough to tell him that she was with the feds.

Apparently, she was exactly that dumb. Van Glock dropped the phone on the felt table and glared at me. As if that weren't enough, he pointed an accusing finger. "McCleet's working with the feds. That phone is a direct link to the FBI."

Any slight air of cooperation that had been established dissolved in a Bobish squabble, with everyone talking at once. I wasn't heartbroken about the shift in mood. As far as I was concerned they could blast themselves to Kingdom Come. I didn't need them to search. They hadn't been able to find Jethro Kowalski. Why would they be able to locate the elusive Spanky?

When I strode toward the door Van Glock stepped in front of me. "You're not going anywhere. You're a fed."

"Back off," I warned. "I'm going after Spanky."

"Spanky?" Van Glock was surprised. "You think Spanky robbed the bank?"

Who the hell did he think I was talking about? "That's right, and by the way, Spanky is an undercover agent with the FBI. That's why he's been here in Bob keeping an eye on you people."

"You're mistaken," Petty said. "Spanky was the one who told me about the Ayatollah's submarines."

That figured.

"He's not a fed," Vikki put in. "I know him intimately, and he—"

"I'm out of here." I'd had enough, too much. I strode toward the exit.

"Hold it right there," Van Glock said.

Exasperated, I wheeled around. "Or what? Are you going to shoot me? What's wrong with you people? You came to Bob looking for paradise, hoping you could find a place where you could live without the oppression of the outside world. Instead, you've turned this nice little setting into a lawless village with gambling, pot, untended pregnant women, and murder. This isn't Eden. It's the seventh circle of hell."

I walked away. These people weren't my problem.

Outside, I breathed the formerly clean air of the surrounding forest land, which had been polluted by the stink of humanity. Not my problem.

I had a life, a career. I was going to marry the woman I loved and become a father. All I needed was to clean the slate and apprehend Spanky. Then Max Faverman would be avenged.

Mounting the Harley, I started up the engine and headed into the back country. Searching at night was nearly impossible. Not only was I unable to see very far into the trees, but the noise of the Harley announced my approach.

I rode past the wreckage of Buddy's house and up the hill to the site where Bambi would build. I cut the engine and took advantage of the panoramic view. Somewhere out there, Spanky was hiding, and I was going to find him.

I headed toward the east, maneuvering the Harley along deer trails.

A couple of things still bothered me. For one, Vikki had said that Spanky promised four hundred thousand dollars, but the bank robbery netted almost twice that amount. What was Spanky intending to do with the rest of the money? The smart thing would have been to get out of the FBI and go into treatment, but I doubted that was his plan.

Why hadn't his brother, Abel Brand, acknowledged him? Abel said he had two brothers, and they were both dead. Even though Spanky was into deep undercover, there was no need for his brother to deny his existence.

And I kept coming back to Roger Engersoll. The bank robbery made a certain amount of sense, but why would Spanky kill the old hermit? Engersoll was so secretive that there wasn't any record of his existence. There had to be a significance in that much subterfuge. In the good old USA, land of computers and opinion polls and census figures, it was hard not to be counted. Once I had that connection figured out, I'd have all the answers.

After a couple of hours, I gave up on the search. The only way I'd find Spanky at night was if he wanted to be found. My quest would have to wait until daybreak. I parked the motorcycle and pulled the sleeping bag off the back.

The night was beautiful, with stars overhead and a sliver of moon. Though my studio was on the Willamette River, I didn't get into the back country often enough to really appreciate the natural beauty of mountains and trees. I made a mental note to take my child camping, to build a fire, to listen to the little noises of wind and hooting of a night owl.

It was with a profound sense of peace that I closed my eyes and slept.

When I woke up it was dawn. I saw brilliant scarlet and cadmium skies overhead. I also saw a huge man sitting on a nearby fallen log, watching me. The revolver in his giant hand looked tiny.

"You must've been tired," he said. "I'm Jethro."

"I guessed."

He didn't have the attitude of somebody who'd come to kill me. Besides, if he'd wanted to he could've bashed in my head with a rock while I was sleeping. Still, I was glad that I'd slept with my own gun under the bundle I'd used as a pillow.

"I got a problem," he said.

I probably could have deduced that. He had three pregnant wives, had pulled a bank robbery, and been caught on camera in the act. "What's the problem?"

"Lois said I should come to you. She's a smart one, that Lois." He sighed. "I kinda got talked into a bank robbery."

"Why don't you start at the beginning?"

"Well, Spanky said he needed some help and he'd give me a bunch of money. I needed the dough, what with all these women having babies. But I went to The Bank of Buddy first, on account of Buddy said he might be able to give me a loan. Then I got picked up by Van Glock's men. And it kinda made me mad."

"So you went to Spanky."

"Yeah, that's right." He looked surprised that I had drawn this very obvious conclusion. "He tole me we was gonna rob the bank and needed some distractions. So, I went and set off the alarm at the jail, and I gave Spanky my key to the earthmover."

Jethro slowly shook his head from side to side. "I heard somebody got killed."

"Max Faverman."

"By damn, I don't like that. Not a bit."

"What happened after you created the diversions?"

"We robbed the bank. I just did what Spanky told me to do. And he gave me fifty thousand dollars." He held up a canvas bag that had been resting on the ground beside him. "I wanna give it back."

I appreciated the sentiment, but it didn't let Jethro off the hook. "Are you willing to be a witness against Spanky?"

"Whatever it takes. I'm sorry for what I done. It was wrong. Do you think I can come back to town now?"

"I can't promise that you won't be arrested. You'll have to testify."

"I can take my medicine." He stood up, towering over me like a redwood. "I'll be seeing you, Mister McCleet."

"Hold up, Jethro. Where can I find Spanky?"

"Damned if I know. He sneaks off like a shadow sometimes. If it wasn't for Lois I probably would've starved out here and burned the money for heat."

As he lumbered off into the woods it occurred to me that I should chase him. But Jethro wasn't the man I wanted.

I stashed the money in my saddlebag and started searching again. It didn't take long for me to decide that combing the woods was futile. Spanky had a talent for showing up where there was a disturbance, and that meant town. I checked my wristwatch. It was eight-thirty. Unless things had changed drastically, the gates of Bob would be thrown open for gambling in an hour and a half. I suspected that Spanky would be near there.

I returned to the casino. Though I was empty-handed, several other people weren't. Apparently, Vikki had opened the doors to the Bobites for a preview before the rest of the outsiders were welcomed inside. Though I didn't see Vikki, I spied two familiar faces. The undertakers, Jimmy and Tammy Light, were sitting side by side at two slot machines, plugging in quarters. Their presence surprised me. From seeing their trailer, I thought these two blond kids were barely scratching out a living.

When I approached, Tammy giggled and waved. "Isn't this fun?"

I wondered if she was twenty-one, then dismissed the

thought. This was Bob. Very likely, there were no age restrictions. Toddlers could play the one-armed bandits. "Be careful," I warned her. "You could lose a lot of money like this."

"Well, I have a lot of money. Last night, when we came home from working here, we found a huge sack of money on our doorstep."

"How much?"

"Hundreds of thousands," her husband said. "I don't know where it came from, but it must be the Lord's will. My Tammy was rich before, a regular society gal, and I always felt kind of bad about—"

"Society gal?" One of the people Margot would know. "What was your maiden name, Tammy?"

"Brand."

"Abel Brand is your father?"

"That's right," she said brightly. "But I was adopted, so he's not my birth father. Do you know him?"

"Do you have an uncle, Tammy?" She might be the last link. "Maybe you haven't seen him for a while?"

She rolled her innocent blue eyes. "Daddy said I was never to speak of him again, but I had a favorite uncle when I was growing up. When he came to visit he always brought me presents from all over the world."

Considering Spanky's profession as an undercover agent, that made sense. I prompted, "And his name was?"

"Kenneth. But everybody called him Cain. You know, like Cain and Abel. He was kind of a black sheep."

"I thought he was an FBI agent," I said.

She giggled. "Boy, have you got the wrong family. Daddy never told me all the details, but I think our family was involved in organized crime in Chicago. When Daddy and Mom moved to Portland they started totally fresh. That was when they adopted me. I guess I was five or six."

She had to be mistaken. Spanky was Gosinia's under-cover agent inside Bob. "Thanks, Tammy. Have fun with your money."

"I really liked Uncle Kenneth," she said. "When I was just a little girl he told me I should never ever be afraid because he would always be watching over me. Like a guardian angel."

How sweet of Uncle Kenneth, alias Cain Brand, alias Spanky. Too bad he had to rob a bank to take care of his niece.

I didn't see Vikki or Van Glock or any of the others, so I went outside to the parking lot to watch and wait. I figured Spanky would show sooner or later. He liked to play the role of protector, and this was where the action was taking place.

I saw Petty standing near the far end of the parking lot. Bambi was also there. Her back was turned to the reverend, and she was about ten yards away from him. A black van with tinted windows zipped into the parking lot and headed toward them. It had to be Spanky.

Checking the gun in my pocket, I jogged toward them.

Van Glock emerged from the driver's side of the van. "Well, here it is," he said. "I hope you're all happy now."

I'd just reached them. "Here what is?"

"The Chemalmeister Seven thirty-one. It's in the back of the van."

I couldn't believe the stupidity. "You brought it into town? Where all these people are?"

Van Glock went around to the rear of the van and opened the rear gate. Laying inside was a black metal device. As Fishman had said dozens of times, it was big. On the end facing the rear of the van, there was a compu-terized hookup with a digital number display.

Van Glock was consulting his owner's manual. "It's turned off right now."

"Unstable," Petty said. "According to an article I read in the *Worldwide Terrorist* magazine, these devices need to be programmed for deactivation. It sure is a pretty thing."

"Ain't that the truth," Van Glock said.

"May I look at the manual?" Petty was stroking the cold metal.

"Yeah, sure. I don't understand half that stuff, anyhow."

Fishman crept from the passenger seat. He was quivering all over, silently mumbling to himself about how we were all going to die in a fiery inferno, which was a little redundant.

"I suggest you get that thing out of town," I said.

"Shut up, fed," Van Glock said.

He did, however, have my handy-dandy cell phone that had been given to me by Agent Gosinia. Van Glock pulled it out of his pocket and punched in a number. "Hey, Gosinia," he said into the phone. "I've got the bomb and I'm right in the middle of town. Wanted to let you know, just in case you and your men wanted to get cute when we open up the gates."

From overhead, I heard the sound of a helicopter.

Van Glock looked up. "Maybe you didn't hear me. Call off your chopper."

He listened for a minute then turned to us. "It's not the FBI."

I wondered who else would want to join our happy little party here in Bob. The chopper landed. The rear door swung open. Buddy stepped out. He had a cigarette dangling from the corner of his mouth.

Casually, he strolled over to where we were standing. "So what are you *putzes* doing about my father's murder?"

Though I would've preferred for Buddy to stay in Portland, I knew exactly why he was here. The same reason I was. "I have it figured out," I said.

"So? Spill."

This was complicated, and I tried to start at the beginning. "First, you've got to know that Spanky is an undercover FBI agent gone sour."

"What kind of shit is this? Spanky's not FBI, Adam."

"Sure he is. Gosinia told me that he had an agent inside who sent out daily messages in Morse code."

"Yeah, yeah," Buddy said. "The agent was Engersoll. That's why I didn't want to make a big deal about his death. It was an accident, and I didn't need the FBI crawling all over and—"

"Engersoll?"

"Yes," Buddy said. "Are you deaf? I just told you."

My brain readjusted the facts to suit this new information, which Buddy could have told me a long time ago, damn it. Engersoll was an FBI agent. That explained the lack of information on his life. What did that make Spanky, alias Kenneth Brand?

His family had been involved in organized crime. I remembered the story he told me about the hit. Though I'd assumed he'd been the undercover agent in charge, he must have been one of the sons. He saw his father killed on the street and went off the deep end, being disowned by the surviving members of his family.

Spanky found out Engersoll was an agent. He must have done so, because he had to keep sending out those Morse code messages to keep Gosinia at bay.

Maybe Engersoll was the agent who'd caused his father's death. Maybe Spanky had tracked him to Bob. Or maybe he'd come here following his niece, whom he'd promised to protect.

"Well?" Buddy said. "You got an answer for me, Adam?"

"Spanky is responsible for your father's death."

From behind my back I heard the word, "Oops."

I turned to see Petty, standing beside the Chemalmeister Seven thirty-one with the instruction manual in his hand. The digital clock display showed one-eight-zero-zero. As I watched, it clicked down to one-seven-ninety-nine. Ninety-eight. Ninety-seven.

Fishman screamed, "That's seventeen hundred ninety-seven seconds until it blows!"

"Seconds?"

"Less than half an hour," he clarified. "We're all going to die."

"Turn it off," I said to Fishman.

But he was paralyzed.

"Wait," Petty said. "I think I know how this works."

He touched another button, and the digital display scooted to one-five-zero-zero and still ticking.

"Oops," he said.

"Don't touch that again," I ordered.

We had two choices here. Move all the people out of range. Or move the bomb. Neither one seemed like a good alternative. Whoever drove that van was a dead man.

"Okay," I said. "I'm driving that fucker out of town. Petty, you follow me in your car. I'm going to park the van. Then you pick me up and we drive like hell to get away from ground zero."

Buddy objected. "I can't let you do that, Adam. I'll drive the van."

"We don't have time to argue."

I leapt behind the steering wheel and took off. Mentally, I counted the seconds as I headed for the most remote destination I could reach in ten minutes. After all my searching I knew the roads, but I wasn't sure if I could get far enough away.

When I looked in the rearview mirror, I saw Petty following me at a distance. "Speed up, you asshole."

At the top of a rise I swerved to avoid hitting Spanky on his white stallion. "Pull over," he yelled.

The minutes were ticking. Goddamn it, this wasn't far enough. Fishman was right. We were all going to die.

But I did what he said. In the back of my mind, I knew what was coming next.

I jumped out from behind the wheel. As I had expected, Spanky took my place. He knew the roads. He knew how to get the bomb far enough away to avoid devastation.

"You've got seven minutes," I said. "Then pull over. We'll follow. You get in the car with us."

"Don't follow me," he said.

"This thing will vaporize you," I said. "Ground zero is half a mile radius."

"For once in my life, I'm going to do the right thing. For the right reasons."

He saluted and drove off.

Petty, who was still following speed limits, pulled over. "What's going on?"

I wasn't going to let Spanky kill himself. I wanted him to stand trial for the murders of Engersoll and Max Faverman. "Follow him."

Spanky was already too far ahead for us to see the van, but we kept going on the same road. Until we hit a fork. At this point, we were on a one-lane, rutted path.

"Which way?" Petty asked.

I checked my watch. It was four minutes until detonation of the bomb. Even if we'd known which way to go, we couldn't catch up to Spanky in time.

"Go back," I said. "It's too late."

"What?"

"Put it in reverse and get out of here."

In retreat, the reverend drove a hell of a lot faster. We were putting some miles of safety distance between ourselves and the bomb.

At Bambi's property, I told him to pull over. It was less than a minute to detonation.

I got out of the car and stood beside one of the backhoes. A minute clicked by. Then another thirty seconds.

The blast was deafening. A storm cloud of dirt and splintered trees rose from the earth like a volcano. I was pushed back a few yards by a harsh, hot wind, but we were far enough away.

It was over. Max's killer had been executed in a manner more horrible than anything I could have imagined. I should have felt gratified, but the inside of my soul was empty.

"That's going to make a nice clearing," the reverend said.

What a knob! "Maybe you can build a monument to G.O.D."

"I was thinking of a domed community. You know, a bubble to keep out all the impurities that the satanists are pumping into the air from Banff." He shrugged. "Hop in. We'll drive back."

"I'd rather walk."

As he drove away, I decided Petty might be right about a couple of things. This was a crazy world bent on destruction. How could Alison and I bring a new life into this insanity?

I guess we'd have to try to make it a better place.

Six months later, with Alison huge and looking more beautiful and serene than any pregnant woman I'd ever seen, we went to Max's grave, where the stone I'd sculpted had been placed. I'd done what he wanted in spite of my better judgment. His epitaph read: No Business Like Shoe Business. On top of the marker were cherubs in loafers and elder angels wearing, pardon the pun, wing tips.

Alison was placing a little bouquet of violets on Max's grave when Buddy came up beside us. He shook my hand and embraced Alison.

"So," I said, "how are things in Bob?"

"Blissfully sane. No casino. No armed guards. No polygamy. It's a development with sewers and county regulations and state restrictions. It's great."

"And the hemp fields?"

"Plowed under. Bambi is talking grapevines for a winery."

"She might be too far north for a vineyard."

"If it grows," Buddy said, "Bambi can handle it."

"Are you going to stay there?"

"Not much longer. Who can afford it? I didn't earn my billions on Bob, so I've got to move on." He lit a cigarette and exhaled slowly. "You'll like this. Vikki and Gosinia? They're a couple. Vik and Dick."

Buddy glanced at his father's gravestone. "I like."

I nodded.

"Max always liked to have the last laugh," he said.

For me, it was good enough for a whole philosophy. Work hard, play hard, and always have the last laugh.